The Reverend & Angel

A Sequel to *A Calling to Love*

By Anita Wolfe

PublishAmerica
Baltimore

Hardcover 978-1-4489-3127-9
Softcover 978-1-4489-4943-4
PUBLISHED BY PUBLISHAMERICA, LLLP
www.publishamerica.com
Baltimore

Printed in the United States of America

For my Jeffrey, Angie, Jenny, & Weston

Acknowledgments

Thank you to Brenda Turner who helped to edit my book and spent countless hours discussing the story with me and suggested some of the scenes. Thank you to Karen Duchoslav who carefully helped to edit my book. Thank you to Laryssa Pearson for modeling as Angel for the cover of the book. Thank you to Angela Bellivean for taking the pictures for the cover and the author's picture on the back.

Chapter 1

One frigidly cold January night, Rev. Michael Donnelly locks up the church after a long drawn out finance committee meeting. Michael has been the pastor at Trinity in Ambrose, Ohio for seven years which has been his first appointment since becoming a minister. Standing at six foot three, the reverend is a handsome man with thick mop of black hair, dark warm eyes that can melt a woman and a slim muscular build.

The pastor hurries across the frozen parking lot to the parsonage entering the kitchen. A small light above the sink has been left on for him. He finds his pretty little daughters already tucked in for the night and leans in the door checking on them. Robin is four years old and Rachel, who is now sleeping in a toddler bed, is two.

Despite the fact that it is only nine o'clock his wife is also already in bed reading a book. Michael goes to his closet to change out of his suit and into a pair of sweats and a sweatshirt. Looking over at his wife gives him a warm feeling. Sadie may be a preacher's wife and an elementary teacher, but she has a classy yet sexy allure.

Grabbing the remote, Michael climbs into bed to watch TV. When he lays his head down on the pillow something rather large makes a crinkling sound. Reaching under his pillow, he pulls out a package of newborn diapers and stares at it for a moment before tossing it aside. Michael takes Sadie into his arms.

"When are you due?" he whispers in her ear.

"In July," she coos.

Kissing her tenderly filled with happiness, the expectant parents make love.

On a Saturday afternoon in March, Michael returns home from a meeting with his District Superintendent, Bob Kavinsky, finding Sadie in the dining room coloring a big poster that she is making for "Right to Read Week" at Ambrose Elementary School where she is a first grade teacher. Robin and Rachel are at the table with paper and coloring books coloring with their Mommy. At five months pregnant, Sadie's rounded tummy already shows. He smiles warmly at his family whom he loves so deeply.

Sadie notices a look in his eyes that worries her, takes the girls into the living room to watch a DVD, and then pulls her husband into the study.

"What is it? What's wrong?" she frets.

Michael looks at the floor not wanting to tell her.

"What did Bob tell you?" a sinking feeling in her gut tells her immediately. "The bishop is going to move us isn't he?"

His eyes lift to hers, "Yes."

"Did the Pastor/Parish Committee request this?" her chin quivers.

"No, the bishop is simply assigning me to a new appointment," he explains.

"Tell him no," Sadie demands.

Michael reaches out to touch her arm, but Sadie takes a step back. "You know I can't," he reminds her.

"Yes you can. Tell him that your wife is pregnant and due the end of July. I can't do the work required to move the first week of July," Sadie insists, but Michael simply stares at her. She gives up, "Oh, never mind. I keep forgetting that the bishop and the cabinet don't care about the minister's wife or family."

"Sadie," Michael reaches to comfort her, but she dodges his touch again.

"Do you know where?" she nervously asks.

"Shermanfield."

"Oh crap, field is actually in the name. It's in the country isn't it?" Sadie hates living in the country.

"I don't know. I was just about to Google it," Michael sits at his computer and pulls up what he can find. Shermanfield is definitely out in the country and is about an hour and forty minutes from Ambrose, too far for Sadie to commute to work. Sadie will have to give up the job she loves and more than half their income.

Sadie rushes out of the room and upstairs where she throws herself on the bed and cries herself to sleep. Michael walks into the living room and sits on the couch. Soon his daughters crawl up on his lap to watch their princess cartoon movie for the fiftieth time while he holds them.

Michael knows that this is going to be a hard move on Sadie, especially since she is pregnant. Sadie's father, Martin Stevens who is also a minister, had been Michael's mentor before his ordination. As a minister's daughter, she moved around her entire childhood. She had lived in small towns, suburban towns, cities, and out in the country. Suburban towns are her favorite. Living in the country was her least favorite feeling stranded with nothing to do and nowhere to walk or a place to ride her bike.

One time, her father was appointed to a country church that had taken over the tavern and then actually turned the tavern into the parsonage. Sadie lived for three years of her life in a tavern. The downstairs inside actually looked like a house, but upstairs simply had two long rooms for bedrooms with many built in cupboards along the walls. The outside of the house was flat with large windows and red brick looking like a store front.

Ambrose was the first town where she had chosen to live and the nine years that she has lived in Ambrose is the longest she has lived anywhere. Her closest friends, Colleen, Brenda, and Stephanie live here. They see each other practically every day. She is close to the faculty with whom she works and loves the people of their church. Everyone in town knows Michael and Sadie, workers in the stores, the people at the recreation center, and the librarians at the library. She knew when she married Michael that this day was coming, but that fact does not make actually moving any easier for her and it is not easy for Michael to watch.

Sadie sleeps for two hours before she comes down and begins fixing supper. During supper and for the rest of the evening, Sadie avoids looking at Michael and is cold towards him. That night, she prepares her daughters for bed, changing their clothes, brushing their teeth, reading them a story, and singing them a song. Michael leans in the doorway listening to her sing. He loves her voice. After the song, he joins her to pray with the girls and then helps her tuck them in and gives kisses goodnight.

Sadie returns to the dining room to work on her poster. Michael leans in the archway watching her. He hates seeing her in pain, but he hates her attitude even more. When he first met her, she had built a wall around herself to protect her from men after having been hurt by her last fiance and he had a terrible time breaking through to convince her to even date him. Then, while they were dating, a jealous Troy, her ex, had shot her and she again pushed Michael away. At their wedding rehearsal, Michael asked her to vow that no matter what happened that she would never push him away again. She promised and up until today, she had kept her promise. However, since she found out that they are moving, he can feel her beginning to pull away from him again.

Michael walks up behind her placing his hands on her shoulders, but Sadie shrugs them off, "Stop it. I'm trying to finish this."

Michael snatches the marker from her hand slamming it down on the table. Grabbing her by the arms, he turns her around to face him, "Now you listen to me. You knew this day was coming and now it is here. I know that this will be a hard move for you, so you go ahead and cry all you need to, but you cry in my arms. We will do this together. Don't you push me away. Do you hear me?"

Sadie stares at him for moment and then wraps her arms around her husband crying into his chest, "I'm sorry. I'm so sorry."

The next day, Sadie drags sadly around the house. While she does the laundry, she does little else. That afternoon, they sit together in the living room while Michael reads a book and Sadie stares at papers that she needs to grade.

Sadie leans back and wistfully shares a memory, "My mom had this friend who was a teacher and a minister's wife. She had to keep starting over in new schools often spending years subbing. Then one time she received a really good position and worked there for six years before her husband moved. But, the new church was only a forty minute drive from her school, so she continued to commute to work for the next eight years. Then her husband was moved again a little over two hours away from her school. Her children were all grown and out of the house. So, she rented an apartment in the town with her school to stay during the week. She drove to her husband's house on Friday evenings and stayed until Sunday evenings and of course there were the holidays, school days off and summers that she stayed at the parsonage."

Michael stares at her in disbelief, "Would you actually want to do that? You would leave me and live as if you are a child of divorced parents with visitation?"

"Well, no, not now. We have young children. I don't know how I would feel later in life," she clarifies.

Michael is indignant, "Forget it. I would never let you leave me. I think that sounds selfish and horrible."

"Really? I thought it was a loving gesture that after all her years of sacrifice, her husband made a sacrifice for her sake. For once, he made her career and her life a priority," Sadie counters.

"I thought when we decided to get married you said that you would move with me," Michael reminds her hotly.

"Yes I know and I will move with you like I promised. I was just telling you a story that my mom told me," she reassures.

"Yeah, that's all you were doing," Michael scoffs and leaves the house for his church office.

Later that evening after their daughters are tucked into bed, Michael and Sadie awkwardly sit in the living room watching television when Sadie suddenly calls him, "The baby's moving. Come feel."

Michael automatically moves to the couch beside her allowing her to place his hand in the appropriate spot. They both sit frozen for a moment waiting for something to happen. Finally, the baby moves again causing a smile to cross Michael's face. As he sits feeling his child, Sadie stares lovingly at him.

"I hate moving," she begins, "But if I thought for a minute that I could live without you, I wouldn't have married you. Of course I'll always go with you. I'm just mourning the loss of my job. "

Michael smiles warmly at his wife wrapping his arms around her, "I'm so sorry that this is so hard for you."

Cuddling up, Sadie laments, "You know that I moved to Gringham when Colleen and I were juniors in high school and we were together for two years. Then we roomed together all four years of college. Then we both moved to Ambrose and have lived near each other for the past nine years. We have been friends for fifteen years and I've been friends with Brenda almost that long. Moving away from them hurts more than losing my first grade class. I knew that this day was coming, but it still hurts. It really hurts. This just sucks."

Michael kisses the top of her head, "I'm so sorry. I wish I could make it easier for you. I'm so sorry."

They quietly watch TV lost in their contemplation, comforting each other simply by being together and feeling their unborn child's movements.

Chapter 2

On the first Tuesday in April, Michael and Sadie drive out to Shermanfield for what is referred to as an interview with the new church's Pastor/Parish Committee, despite the fact that the church can only give an opinion. In the end, the bishop will decide. Until the bishop announces an appointment officially, the minister and his wife are sworn to secrecy. Sadie and her friends tell each other everything, but Sadie has kept this secret from them for almost a month.

Her best friend, Colleen, is babysitting for Sadie and Sadie had lied about the reason for the meeting. It seems odd to Sadie that a church conference would force a minister to lie to his friends and congregation. It seems rather sinful.

As they drive out toward Shermanfield, they leave towns behind. Fields and sprawling country stretch out on both sides of the road. Sadie complains almost nonstop to poor Michael who points out that the landscape is beautiful and peaceful to which he simply receives a dirty look. Finally, they pass a sign announcing that they have just entered Shermanfield. They see nothing except spread out houses surrounded by fields.

They approach an intersection where two state routes cross with a flashing red light. On one corner sets a gas station with a convenient store, the only store in the so called town. On another corner sets a small diner, *The Hungry Wolf*. Across from the diner, a sign hangs on a tiny building which reads, "Post Office" but looks more like a farm shed.

"I do believe that this is downtown Shermanfield. This is not a town; it's just cross roads," Sadie complains.

Michael drives through the intersection turning left. South Street comes up quickly, so Michael turns left again. South Street is a residential road with rows of small shabby houses on both sides. Soon they pull up to

13

a white New England style church sitting up on a small hill. To the left of the church is a large cemetery with some ancient looking tombstones surrounded by a black wrought iron fence. On the right of the church sets a small yellow bungalow which is probably the parsonage.

"I hate it here," Sadie mumbles as Michael pulls into the driveway. The drive winds around to the back of the church to the parking lot.

Michael parks in the empty lot. They are the first to arrive. Michael turns to Sadie, "Oh sweetheart, about the meeting…"

"Don't worry," Sadie interrupts, "I brought my plastic smile that I keep in my jewelry box just where Mom always said that she kept hers."

"I would prefer a real smile, but any smile will do," he concedes and then offers, "When we are finished here, do you want to look at the elementary school?"

"Sure, but only because Robin will be starting kindergarten. I've been thinking about taking some time off work. With a new baby and the girls are still so young, I thought maybe I should stay home for several years. It will be really hard financially, but the kids are only going to be little once."

Michael quickly agrees, "I think that's a good idea. We will figure out how to manage and when you feel you are ready, I will help you workup your resume and send it out. The Lord will provide you with a job when the time is right."

They climb out of the car to look around. Behind the parking lot is a large recreational field with a pavilion, a baseball diamond, soccer field, a basketball court, and a playground.

"Wow," Michael declares, "this is one fantastic backyard. I wonder if the church owns all of this."

"It is really nice," Sadie agrees. "I have also lived by cemeteries before. It is a nice, quiet place to go to think, read, or take walks. You might like jogging in there."

Michael is relieved that Sadie is finally being positive about this. Bob Kavinsky pulls into the parking lot to take them out to eat so that they can talk before the meeting with the church committee. He apologizes that he didn't allow for enough time to drive to a nice restaurant, so they eat at *The Hungry Wolf*, the small diner.

After they order, Bob informs them that Shermanfield does not have a school, but belongs to a county district, Logan River Schools, which is about a twenty minute drive. The nearest town, which has luxuries such as department stores, grocery stores, restaurants, and a library, is also about a twenty minute drive. The closest mall and hospital is about a forty minute drive.

Sadie shakes her head, "How can you deliver such terrible news with such a cheery tone?"

"Sadie," Michael admonishes her.

Bob seems confused, "What do you mean? I'm just telling you where to find things."

"I mean, isn't there a real town anywhere that needs a new minister?" she pleads.

"Sadie," Michael snaps.

"My dear," Bob encourages, "Many people love it out here. The country is beautiful and quiet, and peaceful. The church has over two hundred families with an average attendance of between one hundred fifty to two hundred people."

"I see…" Sadie seems to calm down, but then lays her head down in her arms to beg, "Please don't strand us out in the middle of nowhere."

"Sadie, stop it," Michael demands and then apologizes to Bob, "I'm so sorry."

Bob laughs, "Don't worry about it. I have been doing these dinners for about eight years now. Sadie is actually calm. At least she isn't crying yet. You should see how a country girl reacts when told that she is being moved to the inner-city especially if she has children facing an inner-city school. They tend to become hysterical."

Michael is relieved that Bob understands, but still asks, "Do I have to take her into the meeting him me?"

Bob pats Michael's hand, "Don't worry. I've never seen a minister's wife carry on in a meeting. Sadie will be fine."

Michael nods, but is unconvinced.

Next, Bob gives them a tour of the parsonage. The little yellow bungalow does turn out to be the parsonage. The living room is much smaller than the one they have now which leads to a u-shaped hall. On the first part of the u are three doors. One is a tiny coat closet. Across from it is one which leads up an enclosed staircase to an open room that is a converted attic with storage cubbies and a walk-in closet. The other door leads to a kitchen. At the turn of the u is a small bathroom with no counter space or storage. It only contains a toilet squeezed between a sink and a bathtub. The other side of the u has two doors which lead to a small bedroom and a linen closet. The u leads into a small-sized master bedroom with a window facing the front of the house.

The kitchen has hardly any counter space and Sadie wonders if they will be able to fit in a table big enough for a family of five to sit around. She is quite upset that there isn't a dining room since she owns a beautiful dining room set.

On the other side of the kitchen is a door with three steps. To the left is a door to the garage and to the right are the steps leading to the basement. The unfinished basement is divided in half. At the bottom of the steps is an open doorway into a large rectangular room with indoor/outdoor carpet which the current family living there uses as a rec room. The other part of the basement contains a washer, drier, utility tub and pantry shelves.

The garage was originally built for two cars, but someone years ago built a small narrow office along the connecting wall to the house. There is room for both a computer desk and a regular desk across from built in shelves. Although the space is tight, Michael likes the room. This leaves room for one car and bikes and outdoor toys.

The backdoor of the garage leads to a cement patio with an aluminum overhang. Years back, a church member donated a picnic table and a wooden glider for the patio.

While things will be squished and tight, Sadie believes she can make it work except for her dining room. She cannot stand the thought of losing her dining room. She hates the thought of putting it into storage for years and how would they even pay for storage with her losing her job?

Next, they go to the meeting to meet some of his new parishioners. The meeting goes very well. The committee seems enchanted with the couple with young daughters and one on the way. Michael is both pleased and impressed by how pleasant and sweet Sadie became once they entered the church. She had told the truth about behaving when it mattered.

After interviewing Michael, Ted Lawrence, the committee chairperson, turns to Sadie, "We are very interested in you as well."

"Oh, how so?" Sadie questions surprised.

"Rumor has it that you play the organ. Our organist wants to retire and it is so difficult to find a fulltime organist," Ted explains.

"I don't have any conservatory training. I had piano lessons and am self taught on the organ. I have subbed for our organist for years, but I am not a professional," Sadie admits honestly.

"You don't need to be college trained. Do you think you can do it?"

"I can do it. Do you plan to pay me the same rate as the last organist, or do you want me to donate my time since I'm the minister's wife?" she inquires.

"Which would you prefer?" Ted counters.

"I'm losing my teaching position to move here and with three children, we could use the income," she responds.

"Well, I don't see why we couldn't pay you the same as Wilma if that is what you want," he agrees sounding somewhat disappointed.

"My baby is due in July so I couldn't take over right away," Sadie informs them.

"I'm sure Wilma will be okay with that," Ted turns to Michael, "Ministers work closely with the organist. How do you feel about working with your wife? I'm not sure I would want to work with mine."

Michael places his arm around Sadie while he brags, "I have never worked without Sadie. She was a very active parishioner in my first church. We began working on a Bible School Program together the very first week we met. We have always worked as partners. She was the Sunday School Superintendent, the children's choir director, Bible School director, a lector, a choir member, and the substitute organist at our last church."

While most of the committee is quite impressed, Liza Piazza questions, "Do you mean that you dated and married a parishioner?"

"Yes I did and trust me; we are a match made in heaven."

The committee laughs.

Rob Monroe, a rather handsome police officer, introduces himself, "I'm the chairman of the trustees. How do you like the parsonage?"

Michael nervously squeezes Sadie's shoulder as she responds, "I think it is bright and cheery."

"Did you notice anything that you would like changed or needs done before you move in?" he offers.

"Well, since you asked…" Sadie begins.

"It's fine," Michael interrupts.

"No, let her ask," Rob contradicts.

"I couldn't help noticing that it doesn't have a dining room and we own a beautiful dining room set."

"Sadie," Michael tries to stop her.

Rob laughs, "I don't think we can build you a dining room in two months."

"Actually, I bet you can," Sadie smiles.

"Don't be silly Sadie," Michael cuts her off.

"What are you thinking?" Rob asks curiously.

"Well," Sadie ignores Michael's efforts to stop her, "there is a large room at the bottom of the basement steps that is already painted white. Could you install a carpet in there like a Berber that you can get at one of those do it yourself warehouses?"

"That's a great idea. I could put on a fresh coat of paint, install a carpet and replace the florescent lighting with nicer light fixtures," Rob offers becoming excited.

"Oh, we don't need all of that. I just want better quality carpet to protect the furniture from the cement floor," Sadie assures humbly.

"Don't you worry; you just leave it to me," Rob promises.

"Why, thank you."

Michael smiles to himself as Sadie works her minister's wife magic of making a parsonage work for her family.

On the drive home, Michael asks how she knew that they wanted her to volunteer for a paid position to which she replies that she was raised by a minister's wife. Churches seem to always feel that the wife should volunteer all of her time to her husband's church, but they are going to need the money which will still be a fraction of what she is making now.

Michael squeezes her hand telling her that she is wonderful and that he loves her, but Sadie states with a big smile, "I'm going to hate living out there, but I love you too."

Michael just shakes his head.

Chapter 3

By the end of April, the bishop makes the appointment official allowing Michael and Sadie to finally tell their friends, family, and parishioners about their move. While their friends knew that this day was inevitable, they are still surprised. When Michael arrived in Ambrose, Aidan, Steve, Colleen, Brenda, Stephanie, and Sadie became close friends and spent much of their time together. Quickly, Michael had joined this group exercising several mornings a week with Aidan and Steve and spending almost every Friday night with the group. Soon, the entire group began attending church regularly as well.

Within a year, Stephanie had begun dating Michael's childhood friend, Graham. When they married a year later Michael performed the wedding. This close group of friends began their families together and constantly shares everything. Colleen even babysits fulltime for Sadie. This move will be hard on everyone, including their children who have been raised together.

The church people feel distraught about losing their beloved minister and Sadie. The last couple months are difficult.

Sadie attempts to pack a little at a time beginning with the storage and holiday boxes to make sure that they are secured for the move. However, her pregnancy leaves her fatigued and she continually falls asleep.

June quickly arrives and school ends, working in the first grade at Ambrose Elementary ends. Her friends and colleagues throw her a farewell party. An important part of her life ends, but the present pushes on. Sadie, seven months pregnant, forces herself to pack more boxes.

One evening, Michael runs to the store to pick up milk. While standing in line at the checkout, he runs into Kathy Clark, the school secretary.

"Hello, Reverend. Boy, we are going to miss Sadie. She is wonderful with the children and so much fun to work with."

"Thank you. She will definitely miss all of you too."

"I was surprised when she handed in her forms requesting a two year parental leave. I would have thought that she would resign. Are you planning to return in a couple of years?" Kathy inquires.

Taken off guard, Michael attempts to act as if he knows what she is talking about, "That is what she wanted to do for now, but we aren't coming back."

Returning home, Sadie notices that something is bothering him, but he waits until after the children are tucked in for the night to broach the subject with her.

"Sadie, I ran into Kathy at the store. She mentioned that you requested a two year family leave instead of resigning. Why didn't you resign and why didn't talk to me about this?" he demands.

Sadie sits uncomfortably in the recliner having difficulty breathing with her large belly and the baby pushing up under her lungs, "I was planning to talk with you about it."

"You did it almost two months ago and school is out. When were you planning to have this discussion?"

"In two years. I'm sorry dear. I'm just not ready to resign yet. I can resign in two years," she apologizes.

"What is the point in waiting?" he asks suspiciously.

"You never know what could happen. My family only lived in Senecaville for two years and moved. What if we move again close enough for me to commute? Maybe we could work something out," she explains as she struggles to pull herself out of the recliner.

"What could we possibly workout?" Michael asks as he helps pull her out of the chair. Then he glares at her. "Are you still thinking about renting an apartment here and living away from me during the school week?"

"No, I'm just not ready to quit. It hurts too much. I thought in a year or so, once we have settled in, I'll be able to do it. I'm just putting it off."

"I suppose it doesn't hurt anything, but I don't like it. I don't like that you didn't tell me. Sadie, we are in this together and you have to talk to me. I didn't like finding out from an acquaintance at a grocery store," he reprimands.

"I'm sorry," she apologizes again as tears form.

Michael wraps her in his arms and holds her for a while promising, "It will be okay. God has a plan for your life and reason for having called you into teaching. Try to relax and just trust."

Michael, Sadie, and their girls attend only three out of five days of their denomination's annual conference the third week of June at a small resort town. They stay with Sadie's parents in her parents' cottage. Martin and Joy sympathize with Sadie's emotions. They have faced these moves more times then they wish to count. They can feel the stress between Michael and Sadie. Every minister moving this year will move out on the first Monday in July and move in on Tuesday. Sadie is not the only minister's wife at conference filled with dread and sadness. The day is almost here.

They return home early to prepare for the move. They plan for Michael to tape boxes together and bring everything to Sadie for her to pack and then he will do all the lifting a stacking. The first day they work like clockwork just as they always had, but Sadie has difficulty breathing and tires easily. She feels stressed because they are way behind.

The next day, Michael leaves to work in the office for three hours and suggests that Sadie rest while he is away. Worried about being behind, Sadie goes to the girls' room and has them help her work on their toys. She has them choose toys for a small box to keep out until the rest of their toys are unpacked next week. She sits on the bed and has them bring her toys to place in boxes for moving and some in boxes for Goodwill.

After two hours, Sadie becomes tired, but perseveres. Her daughters are too small to move boxes, so Sadie drags them across the room. Over the past several hours, Sadie experiences Braxton Hicks, light contractions. She had these often during the last month of her other pregnancies and doesn't think anything of it. Sadie tapes together another box and places it beside the children's bookshelf. She fills the box with their books, but plans to leave it set where it is until Michael comes home.

Unable to reach several books because the box is blocking them in, Sadie takes hold of the box and slides it about a foot out of her way. A sudden sharp pain shoots through her stomach. She drops to her knees. The Braxton Hicks turn into stronger contractions. Terrified and panting, Sadie instructs Robin, who just turned five in May, to go to the church and get Daddy.

21

Scared, Robin runs down the stairs, through the house, and out the backdoor. She tears across the parking lot and into the church screaming for her Daddy as soon as she hits the breezeway's door.

Michael comes flying down the stairs, "Baby, what is it? What's wrong?!"

"Come quick! There's something wrong with Mommy!"

Michael snatches the child up in his arms and races home with Sue Anderson, the church secretary following them. Setting Robin down in the kitchen, he runs upstairs to where she told him Mommy is and discovers her on her hands and knees crying.

"Michael, I'm in labor!" she panics.

Michael drops to his knees, "Okay sweetheart, it'll be okay. Let's get you to the hospital; just lean on me."

Rachel hangs on his leg as he pulls Sadie to her feet. Freeing himself from Rachel's grasp, he carefully helps his wife down the stairs. Sue encourages Michael to just go and offers to stay with Robin and Rachel. She picks up Rachel, peeling her from his leg again. Michael manages to get Sadie in the car as she suffers contractions every couple minutes.

"It's too soon, Michael!" she cries. "It's five weeks too early!"

Soon, they reach the hospital and Sadie sits on a table as they strap monitors over her swollen belly. The nurse begins IV fluids and gives her a burning shot to stop the contractions. The doctor checks her several times and monitors her contractions. She is effaced and almost four centimeters.

After four hours, the doctor comes in to talk with them, "I believe that we have stopped the contractions. I want you to try to hold onto this baby for at least one more week, preferably two or three. You will need to be on semi-bed rest."

"Semi-bed rest?" Michael questions.

"Yes, she can get up to use the bathroom or to eat in the kitchen, but she needs to rest and stay off her feet until the baby is born. No picking up your daughters and avoid stress," the doctor instructs.

"But we are moving next week," Sadie protests.

"Well, you will have to decide what is more important to you," he poses in a cocky tone. "I want you to stay here for a couple more hours for observation before we send you home."

As the doctor leaves, a tear rolls down Sadie's face, "What are we going to do?"

"I'll figure something out," Michael promises holding her hand.

"Why is God doing this to us now?" she grumbles bitterly.

"Sadie, you know better than that. Don't blame God and be angry. Turn to Him for help. Pray for our baby," Michael reminds her.

Sadie rolls her eyes.

The next morning, Michael, Sadie, and their girls sit around the kitchen table eating breakfast and attempting to come up with a plan. Sadie wants to go back to sitting on a couch and packing while Michael does all the lifting and fetching. Michael disagrees. He wants Sadie to just go to bed and let him pack by himself.

"You don't pack carefully enough. Things will end up broken or lost," she complains.

"Maybe," he agrees, "but they are just things. You need to take care of yourself and the baby."

"We don't have a chance of being ready in time," Sadie worries.

"Have faith," he reminds her.

There is a knock at the door and Michael answers it. In walk Sadie's parents, Martin and Joy, with her sisters, Mary and Lucy, as well as, her sister-in-law, Judy.

Joy touches her daughter's face, "My dear, you helped us with so many moves. You go straight upstairs, go to bed, and take care of our grandchild. We are going to pack up the house with Michael. Judy is going to take care of the girls. I talked to Colleen. We are going to pack you up, and Colleen, Aidan, Brenda, Steve, Stephanie, and Graham are going to unpack you on Tuesday."

Michael smiles with relief at Sadie, "I told you God would provide."

Sadie tears up as she hugs her mother tightly. It feels odd to lie in bed while her family works all day to pack them up. Martin and Michael go to the church to pack up his office while Sadie's mom and sisters attack her kitchen and dining room. In two days, they are packed and ready to go.

The next Monday, Sadie sits on a couch in the church lounge out of the way, as the movers load up the truck with everything they own. Michael has strict orders to make sure that the piano is not scratched or damaged in anyway. Halfway through the morning, the movers take a break. Michael comes around the side of the house and sees Robin through a side door on the moving van sitting in a child-sized rocking chair holding her chimpanzee doll. The scene tugs at his heart.

Soon it is time to leave. It feels odd and scary to have everything they own on a truck which is driving away. When Sadie was a little girl, she used to watch the moving truck pull away and then have nightmares that it would go crashing off a bridge into a lake and all of her toys and family photos would be gone.

Michael, Sadie, and the girls walk through the empty house one last time. They want the girls to see the house empty so that they know that nothing of theirs had been left behind. Michael remembers moving in as if it were yesterday. He had hardly anything. The church men had helped him unload a small u-haul truck. He had only ordered a living room set and one bedroom set from a furniture store. The church men had brought over a long rectangular table that seats eight with gray metal folding chairs to go with it from the fellowship hall for his dining room.

Sadie, whom he only met a week earlier, came over to help Michael. She made a list of everything that he needed, helped him shop, and helped him unpack. He doesn't know what he would have done without her. A year later, they were married. Now it is time to say goodbye to their first home.

His daughters break his heart as they whimper and cry. They stop in the empty living room standing in a circle holding hands as Michael prays. He prays thanks for their happy times in Ambrose and for help in their transition to their new home as well as comfort on this difficult day. Their friends stand outside tearfully saying goodbye, as all of their children tear around.

"It's not goodbye," Michael reminds them. "We will be less than two hours away. Between e-mail and our cell phones, we will keep in constant contact and we will come back for some of our Friday evenings and you are always welcome anytime."

Sadie reminds him, "You know, Conference Law dictates that we are not allowed to visit with people in our old church for a year after a move."

"This group doesn't count," Michael states firmly. "These are our personal friends, our family, outside of the church and we will visit all we want."

Aidan smiles, "What is with the tearful goodbye? We are meeting you at your new house tomorrow to spend the entire day unpacking."

They laugh and hug. Michael loads his family into the car and pulls out of Ambrose to begin a new life in a new home, in a new church. They head for a hotel for the night in the town with the mall that is still forty minutes from their house. Michael takes the girls to the pool while Sadie remains in bed.

The next day is filled with a flurry of activity. The sky is clear with no signs of rain. How many times did it seem to rain on moving day for Sadie with her parents? Stephanie and Graham take Robin and Rachel and five of their little friends to the playground behind the church, while the parents work. Sadie stays with Brenda and Colleen as they unpack her kitchen so that Sadie can decide where she wants things. Michael works with Aidan and Steve to unpack. With so many helpers, the house quickly takes shape.

Rob Monroe stayed true to his word doing a beautiful job turning the basement room into their dining room. He put a fresh coat of a bright glossy white paint on the walls, laid down new Berber carpet, and hung etched glass, golden light fixtures. His wife had sewn and hung white drapery material with embossed roses over the small rectangular windows which are close to the ceiling. With the furniture in place, Sadie is satisfied.

Michael carries another load of packing paper and garbage to the church dumpster when an elderly lady approaches him, "Excuse me sir, are you the new pastor?"

Michael, sweaty and dirty, wearing old faded jean shorts and a t-shirt, wipes his brow with the back of his hand as he answers, "Yes, I'm Rev. Michael Donnelly."

She gives him a disgusted appraisal as she continues, "I'm Ernestine Smith, one of your new parishioners. May I ask who and why these people are coming in and out of the parsonage all day? And where did all of the children come from?"

"Well, Mrs. Smith," Michael explains, "Six of our friends came to help us unpack and move in. They brought their children to play with our kids."

"You mean that you brought people from your last church to help you? We could have helped you if you had asked," she sounds offended.

Surprised by her attitude, Michael explains further, "No, these aren't just people from my old church. They are personal friends." Michael points toward the playground and Graham, "See that man over there? He has been my closest friend since kindergarten. One of the women inside has been Sadie's best friend since high school."

"Well, some of the ladies and I prepared a lunch to help you out today, but we didn't expect so many people. We don't have near enough," Ernestine frets.

"I'm sorry. I didn't know about a lunch. Nobody told us about it," he apologizes.

"I don't think I ever remember a minister bringing so many people to help move in," she continues amazed and apparently, annoyed.

"You have to understand, Sadie is eight months pregnant and on bed rest. We needed special help for this move," Michael states attempting not to sound annoyed.

"You should have called us. We could have helped you," she persists.

"Well, we haven't even met anyone here yet," Michael attempts to reason, but apparently offends.

"Well, you and your family are welcomed to come and eat, but we don't have enough food for all of these people," she stipulates.

Michael is surprised that she thinks that he and Sadie would eat without their friends who are working so hard for them, "We appreciate the thought, but we only have one day to move in and we need to keep going. Don't worry about our lunch. The girls packed a picnic for us."

Ernestine turns leaving in a huff. When he tells Sadie about the encounter, Sadie only rolls her eyes. She has encountered this attitude in other churches. Although, Michael is the minister, Sadie still knows more about parsonage life than he does.

The living room is definitely crowded with their black leather couch, loveseat, recliner, and piano. Sadie shakes her head. This church provides the minister's family with a small storage room in the basement of the church for which only the minister has a key. Sadie suggests that the guys carry the coffee table to that storage room to create more space in the living room for them. Michael agrees.

At noon, the sounds of bells playing *Amazing Grace* can be heard playing loudly. The children run to Michael and everyone looks toward the church. The church owns a carillon with speakers in the steeple which can be heard for over a mile around. Every day at noon and again at six pm they play a variety of old hymns such as *Amazing Grace, How Great Thou Art, Rock of Ages, The Old Rugged Cross, Morning has Broken, Blessed Assurance, In the Garden,* and *What a Friend We Have in Jesus.* Sadie and Michael stand and listen to the strikingly beautiful music. This is something that they will enjoy.

The last thing their friends do, before they head home, is hang a painting above the couch. The day Michael moved into his first parsonage, Sadie had shown up with a present for a combination ordination and first appointment gift. The painting depicts Joseph working in his workshop while Jesus as a toddler plays in a doorway. As Joseph lifts a hammer, a shadow which looks like a cross is cast over Jesus. This signifies that Jesus had been raised in the shadow of the cross. The house feels more like their home now, sort of. They hug and kiss each other goodbye. Colleen, Brenda, and Sadie hang onto each other crying until the men finally pull them apart.

By eight o'clock the moving day finally ends. Their friends are headed home, the girls are tucked into bed, and Sadie has fallen sound asleep in the recliner. Michael steps outside for a breath of fresh air. The evening is warm, still, and pleasant.

Michael strolls with his hands in his back pockets across the parking lot and into the large recreational field. He learned today that the church has built it up over a period of years. Leaning his back on the pole of a basketball hoop, Michael silently prays, "Well Lord, here we are. I picked up my family and moved here with Sadie eight months pregnant and all. The Bishop believes that You want me here. I believe that You sent me to Ambrose to meet Sadie and because the church was in financial crisis and I have a business degree. Well, I married Sadie and the church is financially healthy, so I suppose it was time for me to move on.

"So, what do You want me to do out here in Shermanfield? Any special reason You want me here or are You just messing with Sadie for the fun of it?"

The sound of a chain clanking on a pole interrupts his meditation. Scanning the area, he notices someone sitting down on a swing. Curious, he walks toward the playground. There he discovers a young teenage girl.

The girl is a sight. Her light brown hair is streaked with green and her long bangs cover half her face completely hiding one of her eyes. The eye that can be seen is surrounded with a thick line of black eyeliner and she wears blood red lipstick. Her faded jeans sport large holes in the knees and her thin top has spaghetti straps allowing her bra straps to show.

The teen notices him, "Hey, you're the new preacher dude ain't ya?"

"Yep."

"You don't look much like a preacher."

Walking closer and leaning on the pole of the swing set, he inquires, "Really? What do ministers look like?"

"The last one was short, pudgy, and almost bald with grey hair and glasses and was boring as hell," she describes.

Michael laughs, "Well, we all come in different shapes and sizes."

"So, what are you going to do? Try to save our souls or something?"

"Something like that," he smirks.

She stands, "I guess I'll see you Sunday morning."

"You attend church?"

"Don't sound so surprised. What'd ya think that I'm out in some barn kneeling by a pentagram? "she acts offended.

Michael laughs, "Sorry, so, what's your name?"

"Angel Heckathorn."

"Seriously?"

"Oh my god, are you making fun of my name now? What kind of minister are you?"

"Is that really your name?"

"Yes, it is," Angel insists.

"If you say so," Michael concedes.

"So what's your fantastically wonderful name?"

"Rev. Donnelly."

"I saw your wife today. She's as big as house."

"She's pregnant," he informs her.

"Well I didn't think she was smuggling a watermelon. I've gotta go. See ya later Rev. Dudley."

"Donnelly," he corrects.

"Whatever," Angel walks away waving her hand over her head.

Chapter 4

The first Sunday at Grace Church is another beautiful summer day. Sadie dresses in a light blue maternity skirt with a short sleeve white blouse with large pastel buttons. The baby is pressing up under her ribcage causing her to be short of breath and uncomfortable.

The first service for a new minister usually attracts a large attendance because everyone is curious about the new pastor and Shermanfield is no exception. The church is filled to capacity with a buzz of excitement in the air. Sadie finds the sanctuary beautiful. The pews are white with polished wooden trim and red seat cushions. She can't stop looking at an ornate pipe organ that a very wealthy man had reportedly donated to the church. The elegantly sculpted pulpit has several steps to climb up into it. The large windows are plain glass but are blocked off into smaller squares by thin wooden trim. The sanctuary has a Tom Sawyer look to it, complete with a large balcony in the back.

There are large beautiful paintings of Jesus hanging around the sanctuary like Jesus in the Garden of Gethsemane, Jesus the Good Shepherd, The Road to Damascus, and The Head of Christ. Sadie is also impressed with the shiny black grand piano. The ceiling boasts four large, golden chandeliers with flame shaped light bulbs.

Sadie is actually becoming excited about playing the beautiful organ and grand piano and about working closely with Michael. Although the choir disbanded for the summer, they came together for the Donnelly's first service. The fifteen members in the choir sing beautifully.

Robin and Rachel miss their friends especially Colleen's children, Jordan and Autumn who are the same ages. Since Colleen had been their babysitter and their parents are such close friends, they were raised together and miss them terribly. They are also close to Brenda's boys, Tyler and Dylan, and Stephanie's son, Korey. Now, sitting here in this new church without any of their friends makes the girls feel miserable. They fuss and are cranky. Sadie struggles with the girls especially since she is under strict orders not to lift them.

When Michael introduces his family from the pulpit, the girls are crying and Rachel begs Mommy to go home calling out that she hates it here. The congregation has a poor first impression of their sweet girls as uncontrollable brats. During the sermon, Sadie attempts to quiet the girls by giving them a baggy full of Cheerios. At first it seems to be working until the girls begin to fight over the bag. Each taking a firm grip, they lean back pulling the baggy in a tug of war until the bag bursts open sending Cheerios flying in every direction. Michael looks up just in time to see the Cheerios raining over his daughters' heads. Distracted for a moment, he has difficulty finding his place. Some people are annoyed while others laugh. He notices Angel laughing and sitting with an older woman.

Michael attempts to ignore his family and focus on his sermon. Rachel manages to climb down off the pew dropping to the floor. Sadie's large belly prohibits her from bending over enough to reach her. Rachel crawls under the pew away from her Mommy. Sadie is embarrassed and frustrated as their three year old daughter stands and runs to the front of the church crying, "Daddy, Daddy…"

Michael stops preaching and climbs down out of the pulpit. He reaches out for his daughter as she runs to him scooping her up.

"Daddy, wanna go home now?" Rachel pleads pitifully.

"Not yet darling," Michael looks at Sadie who mouths the word 'sorry'. Michael looks back at the pouting Rachel, "Do you want to stay with Daddy?"

Rachel nods with her bottom lip sticking out. He pats her on the back. Michael climbs back up into the pulpit. Rachel curls up on Michael's shoulder as he returns to his sermon. Michael's only comment to the congregation about his daughters' behavior is, "Our girls need a little time to adjust to their new home, but they are actually very sweet and well behaved little girls."

While Michael finishes the service holding Rachel, Robin rests her head on her Mommy's arm. Finally the service ends and the Donnellys are welcomed by a reception for the new pastor and his family. They serve a surprisingly good dinner. The women's group provided the food and the guests enjoyed soups and sandwiches, pastries, chips, veggies and dip, and a large cake with a cross made out of flowers.

Ernestine Smith makes rude comments that ministers who can't control their own children shouldn't be able to tell a congregation how to live. Heat from anger flashes in Michael's face, but he fights not to allow his emotions to show. Instead, he points out that they have only been here for four days and that this is a huge change for such young children. She walks away with her nose in the air.

Ted Lawrence also seems concerned about how poorly he feels the service went this morning. Michael never had such a poor response to one of his services in Ambrose, not even the morning he had preached with a black eye and a fat lip from a fist fight with Graham at his bachelor party.

Despite all the negativity, many people are friendly and comforting. They have children too and they assure him that his girls are precious. Many thought it was sweet that he preached with his daughter curled up on his shoulder.

An older woman approaches Michael with Angel in tow, "Good morning Reverend. I'm so glad to meet you. You are so sweet with your daughters. I loved that you preached while holding her. Your poor wife looks as if she is ready to pop. My name is Garnet Heckathorn and this is my granddaughter, Angel. We live across the street from you. We're neighbors."

"How nice to meet you. I met Angel Tuesday evening," he informs her as he looks at Angel who is dressed in low ride jeans and a tight blouse. Her brown and green hair still conceals one of her eyes.

"I told you my name is Angel Heckathorn," she snorts.

Michael smiles at her.

Sadie sits with Liza Piazza whom she met at the interview. Liza picks up Rachel and plays with her. Rachel notices others have cake. Sadie excuses herself to go get a piece for her. People stop to greet Sadie along the way, making the walk to the cake table and back longer than she anticipated. She is exhausted, but attempts to look perky.

When Sadie finally returns with the cake, Rachel is gone. Liza simply states that Rachel wanted down. Sadie sets the cake on the table and looks around. Robin sits with some other children eating cake. Sadie begins to search for Rachel scanning the room and looking under tables.

31

Michael is in midsentence with Rob Monroe when he notices Sadie peering under tables. He excuses himself and hurries to Sadie who nervously informs him that she can't find Rachel. Rob inquires if something is wrong.

On hearing the problem, Rob attracts everyone's attention, "Excuse me, has anyone seen Rev. Donnelly's youngest daughter, Rachel?" No one answers. Being a police officer, he quickly takes charge, "Please look around for her. Hey boys," he calls to three teenagers including his son, Cole, "Go outside and take a run around the church to make sure she didn't get out. Check the playground and the yard by the parsonage," He turns back to Michael, "Come on Reverend. We'll search the building. She couldn't have gone far. Sadie, you just sit here and wait. We'll find her."

Sadie nervously sits. She is also a little annoyed that Liza is not apologetic for offering to hold her daughter and then losing her. Then she didn't even offer to look. Rob and Michael run off to search. In the hall, Ernestine stops the two men, "You have no control over your daughters at all, do you?"

Michael does not bother to hide his anger this time simply barking, "Excuse me."

As Rob and Michael part ways, Rob comforts, "We'll find her and ignore Ernestine. She isn't nice to anyone."

Michael and Rob run up and down the hall with the Sunday school rooms are located, looking under tables and in any space that she might crawl into. They call her name over and over. Michael enters the back of the sanctuary and begins to search the pews.

He calls out, "Rachel, baby, come to Daddy."

A head pops out from behind the pulpit. It is Angel. She nods toward the ornate lectern. Michael rushes to Angel finding Rachel curled up inside the pulpit.

Michael sits on the steps, "Hey baby, what are you doing?"

"I hate it here. I wanna go home," she whines.

"I know cupcake. You will get use to it here. You just have to give it a chance," he promises.

"I wanna play with Jordan and Autumn and Tyler and Dylan, and Korey," she lists her friends.

"We will still visit them and you will make new friends here too," he coaxes.

"No new friends," she cries.

Angel agrees with her, "I know how you feel kid. I hate it here too."

Michael glances up at Angel, "Thanks for finding her." He turns back to Rachel, "Listen to me, whatever is wrong, don't you ever hide from Mommy and Daddy again. You scared us to death. Come on baby, Mommy needs to see you."

Michael holds out his arms, but Rachel whines, "I in twouble?"

"No. I understand, but don't you ever runaway and hide from me," he repeats.

"I sorry," she crawls out reaching for him.

Angel watches Michael hug and kiss his little girl. He seems like such a good dad. She longs with all of her heart that she had a good parent and wishes she had someone to love her. She wishes that she knew who her father is.

Michael hurries to Sadie to relieve her worries. He lets everyone know that they found Rachel and then he collects his family to head to their new home. Once outside, Michael waves to Rob. Michael reports what happened and thanks him for his help.

Michael has a good feeling about Rob, a tall man with a buzz cut and a muscular build of a weightlifter. He did a beautiful job on the dining room. Rob's wife, Jonel, has shoulder length blond hair and a full figure. Their daughter, Cassie, is only one year older than Robin. They also have two teenagers, a boy and a girl. Michael feels hopeful that his family may find new friendship with the Monroe's and their teenagers as possible babysitters.

Wednesday morning, Michael works in his new office. His new secretary, Grace Hudson, is nice but seems to be a bit of a gossip and busybody. She is in her sixties with salt and pepper short hair and is rather plump. She offers to be available over the next three weeks to babysit the girls when Sadie goes into labor.

Garnet Heckathorn stops by the office to meet with Michael, "Excuse me, Reverend. Do you have a minute for me?"

Michael stands welcoming her in. His new office is much bigger and nicer than his last office. His desk is beautiful and he has a full computer desk. The wall is covered with built in bookshelves. The room is large enough for a conference table with chairs and can be used for smaller meetings.

Garnet sits in a chair and Michael sits in the chair beside her instead of sitting behind his desk. He finds sitting closer to his parishioners brings about easier conversations.

Garnet shakes her head, "I'm sorry Pastor, but I have some bad news. I'm your Sunday School Superintendent, but I need to resign from the position. I have been looking for a replacement for a month, but no one is interested. Liza said that your wife held the position in your last church."

"I see. Well, Sadie needs time to have her baby and take care of things. I'll take care of the duties until we find someone to replace you or until Sadie feels ready to take over the position if she wishes. May I ask why you are stepping down?"

"I have lung cancer," she confides.

Michael takes her hand, "I'm so sorry to hear that."

"Oh Reverend, I don't know what I'm going to do," her chin trembles.

"Is there anything I can do to help?" he offers.

"I don't know. I have been trying to raise my granddaughter, but I'm too old. Now I'm too old and too sick. I did a terrible job with my own daughter and now I'm failing Angel."

"I think you are being too hard on yourself," Michael soothes.

"No, I'm not. My daughter partied hard in high school, drugs, sex, and rock-n-roll. She fell in with the wrong crowd and turned wild. I had Tara when I was forty. I guess I spent too much time at work. I gave her way too much freedom. Angel was born when Tara was only sixteen. Now Angel is falling in with the wrong crowd. She is constantly in trouble at school and she has a scary boyfriend.

"I may have to eventually move into a nursing home to be cared for, but what would happen to Angel then? She would end up in foster care. Have you seen her? Who would want to take her in? She could end up in some group home. She was the sweetest little girl. After my husband died, things became so tough on us. I keep praying for a miracle," Garnet shares.

"Where is Tara now?" he asks.

"She is serving time for dealing drugs in prison," Garnet admits staring into her lap.

"Where's Angel's father?"

"Oh Reverend, I'm so embarrassed to tell you, but we don't know who the father is," she continues to stare into her lap.

"Don't be embarrassed. You can tell me," Michael persuades.

"One night at some party, apparently my daughter was stoned out of her mind and a line of boys formed at a bedroom door. She doesn't even know how many boys she was with that night let alone who. I will give Tara credit for one thing. It was so hard on her, but she never took any drugs while she was pregnant. She may be a mess, but she has always loved her baby.

"Angel doesn't take drugs, but she drinks and I bet she is sleeping with her boyfriend even though she denies it."

"How old is Angel?"

"Fifteen," Garnet shakes her head. "Please pray for us, because I have no idea what I am doing. I'm sixty-nine, tired and sick, but I love her."

Michael hugs her. He prays with her for her health, for guidance, and for Angel. Garnet again prays for a miracle, not for her own health, but for her granddaughter to return to being the sweet little girl that she had once been.

The rest of the day, Michael cannot seem to get Angel off his mind. That evening, he tells Sadie everything he knows about the girl. Although he probably shouldn't because of confidentiality, he often shares information with Sadie. She never breeches his confidential information and it helps him to talk things over with her. She is not only the love of his life, but she is his partner in ministry. He teases Sadie that it seems that God sent them to Shermanfield, not for his ministry, but because they need her to be the organist and the Superintendent of Sunday School.

The next afternoon, Michael, wearing shorts and a t-shirt, heads out for a jog. He enjoys running in the cemetery like Sadie had suggested. He notices that across the street Angel and a girlfriend are sitting on the stoop smoking cigarettes. He jogs across the street and walks up to the two girls.

"Good morning ladies. Is your grandmother at home?" he is surprised that they do not even try to hide or are embarrassed by the fact that they are smoking.

"Good morning Reverend. Grams's at a doctor's appointment. She won't be back for awhile," Angel greets him.

Michael reaches over confiscating her cigarette.

"Hey," Angel complains.

Ignoring her, he turns to her friend, "And what's your name?"

"Becky," she replies. Becky is a skinny girl with straggly blond hair and appears to be the kind of girl whose idea of fun is looking for trouble.

"Hello Becky. I'm Reverend Donnelly," he introduces himself as he confiscates her cigarette as well.

"What the hell?" she admonishes.

"I believe you two are too young to smoke," he declares as he drops the cigarettes on the ground rubbing them out with the ball of his foot.

"What's it to you? I thought you were just supposed to worry about my soul," Angel sasses.

"Well, I believe I'll start with your lungs. Doesn't your grandma's cancer mean anything to you?"

Angel only rolls her eyes, or at least the eye he can see, and crosses her arms over her chest huffing. Michael reaches over brushing the hair out of her face for a moment and then allows it to drop back into her face.

"What are you doing?" she asks annoyed.

"Looking to see if you have another eye. I was just curious," he explains.

"This is messed up. You have some nerve coming over here uninvited and pestering us. Who do you think you are anyway?" she rebukes.

"Your Pastor," he simply states.

"Well, you can't stop us. We'll just light up another one," Angel states smugly as she holds up her pack.

"Thanks," Michael snatches the entire pack, "I'll see you later."

As he begins to jog away, Angel calls after him, "Hey, you owe me the money for those!"

Turning and jogging backwards, he dares, "Try to get it from me."

"Asshole!" she yells after him, but he just waves.

That night, Michael locks up the church after a late meeting. A storm hangs in the air threatening to hit at any moment. The wind pushes Michael along as he heads home. The storm clouds block out the moon and stars creating a stark blackness to the night. Michael notices that the pavilion lights are on and what looks like a group of four or five teenagers are messing around. Worrying about vandalism, Michael heads out to the pavilion to shoo the kids away.

Soon, he hears rap music playing and the kids appear to be smoking. The teens do not notice his presence between the darkness and the loud music. As he approaches, he recognizes Becky, Angel's friend. He stops to watch and appraise the situation not seeing Angel at first.

A tall, skinny boy with shoulder length, black, greasy hair is kneeling on a picnic table. Michael hears him sneer, "Hey, this would be a good position for a blow job, don't you think? How about I take off my pants and you do me right here and now?"

"Get off me!" Michael recognizes Angel's voice. Stepping closer he sees Angel pinned on her back with the boy straddling her face.

Michael enters the pavilion startling them, "How romantic; get off of her."

The boy jumps down and faces Michael, "Who the hell are you?"

Michael steps forward staring the teen in the eye, "I'm Rev. Donnelly, the pastor of this church and this is church property. Go home."

"Make me," he dares holding out his hands and curling his fingers as if to dare Michael to a fight.

Angel steps in between them, pushing on the boy, "Knock it off, David."

"It's late. I think you girls should come with me," Michael jesters for them not wanting to leave Angel and Becky with these three young men.

"I don't think so," David spits.

"I'm not leaving these young ladies out here with you," Michael states firmly.

"Ladies? Ha! Who are you kidding?" David sneers.

"It's okay David. It's past my curfew anyway. Grams will be mad if I don't go home soon. I'll see you tomorrow. Come on Beck," Angel walks to Michael with the wind whipping her hair in all directions.

Michael goes to the electric box shutting off the lights, "Go home" he orders again leaving the three boys seething.

As he walks the girls to Angel's house, he questions her, "So, who's the jerk."

"He's not a jerk. He's my boyfriend," she defends him.

As they pass under a spotlight shining from the side of the church, Michael stops and takes hold of Angel by both of her arms forcing her to face him, "Listen to me. That boy is going to hurt you."

"God, take a chill pill man. You only met him one time for a minute. You don't know anything about him. He loves me," she defends her boyfriend.

Michael holds onto her, "He doesn't love you. He owns you. You are his possession. Wanting a blowjob in front of two other guys while pinned uncomfortably to a table is not exactly a loving gesture."

"Relax, god, he was just joking," she protests.

"It wasn't funny," Michael persists.

"This is none of your damn business! First you take my cigarettes and now you're judging my boyfriend! Seriously, how is any of this any of your business?! Leave me alone or I'll call the police for harassment," she threatens.

"I'm just trying to take care of a member of my flock," he poses.

"Fine, I'm not coming to church anymore. I quit! Now leave me alone! Member of your flock, well flock you," Angel jerks free from him and runs home with Becky following her. As Michael turns to head home, he sees David and his friends leaning on a car in the parking lot with the headlights on. David aims his finger at Michael as if it is a gun pretending to shoot which makes Michael nervous remembering Sadie being shot.

As Michael hurries home with thunder rumbling in the distance, he prays silently that God will guide him on how exactly to handle this without endangering Angel and his family. David is trouble, serious trouble. He can feel the evil dripping off the boy. He can't walk away from Angel and he can't endanger his family. He prays for help.

Michael finds Sadie asleep in the recliner. She finds it more comfortable to sleep sitting up at this point. He kisses her and lies on the couch to be near her. Lightning flashes through the windows as a torrential rain pounds at the little house. Michael remembers their wedding day when a thunderstorm had raged during their ceremony. Sadie had smiled and teased that Michael is natural born preacher and that she was not surprised that He had showed up for their wedding. Now, every storm reminds him of their wedding day.

Soon the girls come running down the stairs scared of the storm. With no attic, the girls' ceiling is just under the roof causing the storm to loudly rage on top of their heads. Michael takes them into his bedroom allowing them to sleep with him. He lies awake listening to the storm, looking at his precious little daughters. His mind keeps wandering back to Angel. He can't explain why, but he can't seem to get her off of his mind.

Just as he begins to drift off, the storm blows directly overhead. The thunder claps loudly just seconds following bright flashes of lightening. The wind punishes the little house. Robin sits up terrified and Michael holds her tightly promising that it will pass soon. Suddenly the room lights up with another brilliant flash just as another clap of thunder booms followed by out of tune organ music.

"Daddy, do you hear spooky music?" Robin quivers.

Michael jumps up, "The lightening must have hit the carillon. I have to go check on the damage."

Scared of being left alone, the girls follow their daddy into the living room. The storm had awakened Sadie who moves to the couch to sit with the girls while Michael runs across the parking lot to make sure that the church didn't catch fire. Michael grabs an umbrella and braves the pounding rain. However, with the rain blowing sideways, it is little help as he quickly becomes drenched. Half way across the slippery parking lot, the wind blows his umbrella inside out. Michael struggles to turn it right and then puts it down.

The empty church at night in the storm seems spooky even to Michael as he makes his way to the steeple. He uses his umbrella to hook and pull down a thin ladder. He climbs into the steeple and looks around finding nothing smoking, but unplugs things to be safe and so out of tune music doesn't play again tomorrow at noon.

As Michael climbs back down, he is startled to bump into another man, the custodian.

"Oh, Ed, you startled me."

Ed chuckles, "Sorry about that preacher. I woke up and figured either I'm in a slasher movie or the church was hit by lightening."

The men talk for a moment before heading back out. Once outside, the storm has calmed leaving a steady gentle rain. Michael circles the church once to be safe. As he rounds the corner, he spots Angel sitting on her stoop watching the rain and he crosses the street to her. Angel wears a Pittsburg Steelers football jersey nightshirt.

"Hi Reverend, don't you know better than to go toward the eerie music? Have you never gone to see a good movie?" Angel teases.

Michael laughs, "So are you done being angry with me?"

"Are you going to give me my cigarettes back and stop bugging me about my boyfriend?" she challenges.

"Probably not," Michael smirks.

Angel stands and saunters into the house, "Goodnight Reverend."

Michael returns to his house where his family laughs at him for being drenched. He grabs a change of clothes and goes into the bathroom to dry off. Then he kisses Sadie goodnight leaving her in the living room on the recliner and returns to his room to discover his daughters waiting for him still wanting to sleep with Daddy. He sighs and rearranges the girls so that he can manage to crawl into his bed.

Chapter 5

Friday morning, Michael wakes and finds Sadie in the kitchen writing out a detailed list, "Darling, can you go to the grocery store before you go into the office? We need so much. I wrote out everything I need with the brands and could you please take the girls with you?"

"Why do you want me to take the girls? I could go so much faster without them," Michael complains.

"I can't lift Rachel and I am so tired and achy. I feel just awful today. Please, take the girls with you," she pleads. "I'd have you take them to the office with you too, if I thought I could."

"Okay sweetheart," Michael collects the girls and begins the twenty minute drive to the grocery store. He thinks about his sermon as he drives. Michael wants to make sure that his second service in his new church goes much better than his first. He thinks about sermons that went well at his last church that he can revamp to use. At this point in his career, he has never reused a sermon, but he figures that no one in this church has heard any of his previous sermons. Also, he is helping out more at home with the kids and he is on his own to finish unpacking and hanging the pictures where Sadie directs him. He even attempts to make suppers, and cooking has never come easy to him.

Michael plans to invite Colleen and Aidan to the service so that they can help with the girls if Sadie needs help. The girls will be happy to be with Jordan and Autumn and hopefully will behave. He needs this Sunday to go better.

At the store, Rachel doesn't want to sit in the cart, but Michael doesn't want to chase her all over the store. She screams as he straps her into the cart's seat. He talks calmly to her trying to soothe her. Finally, he speaks firmly with her to knock it off. She sits whimpering as he begins shopping while keeping an eye on Robin. Robin wants to be a good helper which slows the whole process down, but he allows her to help anyway.

Both girls want to buy extras and goodies, but Michael needs to stick to their budget now that they are without Sadie's income. He hates shopping especially for groceries. Rachel keeps swinging her legs, so he keeps getting kicked.

He wonders about the new baby. He and Sadie decided to wait, so he still does not know if they are having another girl or if it is a boy. Part of him hopes for a boy, but he loves his girls and knows that he will be happy with a third daughter.

His mind wanders back to Rachel's birth. On a Sunday morning, two weeks before her due date, Sadie sat in the third pew with their friends, Aidan, Colleen, Steve, and Brenda along with their babies. Aidan held two year old Robin for Sadie. Before the sermon, the congregation stood to sing the preparation hymn. As Sadie stood, her water broke. Grabbing Colleen's arm, she points out what has happened.

Aidan and Colleen hand the babies to Brenda and Steve. Colleen took hold of Sadie's arm and headed out of church. Aidan walked right up front to Michael who had already come out from behind the pulpit and informed Michael about Sadie's water. As Aidan hurried to help Sadie to the car, Michael requested that the organist, Donna, stop the hymn.

Michael announced, "I'm sorry, but I need to leave. Sadie is in labor. Please finish the hymn. Eloise, please finish the parts of the service that you can and we will skip the sermon this week and you will all just get out early today. I'm sorry for any inconvenience. Oh, and Don, there is a bit of a mess on the floor by the third pew."

Don, the custodian, immediately heads out of the sanctuary to fetch the needed supplies as the rest of the congregation laughs. Eloise heads to the front as Michael runs to take his robe off. As Michael removes his robe he overhears Eloise, "Please join me in a prayer for Sadie and her baby as she faces labor."

By the time Michael reaches the car, Aidan already has it running. As Michael climbs in the back with Sadie, Colleen comes running from the house with Sadie's pre-packed bag. Six hours later, Rachel was born.

Waking from his reverie, Michael finishes in the produce section and heads down the first aisle when he hears his name being paged to the customer service. When he arrives at the desk a clerk hands him a phone.

"Oh darling, you forgot the cell phone," Sadie informs him.

"I'm sorry dear. What do you need?"

"My water broke fifteen minutes ago," she informs him calmly.

"What?"

"Don't worry; the contractions aren't that bad yet. I was at the hospital with Robin for over twenty-four hours and six hours with Rachel. We have time, but please come home. I'll call Grace and the doctor," she comforts.

Michael leaves the cart with the clerk and rushes the girls to the car facing a twenty minute drive home and a forty minute drive to the hospital. This part of Sadie's complaints about living out in the country is true. She sounded so calm while his heart is racing.

Five minutes after talking to Michael, the contractions hit Sadie like a baseball bat. She had never experienced contractions like this having always been in the hospital with an epidural. For Robin, a nurse had to break her water with what looked like a crochet needle and she had been put on an epidural again for Rachel before the contractions reached their full strength.

Trying to remain calm, she sits on the edge of the couch attempting the breathing techniques that TV characters are always using, but the pain is overwhelming. She is alone and scared. Sadie can't stop herself as she begins screaming and yelling.

Sadie called Grace who is at the mall and it will take her longer to get here than Michael. She doesn't know who else to call and she doesn't think she can wait. Someone knocks on the front door, but it can't possibly be Grace.

Using a guttural tone, Sadie yells, "Who is it?"

The door opens and Angel runs into the living room, "Are you alright? I can hear you screaming from across the street," Angel informs her.

"I'm fine," Sadie breathes heavily. "I'm in labor and I'm waiting for my husband to come back home."

Despite her best efforts, Sadie begins yelling again. Scared, Angel offers, "Do you want me to call an ambulance?"

As the contraction subsides, Sadie checks the clock, "No, Michael should be here in ten minutes. I'll be fine."

"Can I get you anything, a glass of water maybe?" the teen tries to help.

"No, no, I'm fine," Sadie assures her.

Awkwardly Angel sits on the recliner, "Well, I'm going to, like, stay with you until the Reverend gets here, okay?"

"Thank you dear. I'm sorry about all of the screaming," Sadie apologizes as a wave of pain takes her again. Angel begins timing the contractions which are only two minutes apart.

Michael races into the house with the children hearing Sadie yelling at the top of her lungs surprised to find Angel sitting on the couch holding her hand.

"What's wrong?" Michael asks having never seen Sadie like this.

"She's in labor, duh," Angel answers.

"What are you doing here?" Michael asks.

"I could hear her screaming from across the street. You better take her and go," Angel pushes.

Looking around, he asks, "Where's Grace?"

Angel answers, "She was at the mall. She won't be here for at least twenty more minutes. You better not wait. I'll stay until she comes."

Michael doesn't know what to do. He looks down at his sweet little girls, then at Sadie who fights not to yell out in front of her daughters, and then at Angel in her short shorts and tank top with only one eye returning his gaze. Desperate, he decides to leave the girls with Angel. After all, it would only be for twenty minutes. He runs for his cell phone.

He pulls Sadie to her feet, but Sadie cannot walk. She pants to give her a minute for the contractions to subside. They all stand simply waiting. "Now," she snaps and shuffles out of the house. Michael pulls out and begins his forty minute trek to a hospital with Sadie yelling and trying to lift herself off the seat. He speaks soothingly to her and encourages breathing.

The contractions are on top of each other now and the pain is searing. Twenty-five minutes into the drive, Sadie feels a burning ring of fire and declares, "Oh God, Michael, I think the baby is crowning!"

"I'm going as fast as I can," he promises.

"We're not going to make it! The baby's coming!" Sadie declares.

They are on a state route with fields and houses few and far between. He slows and pulls into a driveway of a farm house that sets far back off the road. Michael parks near the road. Jumping out of the car, he runs to the passenger's side. Opening the backdoor, he unbuckles and pulls out Rachel's car seat. Next, he pulls Sadie out of the front seat and helps her lie down in the back. She props herself up on her elbows screaming. Michael calls 911 on his cell phone.

"Help me; my wife is having a baby in a car. We are heading north on State Route 60 several miles north of route 137." Michael runs to the mailbox on the street giving her the address of the house that owns this driveway. The dispatcher calls for an ambulance. "I'm going to set the phone down now and check on my wife. I'll be right back."

Michael pulls off Sadie's shorts and underpants to have a look. Sadie was right. He can see the top of the head. Sadie is wailing at the top of her lungs. Michael looks through the car realizing that they don't have anything to use for a blanket. They hadn't even remembered to bring Sadie's suitcase. Suddenly, Sadie becomes quiet. Clenching her jaws, she pushes. Michael's heart pounds loudly in his chest. The only prayer he can muster is, "Oh God, help us!"

Quickly, Michael pulls off his t-shirt and lays it on the car seat between her legs. He reaches out to catch the baby. Sadie stops pushing and begs him to help her sit up. Taking her hands, he pulls her up. She wraps her arms around her legs and pushes. The baby is coming out. Michael is scared of dropping it. He is relieved that it is a hot July day so the baby isn't too cold when he or she arrives. He tries to help the baby get the shoulders free. Then the baby slips out into his arms. He wraps the tiny infant up in his t-shirt the best he can. Pulling out his handkerchief from his back pocket, he cleans the baby's face, eyes, mouth, and nose.

Sadie drops back, shaking and trembling. Michael lays the baby on her tummy deciding not to try to cut the umbilical cord.

"It's a boy," Michael beams rubbing the baby's back.

Michael picks up the cell phone. The operator is still on the line and he recounts what just happened. She assures him that the ambulance is on the way. He waits with Sadie who is uncomfortable in the backseat.

Michael hears the siren. With a bare chest, he walks to the end of the driveway waving his arms. The paramedics help Sadie onto a stretcher and cut the umbilical cord. Wrapping the baby in a real blanket, the man, laughing, hands Michael his gooey shirt. Then a paramedic hands him a scrub top.

Michael follows the ambulance to the hospital where he sits next to Sadie's bed while she nurses the infant for the first time.

"So, what are we going to call him?" Sadie coos. They have a list, but never agreed on anything except that if it were a girl, Kelly.

"I still want to name him Peter. What's your top choice?" Michael requests.

"Peter? Are you naming our baby for your favorite disciple?" she questions, but Michael only smiles at her. "You are such a minister. Okay, Peter it is, Peter James."

"I'm so sorry that moving out here caused you to be so far from a hospital. I'm so sorry that I forgot my cell phone, or I would have been back in five minutes instead almost an hour," he apologizes.

"I'm not. We will always remember that Daddy delivered our son," she beams at her husband. "I love you and I will live with you anywhere."

After they share a kiss, Michael and Sadie call family and friends with the good news and sharing their story of the crazy delivery. Their friends simply comment that it is always drama with these two and life is boring without them around. He calls home to talk to the girls and is surprised when Angel answers.

"Hello Angel. Didn't Grace ever come?"

"Sure, she's here. Do you want to talk to her? I hope you don't mind. I've been playing with the girls and just didn't leave."

"That's okay," he assures her.

"So, what happened?"

"It's a boy. Would you believe that we didn't make it to the hospital and I ended up delivering the baby in the backseat of my car in someone's driveway?"

"Shut up, no way," she laughs.

Michael speaks with Grace and then to each of the girls announcing that they have a brother. Grace informs Michael that when she arrived Angel and the girls had brought kitchen chairs into the living room and stretched blankets and afghans all over creating 'caves' and they had stuffed animals all over. Michael smiles picturing Angel playing with the girls like that. He shares the image with Sadie and then holds Peter while Sadie drifts off for a well earned nap. Michael cherishes the quiet moment with the newest member of his family, a son, his son and silently offers prayers of thanks that everyone is safe and healthy.

Chapter 6

Michael needs to bring the baby home on Sunday, but first he has to preach a sermon that he never spent any time preparing. He stays up late on Saturday night at his computer pulling up and reviewing notes on an old sermon that he preached during the last month in Ambrose.

Sunday morning, Angel and Garnet head across the street to church and stop when they notice the church sign. Michael had taken down the letters and numbers which lists the Sunday school and service times replacing it with "IT'S A BOY!" Laughing, Angel and Grams continue to church.

Colleen and Aidan come Saturday and Sunday to help with the girls while Sadie is in the hospital and to meet the new arrival. Robin and Rachel are thrilled to be with their friends and behave perfectly during church sitting between Aidan and Colleen. Michael also notices Angel sitting with Garnet. She didn't quit his church after all.

The next week is busy between nursing the baby every two to three hours and all of their friends and family coming to visit and meet Peter, whose sisters adore him. Plus, Michael and Rob, signed up Robin and Rob's daughter, Cassie, for swimming lessons to which they will car pool.

The Friday after the baby's birth, Michael's brother, Sean, and his partner, Jeremy, arrive to meet their new nephew. The girls love their uncles and run to them jumping up and down calling, "Uncle Sean, Uncle Jeremy!"

Of course Uncle Sean and Uncle Jeremy are carrying big, colorful gift bags. There is a present for the baby, a present for each girl, and a spa bag with goodies just for Sadie. The girls squeal as they excitedly open their gifts. They jump up onto their uncles' laps for hugs and kisses as their uncles beam with joy.

Next, Sadie hands Peter to Sean. He gazes lovingly, longingly, down at the tiny infant. Michael watches his brother's expression carefully noticing that there is something else going on than simply meeting his new nephew. Sean holds and cuddles Peter as if unaware that anyone else is in the room. Jeremy finally insists on having a turn bringing Sean out of his trance like state. Jeremy, too, seems moved by the baby as he gently rocks and coos. He excitedly announces that Peter is holding his finger.

The girls take their new toys up to their bedroom at their father's request. Michael suggests that Sadie takes advantage of these men wanting to hold and fuss over Peter for her to take a nap. Peter won't need to nurse for over an hour. Tiredly, Sadie agrees and excuses herself.

Michael watches his brother and Jeremy sitting close together on the couch completely captivated with his son. Michael regrets that years ago, when Sean had come out to his family about his homosexuality, he had not taken it well. Sean had been in college and Michael was already in seminary.

Michael and Sean got along well while growing up, but were not that close. Michael had been all about sports, a complete athlete. He played tennis, golf, billiards, ran track, rode horses, enjoyed swim team, and diving, and loved skiing. Even as a young child, Michael had played little league and soccer. Sean, on the other hand, loved to draw, sing in choirs, played in the school band, and read. Sean could always be found off by himself reading or sketching. The only things the brothers enjoyed doing together was riding horses and playing pool.

Shortly after coming out to his family, Michael and Sean had an argument because Sean could tell that Michael had become uncomfortable with his own brother. During the unpleasant exchange, Michael pointed out that in the Bible, Corinthians states that homosexuality is a sin as well as several places in the Old Testament. This hurt Sean deeply. His parents were angry with Sean and now his brother was against him too. The only one in his family who accepted him had been their older sister, Carol, who has always been the glue that held their family together in troubled times.

Carol had convinced Sean not to give up on his family. She told him to come to all the family events, even though it was uncomfortable, in hopes that one day he would again find the acceptance that he so longed for. Eventually, his parents did accept his presence, but he was not permitted to bring his boyfriend, Jeremy to their home. Sean had been tempted to

THE REVEREND & ANGEL

walk away from his family and simply tell them to go to hell, but both Carol and Jeremy encouraged him to be patient and his family would come around. Several years passed, and Sean waited patiently, hopefully.

It seemed the family was being torn apart. His parents were furious that Michael had refused to go to Harvard Law School and went to a seminary. His wealthy parents did not want Michael to live the simple life of a minister and to live on a minister's salary. There was tension between the parents and both of their sons, as well as, tension between the brothers. Carol suffered from years of trying desperately to hold the family together.

Then one year, Michael met Sadie. When Sadie learned that Sean is gay and that Michael didn't approve, she immediately took Sean's side in the matter and quickly helped bring the brothers back together. Thanks to her, Michael soon accepted his brother and his partner.

Michael started inviting Sean and Jeremy to events at his home which forced his parents to come face to face with the fact that this wasn't going away. Jeremy was indeed their son's partner. In a heated argument with his mother, Michael insisted that Sean should be allowed to bring Jeremy to Michael and Sadie's wedding and the bachelor party. In the end, Jeremy actually ended up in the wedding party. Thanks to Carol and Sadie's efforts, Sean's dream had come true as his family finally accepted him for who he is and that they accepted Jeremy into their family.

Now, Michael watches his brother and Jeremy soak up every moment that they are spending with Peter with almost a longing. The two men had always been very good with his daughters who adored their uncles. Sadie and Michael trust and feel completely comfortable with both Sean and Jeremy spending time with their children.

Finally, with tears in his eyes, Sean admits that Jeremy and he want to discuss something with Michael. The men both desperately long to be daddies and to have a family of their own. While it is technically legal in Ohio for gay couples to adopt, it can still be difficult. To get started, they are taking the needed courses to become foster parents and they want Michael, as both a brother and a minister, to write them a letter of recommendation. It will still be difficult with the prejudices, but they are considering volunteering to take in hard to place children like young ones who are sick or have disabilities. They are taking extra classes for special needs children.

Michael assures them that he would be happy to write a letter of recommendation for them. He would gladly attest to the fact that they are wonderful uncles and good Christian men. Peter soon becomes fussy and Sadie emerges, almost instinctively, to nurse. Michael teases that this is part of the parenting that probably won't work out for them. Sadie raises her eyebrows and Michael shares his brother's news. She congratulates them and promises to keep them in her prayers.

August arrives. One night after Sadie finishes nursing Peter, the baby remains wide awake. Exhausted, Sadie has difficulty staying awake, so Michael offers to keep the baby and let her get some rest. One o'clock in the morning, Michael sits in the living room playing with Peter and watching an old black and white movie.

The phone rings. Michael answers to find a concerned Garnet, "I'm so sorry to call you this late, but I can see your light is still on."

"Oh, we don't get much sleep with the new baby in the house. Is something wrong?" he questions.

"I hate to ask. Maybe I shouldn't have called you," she stammers.

"It's okay. Go ahead and ask," he encourages.

"I can't drive at night and I'm sick from my treatment today. Angel left with Becky at six o'clock and she didn't come home. I called Becky's mom. She said that the girls went to a party at David's house at eight o'clock. If I give you the address, would you please go get Angel and bring her home? She isn't answering her cell phone and I'm worried sick."

Michael promises to go look for her. Carefully placing Peter in the crib, he wakes Sadie to tell her where he is going. He does not relish the thought of going to David's to dig out Angel. The thought actually makes him nervous, but he is determined to go for Garnet.

David's home is a small dirty white house with a sagging porch that seems to be falling apart. The blasting music can be heard from his car. The house is dark except for the flickering glow from a large television. The front door is open. Michael knocks on the screen door and he recognizes the teen that comes to the door as one of the boys who was with David in the pavilion.

"Hey, the preacher's here. What do you want, dude?" the kid slurs.

"Mrs. Heckathorn sent me to pick up Angel for her. Could you please tell her that I'm here?"

"I haven't seen her, sorry," he obviously lies.

Michael opens the screen door to let himself in, "You don't mind if I take a quick look around do you?"

The kid shrugs appearing to be drunk as he staggers back into the cluttered filthy room. Beer bottles are strewn about and about eight kids are hanging out. He spots Becky sitting on a boy's lap on a recliner. He scans the room for Angel. There is a boy lying on a dilapidated green couch on his side that Michael believes is most likely David. Michael notices that the boy appears to have three legs.

Approaching the couch, Michael can tell that David is heavily making out with someone and reaches out tapping on David's shoulder, "Excuse me, do you have Angel under you?"

David looks over his shoulder and cringes, "Oh Christ, it's you again."

"I'm not Christ. I'm just your friendly neighborhood preacher," Michael attempts to keep the atmosphere light.

Michael notices as David sits up that he pulls his hand out from under Angel's shirt. Angel appears disheveled and embarrassed as she too sits up. David demands, "Why the hell are you here?"

"Angel's grandmother called and asked if I would pick Angel up for her since Angel is over two hours late for her curfew. Her grandmother is too sick to come herself. Come on Angel, your Grandma is worried sick."

"Yes sir," Angel begins to stand, but David tries to hold onto her. "Let me go. Grams wants me." She pushes him away and stumbles across the room apparently somewhat tipsy almost tripping on the clutter and stepping over people stretched out on the floor. Michael takes hold of her arm to assist with her balance.

He stops in front of Becky, "You seem to be a bit drunk. Would you like a ride home?"

"Bug off, you're not my pastor," she sputters.

"You aren't planning to drive home are you?" Michael worries.

"Nah, I'll just crash here," Becky lays her head down on the boy's shoulder while he is caressing her thigh.

Michael shakes his head wishing that he could forcibly take Becky out of here as well, but he does not want to start trouble with this many boys around who are the sizes of men and definitely do not like him. He feels relieved that he is able to walk Angel out as easily as he had.

He places Angel in the car and hurries around to the other side. As he drives home, Angel curls up on the seat. Michael reprimands, "Are you drunk? I can smell the beer on you."

"No, I didn't have that much. I'm just tired," she slurs.

"You shouldn't be drinking beer at all at your age and why do you let that creep get on top of you and paw you like that?" he demands.

"He's my boyfriend. That's what boyfriends do," she responds matter-of-factly.

"No, it's not. That is not how a boyfriend should treat his girlfriend, especially in high school," he informs her although he knows that she does not care what he thinks.

When they reach her home, Michael accompanies her into the house. Grams gives her a hug and sighs, "Child, what am I going to do with you? You scare me to death. Go to bed."

"I'm sorry Grams," Angel kisses her cheek and begins to leave the room.

"Oh no, sit," Michael orders Angel who listens, and then he turns to Garnet, "What are you going to do? This child was out over two hours past curfew, drinking beer, and making out with her boyfriend, heavily, inappropriately."

"I told you that I'm sick. My head has shooting pain and my throat burns so badly I can't eat. I just want to go to bed," she complains helplessly.

"I understand, but what kind of consequences do you usually use?" he urges.

"I usually ground her, but it's hard for me to enforce right now. Will you please punish her for me this once? I need help," she pleads.

Michael cannot enforce a grounding from across the street. He remembers a time at Ambrose when he taught a teenage boy a lesson for gambling on a pool game at a bar by winning his money back and then having him earn the money back by working at the church.

"How about doing some volunteer work at the church as penance? Tomorrow you can scrub the pews. They could use a thorough cleaning," he suggests.

"No way," Angel refuses.

"No arguing, you listen to the preacher. Now go straight to bed," Grams orders as she coughs.

Chapter 7

The next afternoon, Michael works at the picnic table on the patio behind the garage enjoying the summer weather. Sadie joins him setting a glass of lemonade down beside him and then rubbing his shoulders. Robin is at swimming lessons with Cassie and then is going to Cassie's house for a play date. Peter and Rachel are both taking a nap.

"What are you working on?" Sadie asks.

"Sunday School stuff," he bemoans. "Until someone volunteers, I am the Sunday School Superintendent and I have to have things ready for September."

"Oh, give that to me. I'll do it for you. Sunday, announce one more time that we need someone, and if no one else will do it; I'll take over," she offers.

Michael pulls her down on his lap, "Thanks Babe."

He pulls her close kissing her. Enjoying being childfree at the moment, they savor this kiss. His lips travel from hers to her ear and down to her neck as he rubs her back.

While having her neck kissed and nibbled, Sadie glances over Michael's shoulder, "Hello Angel."

Michael stops, looking over his shoulder at the teenager, "May I help you?"

Angel huffs, "You said that I have to wash all of the stupid pews in the whole flipping church today. Grams sent me over to do it."

"Okay, let's go," Michael kisses Sadie on the cheek as she slides off his lap and pulls the Sunday school materials in front of her.

As they walk toward the church, Angel stares oddly at Michael, so he inquires, "Is there a problem?"

"How long have you and Sadie been married?" Angel inquires.

"Six years," he replies.

"It's weird that you two are still all over each other like that. Besides, I never really thought about a minister making out," she muses.

Michael laughs, "Where do you think minister's kids come from? I have three you know?"

"Ooooo, gross," she scrunches her face up causing Michael to laugh harder.

Michael takes her to the basement where he fills a large bucket with soapy water. He carries it to the sanctuary for her and instructs, "Remove the cushions from this side of the church to that side for now. Then be sure to wash the entire pew, the seat, the back, the legs, the ends. When the water gets too dirty, take it down to the utility tub to dump and get fresh water with just a capful of the soap which is meant for wood that you saw me use."

Angel huffs, "This is bogus. Why should I have to do this? This is a lot of work and for what? This sucks. Grams never made me do stuff like this. I was at a party and lost track of time. So shoot me. I don't think this is a fair punishment. How does doing this have anything to do with staying out late? I don't think I should have to do this. I don't know why you have the right to give me a punishment at all. This is messed up."

Michael crosses his arms simply listening to her complain, "If you're finished, you may get to work."

"Why are you making me do this?" she whines.

"You were out over two hours past your curfew and I had to come get you. And you were drinking. There are rules and laws that you are expected to follow and when you don't, there are consequences. Now, get busy. I'm going to check your work later and if it isn't done well, you will have to start over. So, just do a good job the first time," he warns.

Michael climbs up into the pulpit to mark the pages needed for the readings Sunday. He smiles as Angel angrily slaps the rag around harshly scrubbing the first pew muttering and mumbling the entire time.

"At that rate, you're going to wipe yourself out by the third pew. You better pace yourself," he cautions.

She continues to mutter and sputter. Michael organizes the front. He pulls out a small step ladder to climb up to change the hymn numbers on a sign. Not trusting Angel to not vandalize something in the sanctuary, he brings his laptop into the back of the room to work on his sermon so he can keep an eye on her.

Once she finishes the last pew in the first row, she returns the cushions to the seats and removes the second side's cushions. Michael watches as she quietly works. He is actually impressed that once she started, she gave up fighting and just did the work.

She carries the bucket downstairs to empty. Before she refills it, Michael appears behind her, "Would you like to take a break for lunch? You can come home with me if you would like or you can go home to eat. Just be back in an hour."

"You'd give me something to eat?" she snorts.

"Sure, come on," he motions as he leaves. She hesitates and then follows.

Sadie is in the kitchen doing dishes when they enter. Michael greets her with a kiss, "Hi Sweetheart, we came home for a bite of lunch."

"Okay, girls, lunch," Sadie calls as she begins digging in the refrigerator and Michael begins pulling dishes from the cupboard, motioning for Angel to have a seat.

"Daddy!" Robin runs into the kitchen.

Michael scoops her up, "Hi Cupcake; how was your play date?"

"I had fun. Cassie loves horses. Her whole room is covered in beautiful horse stuff. She takes riding lessons close to here. Can I take riding lessons too Daddy? Can I? Please?" she begs excitedly.

"Riding lessons? You're kind of young and they're kind of expensive, but you liked playing with her?"

"Yes. Do you think Jordan will be jealous that I made a new friend?" Robin wonders.

"No. It's okay. Friends are like baseball cards. You want to collect as many as you can. I was best friends with Uncle Graham and Uncle Colby growing up, but I still became good friends with Uncle Aidan and Uncle Steve. I'm hoping to make friends here in our new town too like with Cassie's daddy."

Kissing her, he sets her down as Sadie gives them their choices, "We have left over chicken and mashed potatoes, there's some salad, and there is left over spaghetti."

"Spaghetti!" Robin yells.

Rachel grabs hold of her Daddy's pants jumping up and down, "Peanu budder and jelly, peanu budder and jelly, peanu budder and jelly…"

"Okay, okay, peanut butter and jelly," Michael lifts her into her booster seat with a kiss asking Angel, "How about you? Do you want chicken or spaghetti? I highly recommend Sadie's barbeque chicken."

"Yeah, okay," she answers awkwardly as she sits quietly watching the family of her dreams sitting around a table for a meal with smiling excited children, a husband who has kissed his wife and both of his daughters, and a mommy who is fussing around to feed her family something tasty. Michael leaves the room for a moment returning with an extra chair.

Sadie heats the chicken and potatoes in the microwave for Angel and also serves her some salad. Michael helps with all the serving making the sandwich for Rachel and pouring drinks. Angel often drinks soda-pop and energy drinks, but Michael only pours milk for his children and ice water for himself, Sadie, and Angel. Sadie sets a large glass bowl of grapes in the center of the table.

Before they begin eating, the family all joins hands. Robin and Michael each reach out to Angel who awkwardly takes their hands as Michael says grace and then the whole family recites a cutesy memorized prayer for their children.

"God is great. God is good. Let us thank him for our food. By His hand, we all are fed. We thank you Lord for our daily bread."

Angel had always heard of people saying grace, but never sat at table where it was actually said. She feels uncomfortable the entire time and is relieved when they finish and begin eating.

Robin chats excitedly about her swimming lessons, horses and her play date as her parents actually listen to the little girl. Rachel babbles simply for the sake of having a turn to talk and her parents listen and respond to her as well, amused.

It is a loud, cheery lunch which makes Angel feel almost like crying although she is not sure why. Michael and Sadie even direct conversation to include Angel. The baby cries and Sadie fetches him and attempts to eat while holding him. To Angel's surprise, Michael leans over and cuts up Sadie's chicken breast so that she can easily eat one handed.

Michael stares at Angel for a moment and then leaves the room. When he returns, he pulls back Angel's bangs with one of his daughter's yellow butterfly Barrettes, "There, I wouldn't want you to get hair in your food and you can see what you're eating now."

Angel gives him a dirty look as his daughters giggle. Angel reaches up pulling the Barrett back out again. Sadie smirks, "Don't take it personal Angel. He has always been pushy like this." She then turns to her husband, "I talked for a little bit with Jonel when she dropped off Robin. She was on her way to *Curves* to workout. She said that there is a *Curves* just a few minutes down the road. I know money is tight, but I would love a place to go workout with a group of women again. I have all of this baby weight to lose and I always do better going somewhere than trying to workout at home with the kids. Besides, it would be nice to have a place to go and make some new friends outside of the church. Of course, Jonel is from church, but I like her. I wouldn't mind meeting up with her to work out."

"Why don't you stop there and see if you like it and how much it would cost us," Michael agrees.

Robin pipes up, "Can we stop at the ranch and see how much it would cost for horse riding lessons?"

Michael smirks, "We'll see, but don't get your hopes up."

Robin pouts.

After lunch, Michael helps with the dishes before leading Angel back to church to finish her punishment. He again broaches the subject of her need to get away from David which falls on deaf ears.

As she works on the second half of the room, Garnet enters the church to watch her clean. Michael greets her.

"Reverend, can I speak to you in private?" Garnet requests.

Michael accompanies her to his office where she begins, "I laid awake half of the night. I have come to the conclusion that I am not doing that child any favors trying to take care of her. She was missing and I was helpless. Then, I was just going to send her to bed letting her get away with it if you hadn't stepped in. I just can't raise her. I'm almost seventy with cancer. I've decided to give her up and pray that she makes it into a good foster home, but I'm afraid."

Michael feels sick inside to think of all the bad things that could happen to her. She will get away from David, but will probably simply find someone just like him. Michael can't explain why, but he cares. He cares more than he probably should.

Garnet continues, "Pastor, is there any chance that you could take her in? Maybe you could reach her? I've been praying for a miracle and here you are helping so much."

58

Michael is stunned by the request, "I don't thin¹
three children, one who's just a helpless infant. O⁻
us and we are missing Sadie's fulltime teacher'ₛ

"I understand. I receive four hundred dollars ⌐
from the state that I would transfer over to you, if you chaₙₓ
I'm going to wait for at least two weeks before I tell her and beₜₒᵣ⌐
anything just to make sure that this decision sets well and in case you change
your mind. Thank you for all of your help. You were so kind to go out at that
late hour when you have only known us for a month."

Michael returns to the sanctuary and watches as Angel finishes her
major chore. Part of him wants to take her home with him. The thought of
her simply disappearing into the system scares him. Placing teenagers is
difficult and she looks like a target at her age for promiscuity with others
or even by older men. She could end up in an institution. He wonders if he
could reach her or if she would bring nothing but heartache.

The thought occurs to him that on his first day in Shermanfield, he
prayed asking the Lord what He wanted him to do here and that was the
exact moment that he met Angel, Angel Heckathorn. He wonders if
bringing her home with him would endanger his children in anyway. He
cares about her, but he has to protect his family first.

Later that night once the kids are all in bed, Michael recounts the
conversation with Garnet concerning Angel including his response. Sadie
quickly agrees that taking Angel in is not possible. She agrees that there
is no room in the house and she worries about the negative effects she
could have on their children.

Michael has difficulty sleeping. He can't seem to get the teen off his
mind. When Peter cries at three, Michael goes for the baby to cuddle and
kiss. Michael changes the baby's diaper and takes him to Sadie so she can
nurse him in bed. He lies beside them watching and placing his arm
around her. He gently touches his son's little, soft face. When the feeding
is finished, Michael returns the baby to his room rocking him in a rocking
chair for a little bit and softly sings to him before placing him in the crib.

Sadie always sang to the girls and told him that he has a nice deep
singing voice. She encouraged him to sing to his children. She suggested
Christmas carols that he already knows. Songs like *Oh Little Town of
Bethlehem, Away in the Manger,* and *Silent Night* have lullaby tunes

a baby Jesus sleeping in a peaceful night with motherly love and angels
atching. Sadie was right. Those songs are perfect for rocking a baby to sleep
n the night.

The next morning, Michael takes a turn driving the girls to their
swimming lessons. He does laps while the girls take their lesson. He still
cannot stop thinking about Angel's plight, no father, mother in jail, heading
down the wrong path, sick grandmother, dead grandfather, and about to enter
the foster care system as a troubled teenager. He wonders if God is the reason
he can't stop thinking about her.

After lunch, Peter and Rachel nap while Robin lies in the middle of the
living room floor watching a DVD. Michael leads Sadie out to the patio,
"Sweetheart, I can't stop thinking about Angel. I was thinking…"

"No," Sadie interrupts, "We are not taking her in."

"Please hear me out," he begs.

"Absolutely not," Sadie stands firm.

"Just listen for a minute. I'm beginning to wonder if God isn't leading
me to help her and I understand your fears and reluctance. I have them too,
but here's the thing. I believe in your faith and in your prayer life. All I'm
asking you to do over the next few days is pray about it. Would you do
that?" Michael persuades.

"No, I will not. God never lets us take the easy way. Now you listen to
me, I gave up my home, I gave up my career, I gave up living in an actual
town, and I gave up living close to our friends. The only thing I have left
in my life is my happy family and you and God are not going to take that
away from me too. Bringing Angel into this house is like throwing a
wrench into the works. And I'll tell you something else, if anything would
happen to hurt one of our babies, I would never forgive you or God," Sadie
rants.

Michael wraps his arms around her even though she tries to push him
away as he attempts to calm her, "Okay sweetheart, okay, I hear you. I'm
sorry I asked. I won't bring it up again. I'll just pray that she gets into a
good foster home and hope for the best. I'm sorry."

Michael keeps his word, not bringing Angel up for the rest of the week.
Sadie, however, keeps seeing Angel through the window or walking
down the street. It is Sadie's turn to have trouble getting the young girl off
her mind.

Sunday comes, and Sadie sits in church armed with coloring books and crayons to help keep the girls quiet during the service while she holds Peter. Garnet and Angel sit across the aisle. Sadie tries to ignore them, but her eyes keep wandering over in their direction.

Michael comes to the main church prayer. Before he begins, he goes over prayer requests. As he comes to Garnet, he asks for prayer for her health and for a private prayer matter. Sadie's chest tightens and she feels pressure in her head. She orders God to leave her alone.

As Michael announces, "Let us pray," Rachel decides to pray like a big girl. She folds her hands and bows her head. However, the church prayer is rather long. As Michael prays on and on, Rachel becomes more and more restless. Frustrated waiting for the amen, Rachel yells out, "Amen Daddy!"

Michael pauses glancing up and then returns to his prayer fighting the urge to laugh and suppressing a smile. A quiet ripple of giggles can be heard.

After church, Robin and Rachel run across the aisle jumping up on Angel. Sadie watches as the girls hug and talk to Angel who laughs and tickles the girls. She lifts and holds Rachel while Robin slaughters a knock, knock joke. Sadie thinks to herself, "Damn."

Michael greets people after church, many joking about his daughter, the critic. He asks several of the Sunday school teachers if they would be willing to act as the Superintendent, but no one is interested.

Ernestine approaches him, "What are you going to do about the Superintendent?"

"I'm working on it. Are you interested?" he actually hopes that she is not.

"No thank you," she croaks.

"If no one will do it, Sadie has offered to take over," he assures.

"Will we have to pay her for that too?" she snipes.

Anger flashes through Michael, but he tries to remain calm, "Superintendent is a volunteer position while a church organist is almost always a paid position. This church is paying Wilma."

"You would think that a minister's wife would volunteer for her church," she persists.

"That would be nice, but our children enjoy eating and having clothes to wear," Michael defends his wife.

"You would think that a free house would help with that," she insults.

Anger builds in him causing his lips to tighten, "The house is part of my salary. It is deducted as if it were rent. If you would excuse me, I have something I need to do."

Michael walks away thinking, "I need to get away from you before I lose my temper."

Over lunch, Michael rants about Ernestine's comments, "I didn't know that I could have a parishioner who actually drove me more nuts than Mac use to. This old bitty takes the cake. For a Christian, she is awfully nasty. I cringe when I see her coming. It's all I can do to keep from losing my temper." Sadie shakes her head at the rudeness.

"I was talking to Wilma," Sadie changes the subject. "She wants to retire by September. I told her that I guess I could try to work it out. I'm not sure who to have sit with the kids. I thought maybe Jonel could. The girls like Cassie and Jonel also has her two teenagers. It is quite an age gap between Cole and Amber and little Cassie."

"Rob told me that Cole and Amber are from his first marriage. Cassie is Jonel's only child," Michael informs her and then changes the subject again. "Garnet told me that she is sure about giving Angel up. She is going to tell Angel someday this week. Angel's mother has four more years to serve before she can even try for parole, so by then Angel will be nineteen. Angel is probably better off in foster care than with her mother anyway. I hope they find her a good placement."

Sadie nods in agreement, but does not respond. She knows that he wants to plead Angel's case again, but Michael had promised not to bring it up again, and he doesn't.

Chapter 8

Sunday evening, Michael goes for a jog through the cemetery enjoying the peace and solitude. When he returns home, Peter is lying on a blanket in the middle of the living room under a play gym while Robin and Rachel watch TV.

Looking around, Michael asks, "Where's Mommy?"

The girls don't know, so Michael begins to check the other rooms and discovers Sadie in the basement with her arms crossed standing at the opposite end of the room from the laundry machines.

"What are you doing?" he questions.

"There is room here for another room," she comments.

"Another room?" Michael scans the area.

"Sure, if we took all of this storage stuff over to our storage room at the church, tore out this old cruddy wooden cabinet, we could build a closet here and add walls with drywall and drywall the ceiling. We could put a door here and use a nice thick carpet. This could make a decent size room for a computer desk, dresser, and a twin bed maybe over here," Sadie plans.

Michael stares at her for a moment unsure of what she is talking about until he catches the words "twin bed." A smile slowly crosses his face, "What exactly are you getting at?"

"Don't smile. It will be hell if we do this," she warns. "And you have to do most of the work. You deal with the rules and consequences. You deal with the school phone calls and the homework. You can't complain when she is hogging our only bathroom. You chase after her when she doesn't come home. You take her for walks and clean up after her."

Michael grabs Sadie kissing her, "Thank you."

"I must be crazy," Sadie bemoans. "It won't be easy to get the room ready quickly."

"What you're talking about will be expensive and the church just fixed up that room for our dining room. We may need to take out a loan," Michael thinks aloud.

"Michael, what about your trust fund?" Sadie suggests.

"No, I promised myself that I would give that up and live like a minister. I don't want to begin turning to that," Michael puts his foot down.

"Look, your father told me that they kept it intact for you. He said that we can use it to pay for the kids' college and weddings, save some for our retirement and split the rest between our children. Your father could donate the money to the church in his name for this project and receive a tax donation for a charitable contribution. It's win, win. You are the one who wants to bring her into this tiny house. Well, she needs a decent room and you have the means of providing it without bankrupting us," Sadie argues.

"I'll think about it," Michael sighs. "You were so dead set against this. What changed your mind?"

"God's been bugging me, but I'm still scared that we are going to regret this," Sadie laments.

"Me too," Michael pulls her close again. "I will not neglect our own kids and I will do everything I can to protect them."

"I know. I trust you or I couldn't do this at all," Sadie agrees. "Just remember, if anything happens to one of our children, I'll kill you."

"Good to know."

Michael's father owns a prosperous business and Michael had been raised in a mansion. His mother loved her country club where she often took her children. That is where Michael learned and played most of his sports having won many tennis trophies. James Donnelly, Michael's father, had expected Michael to go to Harvard Law School after college to become a powerful attorney. His parents and friends were horrified and angry when Michael decided to attend a seminary and give up his trust fund to become a minister. Michael had felt a strong calling to the ministry during college. It had been Sadie who helped mend the fences between Michael and his parents.

When Michael became a minister, he decided to turn his trust fund over to his parents so that he would live as a normal minister in his denomination that had made his parents furious. Since then, they kept the trust fund for him. Michael doesn't want his church to know about it for fear that they will expect him to pay for all of the church needs and go through it quickly. Michael never uses it except to tithe to the conference.

Before bed, Michael decides to move the garbage cans to the curb so that he doesn't have to remember in the morning and notices Angel sitting on her front stoop. He calls to her, "Good evening, Angel."

"What's so good about it?" she barks.

Michael crosses the road, "Are you okay?"

"No, I'm not okay," she mocks.

"What's wrong?"

"Like you care," she snaps.

"You'd be surprised. Come on, out with it," Michael persuades.

"Grams is getting sicker and moving to a stupid nursing home. I'm gonna have to move somewhere, with someone I don't know and leave what little I got behind and it sucks," she sputters attempting to appear tough.

"Try something for me," Michael suggests. "Try praying and see what happens."

"Oh please, I only go to church because of Grams. You're such a cornball. I guess you won't have to put up with me anymore. I'm out of here," she stomps back into the house.

Michael returns home picking up the kitchen phone and dials, "Hello Dad? I hate to do this but I'm calling for a favor."

Monday night, Michael calls Garnet and requests a visit. She invites him over immediately. Sadie remains at home with the children. They don't want the girls to know until they are sure that it is happening. Garnet invites him to have a seat on the couch. Angel lurks in a doorway and Michael asks her to join them.

"Angel, I am going to make you an offer, but I need you to really think about what you are willing to do. With every offer there are pros and cons, so I don't want you to answer today. I want you to really think about it," Michael begins as Angel stares suspiciously and Garnet stares hopefully. "Sadie and I know that you are about to enter foster care and that placing a teenager can be difficult. You could end up in a group home or an institution. You are welcome to come live with us instead if you would like."

Garnet claps her hands together and Angel's eyes grow wide as she asks, "Are you serious?"

"Yes dear, but there are rules that you need to be aware of. Sadie and I are very strict and we have to worry about the safety of our children. You would be expected to abide by normal every day laws, which I don't think is too much to expect, for example, absolutely no drinking, smoking, or drugs of any kind. You will also attend school every day with absolutely no skipping of classes.

"There would be rules and expectations in our home, for example, no disrespectful language toward Sadie or me and no cussing. You will be expected to keep your room clean and help out with household chores. You would be expected to do all of your homework and to continue going to church. You would also be encouraged to join the youth group at church and to join some type of extracurricular activity at school. There would always be consequences for broken rules as you well know.

"On the positive side, you can remain in your school, town, and church. You can feel safe that we would never hurt you and that you would have all of your needs met. We would take good care of you. So you think about this and let us know what you decide."

Garnet declares firmly, "There is nothing to think about. All of those rules are the way it should be. All of those rules will make you the person you should be. It breaks my heart to leave you and the thought of not knowing if you will be okay is killing me. You would be safe and cared for at the Donnelly's and that is what you will do and you will follow all of those rules which I should have been making you follow all along. Do you understand?"

"Yes ma'am," Angel mumbles, unsure of how she feels.

"There is a problem," Michael informs them. "We will need to build a room for you in the basement. I'm not sure how long that will take."

"I can't get into the nursing home for three weeks. Is that long enough?" Garnet inquires.

"We'll try to get it done. You may need to campout on the couch for a while, but we will work it out," Michael warns, "There is one more thing and you won't like it. There will be no more David or Becky."

"What?! You can't do that!" Angel jumps up. "You can't decide who I date!"

"I won't pick who you date, but at fifteen, I can and will decide who you can't date. That boy doesn't treat you right and he is going to hurt you either by accident or on purpose," he insists.

"I won't do it. I won't live with you if those are the conditions!" she defies.

"Here's the thing," Michael debates, "If you go into foster care, you have to leave them anyway."

Angry and feeling trapped, Angel paces thinking, "Okay, I get David, but why Becky?"

"Becky is who you smoke and drink with. The two of you get in trouble together," Michael reasons.

"I don't care what the Reverend asks. You will do it," Garnet puts her foot down.

Angel kneels dramatically in front of Michael with her hands folded pleading, "Please, not Becky. She's my best friend. She's like my sister. We have been together forever. We are all we have. I'll give up David, but please don't take Becky away from me, please."

Michael thinks about Graham and how they stayed friends despite their differences and their arguments. Michael remembers the fist fight between them at his bachelor party. He thinks about Sadie and Colleen and how important their friendship has been.

Michael sighs, "Okay, I'll give you a chance. You can still spend time with Becky, but if you begin getting into trouble together, serious trouble, she's gone."

"Oh thank you, thank you, we'll behave. I promise we'll behave," she wails.

Michael returns home leaning on the wall shaking his head and tells Sadie, "We are in for a lot of drama."

The next day, Michael calls Rob, as the chairman of the trustees, to stop at the parsonage after his shift. Rob arrives and Michael shows him the area of the basement that they want to remodel, explaining that he and Sadie will be taking in Angel and that his father plans to donate the necessary funds. Rob promises to call an emergency trustee meeting on Sunday, but does not see any problems. Because of the rush, he suggests that Michael go ahead and call a contractor.

Rob then asks if he and Sadie have really thought through opening their home to someone like Angel. As a police officer and as the father of two teenagers, he can't recommend the situation.

Michael smiles, "Trust me, Sadie has explained the pitfalls in great detail, but Angel needs us. Who knows where she could end up?"

Rob admires his new minister, but also believes that this is a bad idea. Wishing him well, he leaves.

The next three weeks, rush by. School begins and Sadie, tearfully, and Michael watch as Robin climbs into the school bus for her first day of kindergarten. They are both there waiting anxiously when she returns home to excitedly share every detail of her day.

The room in the basement is not ready, but well on its way. Angel will move in with them on Sunday. She will leave most of her things at her house until the room is finished and she will have to campout on the couch. Sunday afternoon, Michael and Angel will drive her grandma to the nursing home.

Friday evening, Sadie goes to *Curves* for the first time and is quite impressed. It is a bright room with high energy music playing. Fifteen workout machines are arranged in a circle which works the various muscle groups. The resistance machines use hydraulics instead of weights so that the more a woman puts into the move, the more resistance she has. Between each machine sets a wooden square with a gray mat called a recovery station for the women to either jog or march in place or do different aerobic moves which are suggested on cards setting on the floor in front of each platform.

One thing that Sadie likes about *Curves* is that it is not a class with specific days and times. The ladies simply arrive and do the thirty minute workout by going around the circuit twice on each machine and square and then go to the stretching station for a complete cardio and strength-training. Sadie can go however many days that she can, any time during the day.

The women range in ages from twenties to sixties and their weights vary from slender and fit to obese. Everyone seems to be cheerful and chat as they make their way around the circle. Some jog in place while others march. There doesn't seem to be competition between them or judgment, and it has a friendly atmosphere.

Sadie obtains the information she needs about joining, the onetime membership fee and monthly payments giving Jonel Monroe credit for recommending the business. Just as she is about to leave, Jonel arrives wearing an oversized t-shirt and sweatpants happy to see her minister's wife and glad that she might be joining.

They stand by a wall to chat for a moment. Jonel begins, "You know I have two teenagers. They aren't mine of course, but I love them all the same. It was hard at first for them to accept me, but we get along well now. I've been with their father for over eight years now. They don't see their mother often anymore. The divorce was hard them, but their father always loved them, took care of them, and is rather strict with them. They can be a handful at times.

"Rob told me that you are taking in Angel. My teens are good kids and still a challenge at times. I would be scared of taking a child like that into my home. Her mother is a drug dealer. I don't know if Angel takes drugs or not, but she drinks and smokes. I wouldn't want her friends coming around my house. She goes to school with my kids. They say that she does poorly in school and spends a good amount of time in the office. Are you sure that this is a good idea?"

Sadie shakes her head, "I don't know. My biggest fear is that she will be a bad influence on my girls or that my kids could be hurt somehow. I said no at first, but Michael believes that God wants him to do this. I have always trusted Michael's faith, but this one has me nervous. Please keep us in your prayers. We will need all the help we can get."

Sadie arrives home excitedly telling Michael all about *Curves*. Michael assures her that they can afford it and that it is a reasonable cost. Sadie feels guilty joining when they can't afford to pay for horse riding lessons for Robin. However, Michael insists that exercise is important to Sadie's health and to help her bad hip which always hurts during a pregnancy and for a period of time afterwards.

He also believes that having a place to go and to make new friends in the area outside of church is important. While the church is imperative in their lives, he knows that Sadie needs a life outside of it as well. Decision made, Sadie plans to return in the morning and join.

Chapter 9

Sunday morning, Michael's parents, James and Sophia Donnelly, come to church to see their grandchildren again, to a see the progress on the new room they are funding to build since they decided not to touch their son's trust fund, and to meet Angel, the new addition to the family. Sadie, her children, and her in-laws sit in the second pew in front of Michael. James enjoys holding his first grandson while his granddaughters each sit beside him.

After church, the ladies' group sponsors a coffee hour. That is where Sophia meets Angel for the first time with her green streaked hair covering her eye, black fingernails, and her hole filled jeans. Sophia is visibly surprised and horrified by the girl's appearance. Angel is nothing at all how Sophia pictured a church going teenager.

"Mom, Dad, this is Angel. Angel, these are my parents, Mr. and Mrs. Donnelly," Michael introduces.

"Hello Angel. It is nice to meet you," Sophia nods.

"What's up?" Angel grunts.

"They are paying to have the room built for you," he informs the girl.

"So, like, are you rich or something?" Angel quips.

"As a matter of fact, we are rich," James smirks amused.

Angel goes home with her grandma to help her prepare to leave in a couple of hours for the nursing home. Michael and his family walk to the parsonage for lunch before he needs to leave as well.

When they enter the garage to head for the basement, James stops instead by the minivan giving it a once over, "Son, the bottom of this door and the frame are beginning to rust. How old is this thing?"

"It's fine Dad. Don't worry about it," Michael assures him.

"Since we are building you a room, why don't you let me buy you a new minivan? You are going to need it with two new additions to your family and living out in the country, you will need a good one that will last," James offers.

"No Dad, our van is fine. Come on, I'll show you the progress to the room."

He and Sadie show his parents the unfinished room in the basement. Sophia stops first to comment on a dining room in the basement. Sadie explains that she loves her set and refused to give it up. Besides, where would they entertain company without it? The kitchen is too small for just the family. In order to get into the oven, Michael has to stand and push in his chair and they can barely pass each other between the refrigerator and the table to get from the garage door to the hall.

Sophia turns the corner where the framework for the new walls is already up and the closet is being formed.

"This will be a nice room, but sweetheart, I don't understand why you are bringing a girl like that into your home. She looks like a trouble-maker," Sophia declares with dismay.

"You have no idea," Michael agrees.

"So why are you doing this?"

"She is one of my parishioners and she needs help," he simply states.

"Sadie, aren't you concerned about the havoc she will bring and the environment she will create for your daughters?" she turns her debate to Sadie.

"Oh yes, I'm scared to death about how this is going to affect the children and our home," Sadie readily agrees.

"Then why are you allowing this?" Sophia challenges.

"Because Michael honestly believes that this is what God wants us to do and I believe in Michael's relationship with God. I just pray that God will protect our children from harm and Michael better not let anything happen to them or I'll kill him," Sadie states with conviction.

"So all Michael has to do to have his way is tell you that it is ordained by God?" James teases causing Michael to roll his eyes.

Sadie giggles, "I trust Michael to not abuse this power."

Sophia continues to worry, but knows by now how stubborn her son is. Her son refused to listen to his parents when they pushed him to be a lawyer. When his parents told him that he was forbidden to become a minister, he went to seminary anyway. When his father told him he was not to give up his trust fund, he still had the money transferred back to his parents. Sophia did not want Michael to date Sadie, so he married her. All of his decisions have worked for him so far, but she has her doubts about this one.

He definitely needs someone like Sadie to share his life with the way he lives. Sophia would never have allowed James to bring a child like that into their house for a weekend let alone to live.

They lead his parents to the patio to eat a simple lunch. Robin jumps around telling her grandparents all about Cassie taking riding lessons and how much she wants to take lessons too. Sophia touches Robin's hair enjoying her enthusiasm. Robin then pouts that her daddy will not allow her to have the lessons because they are too expensive. Sophia offers to pay for the lessons for however long the child rides.

"Thank you Mom, but no thank you," Michael turns her down. "We don't want you to do that."

"Maybe we should discuss this," Sadie suggests.

"No, absolutely not, we can take care of the girls ourselves," Michael cuts her off.

Sadie glares at him for a moment before smiling at her mother-in-law, "Thank you for the kind offer, but the Lord and Master has spoken."

Michael's head snaps up at the comment as Sadie stands walking into the house. Sophia and James attempt to suppress smiles. Michael excuses himself following Sadie into the kitchen.

"What was with that crack?" he demands.

"You made the decision without me and when I asked to discuss it, you said no. I just went along with you on a life changing decision and you won't even talk to me about our own daughter," she accuses.

"You know I don't want help. I don't want them to buy us a van or take care of our girls. I want to do this on my own. I already went to them for a large amount of money, and now Mom is going to pay for weekly lessons?" he explains.

"What about Robin's happiness? I gave up my job and now I can't afford to pay for her to have lessons. Her grandmother offers to give her something nice and we say no just for your pride!" Sadie reasons.

"Robin doesn't have to get everything she wants. You were raised by a minister and you did just fine," Michael points out.

"I begged and begged for piano lessons. There were a lot of things I didn't get to do because of the lack of money and I resented it. When you asked me why I refused to date you, I told you that I didn't want to be a minister's wife, remember? You wouldn't understand. You had your lessons. You had swimming, golf, and tennis lessons. You had anything you wanted.

"I'm not saying that we should run to your parents every time we need or want something, but they are the grandparents. I don't see how it would hurt to allow them to do something nice for a granddaughter who was just forced to move away from her home and friends. Something in this sad excuse for a town excites her and you say no with no thought."

Sadie turns her back on him to go retrieve Peter from his crib and carry him out to the patio where she hands Peter to James.

"Well, if it isn't my little Peter James," his grandfather boasts, "my first grandson and my namesake."

Michael returns to the table and sheepishly caves, "Mom, I guess I made a hasty decision. I think we would like to reconsider your offer."

"Good. You enjoyed riding lessons when you were young," Sophia reminds him. "You and Sean used to disappear for hours on your horses."

Sadie and Robin are surprised by this bit of information.

"Son," his father interjects, "I don't want to embarrass you, but in case you entertain parishioners here, you should know that you and Sadie probably shouldn't have loud discussions by the two open windows in your kitchen."

Sadie and Michael's eyes lift to the kitchen windows over the patio and then exchange embarrassed looks.

"Oh my, it is a tight fit in that kitchen. Maybe your table is a little bit too big for the room," Sophia observes.

"It is too big for the room, but we need to seat six now," Sadie agrees. "It's a tight squeeze, but it works."

Michael bids his parents goodbye and then crosses the street to the Heckathorn home where Garnet is waiting to leave. Michael packs his van with her luggage and helps Grams in while Angel climbs in behind her. They cheerfully chat on the way to the old woman's new home.

While Michael and Garnet check in at the receptionist's desk, Angel looks around her. The moment they step into the nursing home, Angel's nose is accosted by the smell common to hospitals and nursing homes. A nurse comes with a wheel chair to transport Grams to her new room. Angel walks behind them looking around as a creepy feeling descends on the girl.

73

They take a rickety elevator ride to the third floor. Many of the doors to the rooms are opened as they walk down the hall. Some residents are sitting in the hall appearing depressed and half dead. Lonely, they stare at the group which is passing by. One woman, desperate for a visitor, for human contact, reaches out touching Angel's arm. Angel jumps away and hurries to walk closer to Michael.

As she passes one room, she hears a woman crying pitifully. They arrive at a room that looks like a hospital room. Angel had thought that a nursing home would look more like a home than this. Grams will have a roommate who is asleep when they arrive. The woman grunts and groans loudly in her sleep. The room reeks of urine. Michael comments on the smell and the nurse responds that the roommate must have wet the bed again.

Grams sits on the edge of her bed while Michael sets her luggage down offering to unpack with her before they leave. Grams agrees and Michael calls Angel over to help. Angel moves slowly, mechanically. Michael sets pictures of Angel, Tara, and Grams's deceased husband on a shelf by the television where she can easily see them.

Angel stares at the pictures and then runs to her grandmother, "Grams, Grams, we don't have to leave you here. We can take you back home and I'll do better. I'll take care of you. I'll wait on you hand and foot. I'll come straight home from school and stay with you all evening. You don't have to live here. I can take care of you."

Garnet pulls Angel close to her rocking her back and forth, "Shh, there, there child. Don't cry. I love you so much for wanting to take care of me, but I need too much. I need chemo and medicine and constant care."

"I can do it," Angel promises.

"Oh my dear, dear child, do you really think that is the life I want for you? No, you go on home with the Reverend. I trust him and his wife to take good care of you. They will do better than I have. You listen, mind your manners, and behave yourself. You follow all of their rules and be the good little girl that I have always loved," she comforts. "Reverend, I can finish that and put things where I want. You better take my sweet Angel home now. I think she needs to go now."

Michael nods and hugs Garnet. Angel hugs her Grams as if she may never see her again. Michael lightly lays his hand on Angel's shoulder as he leads her from the room. Angel feels as if her feet are weighed down with bricks. She feels as if she is leaving her grandmother in a prison to be tortured. She's angry that her mother isn't here. Her mother shouldn't have gotten herself thrown in jail. A mother should be here to take care of her own mother and daughter. She feels all alone in the world as she heads to live with complete strangers.

Once outside, panic seizes Angel. Crying, she turns running back toward the doors. Michael catches her arms. She turns, jerking to pull away, "We can't leave her here. We can't. She doesn't deserve this. She doesn't belong here."

Michael pulls her in close, wrapping his arms around her, holding her until she calms down crying into his chest.

Michael comforts her, "She'll be okay darling. This is the best place for her right now. Here, they will feed her, do her laundry, keep track of the meds, clean up the vomit from chemo. She needs cared for and this place will do all of that."

Angel sputters viciously pushing herself out of his arms, "I can do all that!"

"You're fifteen. You're a child. Let them take care of Grams and I promise that I will bring you to visit. We won't leave her here all alone. I know that some nursing homes have poor reputations, but I have seen many nursing homes. This is a good one. Come on, I'll take you home."

"Not to my home," she snaps.

"No, to mine. Hopefully, it will come to feel like your home as well," Michael holds the door for her.

She climbs in, slumps down in the seat, and turns her back to Michael staring out the window.

That night, Sadie makes a bed on the couch for Angel who awkwardly enters her new home feeling out of place. They place Angel's clothes and things that she brought with her in the basement dining room. She will bring more things as soon as she can move into her room.

She lies in the living room staring at the ceiling unable to stop thinking about her grandmother. She doesn't know if she'll ever feel comfortable here. It all seems so foreign to her and she feels like a fish out of water.

Chapter 10

Monday morning, as Michael and Sadie eat breakfast, Angel shuffles into the kitchen in a tank top which exposes her bra straps and low ride jeans. Michael calmly rebukes her, "No, go change."

"What? Why?" she glares at him.

"You are not going to school with your bra showing and your butt hanging out. Now go change," he directs.

Angel stomps loudly back down the stairs while Sadie and Michael smile at each other. She returns to the kitchen wearing the same clothes simply having added a zipper sweatshirt jacket. Michael stands leading her back down to the dining room. He digs through her clothes until he finds something acceptable, a t-shirt which sports the words, "AS IF," even though he still doesn't like it.

Returning to the kitchen, Michael pulls a pair of scissors out of the kitchen drawer, "Come here Angel."

"What are you going to do with those?" she frets.

"I'm going to cut your bangs so that you can see," he states matter-of-factly.

Angel takes off running into the living room. Michael follows and corners her as she begs him not to cut her hair. Sadie appears taking the scissors out of Michael's hand, "You are not whacking her hair off. Just take her to school as is for now."

"Thank you Sadie. I swear he's crazy," Angel shakes her head.

"Don't talk that way about him. You are to be respectful," Sadie reprimands.

Michael drives Angel to school so that they can meet with the principal. Michael presents him with a copy of a contract that he had typed up and he and Garnet had signed and notarized. He explains that he is taking over guardianship of Angel with the grandmother's permission for now, but plans to petition the court to make it official. Michael is given forms for change of address and contact information.

While Michael fills out the paperwork, Angel heads for class. She finds Becky, David, and Jerry, David's brother, waiting for her in the hall. She had told them that she would be moving into the preacher's house and that he has been forbidden her to date David. However, she promises to sneak around and continue to see David. She pushes them quickly out of sight of the office.

Finished with the paperwork, Michael sits down to have a discussion with the principal, Ronald Moore. Michael wants to know what kind of student Angel is to which Mr. Moore gives Michael a deadpan stare.

Michael laughs, "I can guess, but let's hear it anyway."

Ronald sighs, "She has C's, D's, and F's. She is constantly in detention and In School Suspension. She gets into fights, talks back to teachers, cuts classes, vandalizes school property, steals from other students, and basically drives her teachers crazy. She sits in her classes glaring at the teachers and giving attitude."

Michael runs his hand over his face, "Okay, well, I will do my best to work with you and help turn her around. I don't want to ask you to do extra work, but is there a way to let me know what she is doing without counting on her to bring home notes and actually give them to me?"

"Sure, we have Progress Book," Ronald reaches into a drawer and pulls out paperwork, "We can give you a code which will allow you to go online and pull up all of her information. You will see the zeros she has for not turning in items, you can find the teachers weekly assignments and when the tests will be given, and you can see her attendance for each class. You can also read the school newsletters, calendars, and menus. Also, if I receive responses from you, I or Mr. Foster, the vice principal, can e-mail you with all the discipline issues we deal with here in the office. I can show you how it works if you are interested."

Michael is interested. Mr. Moore calls the secretary to give him Angel's secured access code for Progress Book and Michael gives him his e-mail address. Then Mr. Moore takes his time to show Michael how to use the program. Michael plugs in his own password, "havemercy." Ronald then shakes his hand wishing him good luck; he'll need it. Michael smirks shaking his head and taking a deep breath.

As Michael leaves the principal's office, the first period ends with the halls filling with students. He remains behind the glass walls of the office area watching the students passing by. Most of the students dress much better than Angel, but there are some who share her sense of style. He spots Angel walking down the hall with David's hand in her back pocket and hurries out of the office to catch her.

"May I speak with you?" he requests as he pulls her away from an annoyed David. Angel is surprised that the Reverend is still in the school.

Dragging her back into the office, he requests a quiet place to have a talk with her. Mr. Moore offers his office. Michael recounts his discussion with Mr. Moore including his ability to keep tabs on her through Progress Book to be sure that she is turning in all of her assignments, attending all of her classes and he will know when her tests are scheduled or projects are due. Angel huffs and puffs with her arms crossed, slumped in a chair. Michael insists that she will straighten up if it kills her.

"I also remember a certain girl promising to break up with David. Walking around the school halls with his hand in your pants pocket is not acceptable behavior and it will stop one way or the other. Do you hear me?"

She hears him and refers to him as a tyrannical dictator to which he responds, "You bet."

As the secretary writes Angel a pass for her class, Michael informs the principal that he has forbidden her from dating David. The principal laughs wishing him a lot of luck with that. Michael knew this was going to be hard, but now that it is all in his lap, he hopes he can really handle this.

When Angel arrives home from school, Sadie informs Michael that she and Angel are going out and that she left dinner in the oven for him and the girls. She also points out the bottles of breast milk she left for him in the refrigerator. Sadie takes Angel and leaves without telling Michael where they are going.

Sadie drives Angel over to a parishioner's house. A young woman named Kim Weaver has built a small beauty salon in her garage. Sadie requests that Kim gives Angel a new look; something in style, but is out of her face. Sadie also recommends removing the green, but adding streaks of highlights. To Sadie's surprise, Kim easily removes the green streaks which turned out to be clips with fake hair. Sadie thinks to herself that had Michael known, he would have removed them.

Kim happily begins Angel's make-over. While Angel's hair is up in foil, they wash her face and redo her make-up minus the thick eyeliner and blood red lipstick. When they are finished, Kim turns Angel toward the mirror. Sadie catches a flash of happiness on Angel's face, before Angel remembers to act annoyed. Kim gave her a long layered look with thin bangs that part in the middle and streaks of blond highlights through her brown hair.

Kim refuses any money spouting that she had wanted to do this for two years and that if the Reverend and Sadie were willing to take Angel in, the other church members should help where they can. Sadie thanks her and leaves.

Instead of going home, Sadie takes Angel to the Hungry Wolf for a bite to eat since they missed supper. Angel likes Sadie, but tries to hide the fact.

"Did you take me in just so you and the Reverend can change everything about me? I mean, why take me in if you don't even like me?" she asks honestly.

"We like you. You have to understand that we were once your age, but you have never been our age. If you double your age, it still doesn't quite add up to ours. Angel, we have a better understanding of life and the consequences of certain lifestyle choices. You are on a dangerous road and we want a better life for you. We are trying to help because we do like you and because we do care," Sadie gently and lovingly explains.

Angel rolls her eyes and huffs.

When Angel and Sadie arrive home, Michael is sitting in the recliner rocking Peter. His face lights up when he sees Angel's make-over. She is actually a very pretty girl. They can tell that Angel enjoys Michael's praise, before she quickly covers it up remembering to give them attitude.

Chapter 11

The next morning, Sadie helps pick out one of Angel's outfits that is decent and then helps with her make-up not allowing eyeliner and giving Angel one of her own softer pink lipsticks. Michael is pleased with the result. As he goes to tell her that it is time to go out for the bus, he finds her admiring herself in the bathroom mirror.

"Excuse me," Michael interrupts as her face changes back to her usual annoyed appearance, "the bus will be here any minute. I was online this morning and I want you to bring your algebra homework home even if you swear that it is finished and bring home your History book. I noticed that you have a test Friday."

Angel rolls her eyes, "That test isn't for three days. I won't need the book until Thursday."

"No, you are supposed to study for a test little by little over the course of at least several days. That is why the teacher gives you a week's notice. I will go over your math with you; that is my area, Science and math. Sadie can help you study for history. Reading, English, and History are her areas. Oh, and if you accidently forget, I'll just drive you back to the school to get them," he explains.

Angel responds simply by huffing, staring at the ceiling and stomping out of the house.

Michael calls after her, "Have a nice day."

Ronald Moore stands outside of the office watching his students arrive when he notices Angel. He almost doesn't recognize her and wonders if this minister really can turn her around. After years of working in a high school, teachers and administrators lose a certain amount of hope for some of the tough luck cases that pull at their hearts. Just as he becomes hopeful, he sees David, Jerry, and Becky approach her, obviously making fun of her appearance, and Ronald loses some of his hope as Angel appears embarrassed.

"Aw, look at the sweet little minister's daughter," David taunts. "Where's your Bible sweetheart?"

"Stop it," Angel demands, "Do you think I like this goody, goody look. They're very pushy people and I'm doing the best I can."

"Can you get away tonight for a little bit? It's been days since we hung out," David points out.

"I don't know. I'll try," Angel promises, "But I can't get caught. The Reverend is dead set against us."

Angel arrives home at the same time as Michael pulls in from making his rounds at the hospital. The two enter the house together to find Sadie lying on the couch half asleep.

Sadie sits up wiping her face, "Oh, I'm sorry. The time got away from me. I didn't do anything about supper. The baby was up so much last night. That stupid supper comes up every single night."

Michael laughs assuring her not to feel bad, but Angel offers, "I can fix supper."

"No, that's alright dear. I'll figure something out," Sadie wipes her eyes again.

"No, seriously, I can do it. Grams has been sick for a while. I cooked for us all of the time. I'm pretty good at it," Angel boasts.

"Alright, go ahead. Let us know if you need any help," Michael agrees glad to hear her offer to pitch in.

Forty-five minutes later, Angel calls everyone to dinner having prepared spaghetti, garlic bread, green beans, and dessert cups with apple sauce. She smiles shyly as Michael and Sadie praise her. After supper, Michael insists that Sadie take it easy while he does the dishes and comments to Angel that since she cooked, she shouldn't have to do the dishes. Instead, he suggests that she take the girls out to the church playground for awhile with the promise that when he finishes, he'll take the girls and she can have some time to herself.

Angel agrees as the girls excitedly jump around her. Sadie gives Michael a worried glance, but he just winks at her. Besides, Michael can see the playground across the parking lot from the window.

Halfway done with the dishes, Michael glances out the window in time to see David, Jerry, and Becky walking up to the fence around the playground and is overcome with worry. He watches closely as Angel talks with them for a minute and is relieved that she had obviously turned them away. He can't help checking out the window more frequently.

As he finishes, Peter wakes. Michael changes his diaper and carries him to Sadie to nurse. Michael then walks out to the playground. The girls run to him and are told that it is getting late and to go get ready for bed.

"Reverend, I think I'm gonna go for a walk. I'll be back in a little bit," Angel casually tells him.

"It's a beautiful night, maybe I'll go with you," he suggests knowing that she is planning to meet up with David and friends.

"No, no I would rather have some, you know, alone time," she stutters.

"Alone time, aren't you planning to meet your friends somewhere? You know, the ones you were talking to little while ago?" he lets her know that he knows.

"What, were you spying on me or something?" she accuses.

"I simply saw you from the window. You know that I don't want you with David," he reminds her.

"Look, I did my math, I studied for my history, I wore the clothes Sadie picked, I let her do my make-up, I made your supper, and I played with the girls. I'm trying hard here damn it and nothing seems to be enough for you! What the hell do you want?! I think I've earned some time off for good behavior," Angel rants.

"I want you to be safe. I want you to get away from David," Michael states firmly. "I've seen him pinning you down and talking to you in a disgusting way. I've pulled you out from under him and have found you drinking with him. I know that it is almost impossible to force a teen to stop seeing the boy that she wants to see, but I have to try. He scares me."

"Well, you're right about one thing. You can't stop me. What're you going to do, throw me out of the house for being in love?" she challenges.

"I am not going to get my way by threatening to throw you out. I brought you into our home and you are welcome here. I am however going to constantly pester you. You have no idea just how stubborn I can be," Michael warns. "Besides, look at you. You are panicking because I'm stopping you. You look all nervous. You don't look like a girl who is in love and longing to see a boy. You look scared like he's going to be angry with you for not showing up."

Angel's eyes dart back and forth as she tries to decide what to do feeling trapped. Desperate, she takes off running yelling over her shoulder, "I'll be back soon, but I have to go."

She runs at full speed believing that she has left him in the dust, and that she will deal with the angry preacher later. After all, he just promised he wouldn't throw her out. Soon, to her surprise, she realizes that he is chasing her. She runs faster, but her chest tightens up. She has a cramp in her side and loses her breath. Stopping, she doubles in half grasping her knees. The preacher stops beside her not even winded.

"Come on, is that all you got?" He taunts, "You can't even out run an old guy like me?"

"No fair," Angel gasps, "you jog all of the time."

"It must be all of the smoke in your lungs. We're going to have to get you healthy. Trust me, you'll feel better," he persuades.

"Can't you lighten up and leave me alone for one evening?" she spits.

"Nope."

"Please," she begs.

"You're coming back to the house with me like it or not," he orders.

"No I'm not and you can't make me," she defies him.

"Oh, can't I?" Michael bends over, pulling her waist over his shoulder. He heads back to the parsonage with her draped over his shoulder while she carries on all of the way.

The next morning, Angel climbs onto the bus where she finds Becky waiting for her. Becky usually drives to school, but she is riding the bus to spend time with her friend. Becky warns Angel of David's anger last night about not seeing Angel since she moved in with the stupid preacher. Angel explains that the Reverend knew that she was trying to see David and physically carried her back to the house.

Becky rants and raves about the minister stopping Angel from seeing the people that she loves and what right does he have. Becky suggests that Angel consider leaving the preacher's prison and coming to live with her.

Angel pictures Becky's house which is dirty and smells from her mother's cigarettes. Her mother drinks and there seems to always be a parade of men coming in and out. Angel does not want to admit that she would rather live with the Reverend and Sadie, so she simply explains that

Grams would not allow it and that she is where Grams put her. They are in the process of filing for legal custody.

At school, Angel ducks David heading straight to homeroom. She does not want to face his anger and definitely does not want to miss homeroom causing the office to call the Reverend to find out where she is.

After homeroom, David comes up beside her grabbing her arm. She snaps that she has to get to class, but he forcibly drags her with him leading her to the basement's boiler room.

"You stood me up last night," David accuses.

"I tried to get to you, but the Reverend wouldn't let me go. I ran, but he caught me and carried me back over his shoulder," Angel whimpers.

"What are we going to do about this?" he challenges.

"David, I want it to work out for me there. I don't want to disappear into some institution or foster care. I know there are problems, but right now it is my best bet. Please don't cause problems," Angel begs.

"Why won't he let you out? You're not a baby," he demands.

"He doesn't want me dating you. He found you sitting on my face talking about a blow job and he found us drinking with your hand up my shirt. Hell, why would he like you?"

David sits on an old metal folding chair pulling Angel down across his lap, "Well, he is going to hate this."

Angel struggles, but David firmly holds her. Grabbing the back of her hair, he forces her chin back and begins kissing her neck. Soon, he sucks, sucking hard on her neck.

"Stop it," she pleads. "You're hurting me."

Her begging falls on deaf ears as he continues to suck on her neck in several different areas. When he finally turns her loose, she drops to the floor crying. He leaves her there calling her a big baby. Once she calms down, she wipes the spit from her neck. Waiting for the next bell, she quietly goes to her second period class. Stopping at her locker, she snatches her jacket and pulls her hair around her neck. She spends the rest of the day attempting to cover her bruises.

At lunch, she walks into the restroom peering in the mirror at four large dark hideous hickeys. Tears well up in her eyes. She zips up her sweatshirt jacket and carefully tucks her hair in around her neck. Returning to her table, the others chat as if nothing is wrong. Angel simply stares at her food. Her so called friends make fun of her for becoming a quiet preacher's kid. When the lunch bell rings signaling their next class, David kisses her on the cheek as if they are fine.

Arriving home on the bus, Angel plans to hurry to the basement to find clothes that will hide her neck. It is a hot September day, but she wants her turtleneck and hopes that no one becomes suspicious. She also hopes that the Reverend isn't home. His schedule is all over the place. Some nights he has meetings, some days he has hospital calls, sometimes he works late in the church office. She never knows where he will be. Between Peter and Rachel, Sadie will be home.

As the bus pulls up in front of her house, she notices the garage is shut, forcing her to enter through the living room instead of making a quick beeline for her clothes in the dining room. The Reverend's car is in the driveway, but she hopes that he is at the church office. Pulling her jacket tight and carefully tucking in her hair, she carefully, slowly walks toward the house. Taking in a deep breath, she quietly opens the door sneaking in.

"Hey, there she is," calls Michael with a large smile. He and Sadie had been waiting for her. "We have a surprise for you."

Keeping her chin down, she mumbles, "I need to run downstairs first, okay?"

"Sure, your surprise is downstairs," he chirps happily.

Michael, Sadie, Robin, and Rachel all descend the stairs with her. At the bottom of the stairs, Angel takes a quick left into the dining room and is shocked to find that all of her stuff is missing.

"Where's my stuff?"

"In your new room, the builders finished today," Michael excitedly informs her. "Come on, let's have a look."

Nervously, Angel walks around the stairs to a new door. Opening it, she steps into a freshly painted, very clean room. The walls are light blue with a thick blue carpet. Sadie thinks the color is calming. Angel's own bed is in the corner, but Sadie has purchased new fresh bedding. There is a director's style chair which is covered with shaggy blue fur in a corner. They placed her grandma's old TV in here for her, plus her computer and computer table. They even managed to get Angel's dresser with mirror down here. It looks beautiful and inviting.

Angel mumbles appearing unexcited, "Thank you. It's very nice."

"You can add your own pictures and posters to make it your own. We didn't bring over anything that you had on your walls at home. You can personalize, but just keep in mind that our young daughters will be in here from time to time. You might want to give up the big poster with the sweaty man without a shirt and his thumb hooked on his pants," Michael cocks his head looking at her, "Do you feel okay? You look a little flushed and you're sweating." As he moves forward, Angel backs away, "It's a hot day. Why are you wearing a sweatshirt?" Angel looks away. "Hey girls, why don't you run upstairs for now and give Angel sometime in her new room? You can come back down later."

"Where are my clothes?" Angel asks.

Sadie pulls open a white vented folding door, "in your new closet."

"Thank you. Don't worry about me. I'm fine. I just need to change my clothes. Thank you, the room is beautiful," she mumbles.

"We put in this lighted mirror for you to do your make-up and there is an outlet here by your dresser's mirror so you can do your hair. There are too many people in this house to do those things in the bathroom," Sadie explains.

"Well, we'll give you some time in your new room," Michael begins to leave, but Sadie touches his arm as she questions Angel.

"Sweetheart, why do you have your hair tucked in like that?"

Angel turns her back to them, "No reason."

Michael moves in front of her reaching to move her hair. Angel knocks his hand away jumping back. They stare at each other for a moment. Michael reaches out taking her by the arm and pulling her back to him. He brushes her hair out of her jacket immediately seeing the dark bruising.

"What happened to you?" Michael questions.

Angel pulls away, "It's no big deal."

Sadie gently touches her face to examine her neck, "These look like at least four rather painful hickeys."

The heat of anger flashes through Michael's face, "Did David do this to you?" Angel does not respond, but looks away. Michael takes her arm turning her to face him. "Answer me." She nods without looking at him. "Did you like this? Do you consider this type of pain a form of making out? I know kids like a hickey now and then, but these are huge and very dark. Don't these hurt?"

"Yes it hurts! No, I didn't enjoy it! Are you happy now? This is all your fault!" she accuses.

"My fault?!" Michael snaps back.

"David's furious that he can't see me anymore. He misses me and he did this to get back at you. I begged him to stop, but he wouldn't," she tries to justify.

Michael runs his hands over his face before answering, "I told you he would hurt you. He loves you so much that he is willing to hurt you to prove something to me? So, what did he prove? I'll tell you; he proved that I'm right. He didn't hurt you last night when you were home safe with me."

Angel stomps away throwing herself down on her bed. Sadie calmly sits on the edge of the bed unbuttoning her nursing blouse and exposing her shoulder, "Angel, look at this. You can't win in this type of relationship. I know this for a fact." Angel looks up to see an ugly scar on Sadie's left shoulder and sits up for closer look. "My first fiancé shot me. I broke up with him years earlier, but then he wanted me to forgive him and make up. Instead, I said no and became engaged to Michael. He shot me. Years earlier, the first time I broke up with him, he threw me down a flight of stairs.

"This kind of abuse doesn't stay at this level; it builds. It gets worse. He came after me a third time and tried to kill me. I was married. He knocked Michael over the head and tied him to a chair with a ton of duct tape. He cut Michael with a knife. Luckily and by the grace of God, I managed to get a gun and shot him in the leg and arm to stop him. He's still in jail and I'm still scared of the day that he gets out on parole.

"This type of relationship can cost you your life. We know. That is why Michael picked you up last night and forced you home."

Michael pulls up his sleeve revealing the two long scars from the knife on his upper left arm. Angel stares in disbelief. Michael touches her chin lifting her face toward him, "Think about it little girl. You don't deserve this. You can have so much better. I have never, never hurt Sadie or left any kind of bruise on her, not even by accident. I would never do anything that would hurt her. I do everything I can to take care of her and my family and now that you are part of my family, I just want to take care of you." He strokes her cheek with the back of his hand.

Sadie hugs her and kisses her cheek. They leave closing the door behind them. Angel has difficulty digesting all of this new information. Angel stares at the beautiful room they had built for her with the thoughtful extras like the new stylish chair and the new blue comforter with big colorful dots all over it.

They could have just thrown a rug down and placed her furniture in an unfinished basement. She is unsure of how to react to any of this. The only person who ever treated her lovingly had been Grams and half the time Grams neglected her because of her age, health, and grief over the death Gramps. Overwhelmed, she cries into her pillow, slamming her fists into the bed.

Chapter 12

The next morning, Angel dresses in a turtleneck for school even though the weather remains hot. She had purchased several turtlenecks just for this purpose, only she had never had such painful ones before. When she reaches the kitchen, breakfast is out and Michael and the girls are eating while Sadie nurses Peter. No one mentions her neck.

"So, how did you sleep in your new room?" Michael inquires.

"Fine, it's a nice room. I like it. Thank you," Angel stammers.

"Did the noises from the furnace or water heater bother you? Basements can be full of odd noises," Michael checks.

"Nope, I slept fine. Thanks. I better go or I'll miss the bus," Angel picks up her book bag.

"Don't bother. I'll drive you to school this morning," Michael informs her.

Angel freezes, "Why?"

"I need to see your principal," he states matter-of-factly.

"About what?" she becomes more nervous.

To her horror, Michael plans to tell her Principal about the hickeys. He calls it an assault and he is angry that it happened in the school building. Angel begs and pleads with him not to do it because it will humiliate her. Michael apologizes, but insists that it needs to be done. Angel carries on all the way to school.

Mr. Moore is not available, so Michael speaks with the vice principal, Glen Foster. Michael explains that because he forbids Angel to see David that David became angry and hurt Angel right in the school having dragged her down to the boiler room. Michael is taken aback by the nonchalant attitude of Glen. As far as Glen is concerned, Angel is lying to cover up making out and cutting class and Michael is buying it.

While this attitude does not surprise Angel, Michael becomes furious. He pulls down her turtleneck showing him how bad they actually are and insisting that she did not enjoy being hurt, but Mr. Foster remains unmoved.

"What do you want me to do about it?" he asks.

"Do you mean to tell me that this school has no idea how to keep a young lady safe in the halls?" Michael demands.

"Young lady? You mean how do we keep her safe from her boyfriend who she has been hanging out with for years? Do you realize how often she is in my office? I know you're new here and with her, but don't be played. She is not an innocent angel just because her name is Angel," Foster warns.

Anger floods through Michael with an urge to punch this man with the smirk. Instead, he simply takes Angel by the arm and leads her out of the office without a word indicating for her to take a chair and wait for him. Michael takes a moment to calm down before walking to the secretary's counter to wait for assistance.

"Yes, may I help you?" she greets.

"Yes, I would like a form to withdraw a student from this school," he requests.

Appearing suspicious, the secretary pulls the form from a filing cabinet and then asks, "Where do you want her records sent?"

"I don't know yet. I need to go home and look on the computer and in the phone book for other schools in the area. I will have to get back to you."

"There isn't much open enrollment around here and the only private school is a catholic school, but it is a rather far drive," the secretary warns.

"I don't care how far it is. I need a school where my girl will be safe."

Mr. Moore enters the office overhearing Michael's last remark, "Is there a problem here?"

"Yes, Angel doesn't have a chance here. She needs a fresh start in a different school where people aren't so tired of her that they don't care if she has been assaulted right in the school building. So, I am withdrawing her," Michael announces.

"Please, Reverend, come inside and tell me what exactly happened," Ronald shows Michael into his office.

Angel sits in shock. She never had anyone in all of her years in school stand up for her.

Mr. Moore does not want the minister from the only church in Shermanfield to pull his girl out of their school because he does not believe that she is safe. People respect ministers and he fears the backlash. Also, he had been impressed with Michael at their first meeting and had hoped to help with Angel. Michael recounts the events of the past hours before including Mr. Foster's attitude.

"I apologize that this upset you, but you have to understand that Mr. Foster is in charge of the discipline in this school and he deals with Angel on a regular basis," Mr. Moore reasons.

"This attitude is why there are so many battered women and abused children. I'm not a fool. I know the trouble Angel causes and I know that she is willingly his girlfriend. However, that does not give him the right to attack her. Women and girls can't escape abuse, because no one cares and they have nowhere else to go."

"Are you sure she is telling you the truth?" Mr. Moore checks.

Michael opens the door signaling for Angel. He shows the principal the hickeys and then sends her back to her seat, "I just don't believe that she wanted that. I believe her when she said that she begged him to stop, but even if she is lying, I need to get her away from that boy if she is going to have a chance of doing better."

Mr. Moore rubs his chin, "Okay, I will out of school suspend David for ten days for the assault and tell him that he is not allowed near her at school like a restraining order, but that won't help outside of school."

"I'll do what I can about outside of school. I know that Mr. Foster thinks that I'm naïve, but I'm not. If I leave Angel in this school, I will probably have to come in on a regular basis and she will probably be guilty most of the time. Her mother's in prison, she doesn't know who her father is, and her grandmother, while she loves her, had no idea how to discipline her. Sadie and I are trying to undo years and years of damage that has been inflicted on her throughout her developmental years. We might be fighting a losing battle, but we have decided to fight."

Ronald promises to help all he can and hopes that Michael and Sadie win this battle. He would love to see a hard luck case turned around. It is every principal and teacher's dream to help make a difference in the life of a child in need, but with their dysfunctional home lives, meaningful change seldom takes place or doesn't last. In Angel's case, her home situation has in fact changed, he has hope that she can turn her life around.

Michael sits and talks with Angel before sending her to class. Angel finds it surprising to have Michael explain what is happening to her and to be doing this for her, but she also fears David's reaction. Michael fears his reaction as well. He has Sadie and three small children at home.

On the bus ride home, Becky sits with her telling her about how David laughed. He hates school and doesn't care about the suspension. He just finds it funny that he was able to freak out the minister and wants Becky to assure Angel that the preacher can't stop him from being her boyfriend. Angel begins to wish that David would go away.

Chapter 13

When Angel arrives home from school, Robin runs to her in the front yard jumping up and down excitedly, "Guess what, guess what, Mommy and Daddy have a surprise for you and we were just waiting for you to come home and now we can go."

"Go where?" Angel asks skeptically.

"I shouldn't say. It's a surprise," Robin beams.

"It would be more fun for me hearing it from you," Angel coaxes.

"We're going to the mall to buy you new clothes!" the little girl blurts out.

Angel runs into the house attempting to duck down into her new room, but Michael blocks her way in the kitchen informing her that they are going out to eat.

"Where, the mall? I don't need any new clothes," she sasses.

"I see that you've seen Robin. Why don't you want some new clothes?"

"First, you get me a new haircut and new hair color, and now you are going to pick out clothes that you want me to wear. You didn't just take me in, you are trying to change everything about me including who my boyfriend is and who my friends are," Angle accuses.

"Sweetheart, we have been very upfront that we are worried about the road you are walking down. Yes, we are putting up borders that you haven't had, but should have had. The truth is, people judge you by your clothes and frankly, you dress poorly and too provacatively for a fifteen year old girl. I am going to use the money from your support checks to buy you some new clothes. You are not going to go to school wearing jeans with holes and that don't cover your underwear completely anymore. Now, go get in the van."

Angel slams her book bag down stomping all of the way to the van where she throws herself into the very back with an excited Robin.

ANITA WOLFE

Michael follows her out securing Peter's car seat behind Sadie's seat as Sadie buckles Rachel into her booster seat behind Michael's. They drive out to the mall with Angel sitting with her arms crossed the whole way.

At the mall, Michael and Angel begin walking through the clothing aisles. Michael lifts a pretty pink floral top to which Angel steps back horrified. Laughing, Sadie takes the top away from Michael and replaces it on the rack.

"The tops you pick out for yourself must have sleeves and reveal absolutely no cleavage and no crop tops. Other than that, you can choose what you want, but we have the power to veto," Sadie stipulates. "Also, you need to pick out two or three pairs of jeans as long as they are not low ride or too tight. Go have fun."

Michael and Sadie push the double stroller in which Rachel sits in the front and Peter lies in the back simply following Angel with Robin bobbing all around her. At first Angel wanders around awkwardly, but soon something new takes over. She begins having fun holding up tops and jeans and even finds herself smiling and twirling around despite herself. Michael and Sadie smile nodding their approval and at times, shaking their heads.

Angel finds her favorite top. It appears to be low cut, but has a fake lacy top sown in the right place to adequately cover her. Michael vetoes it as too sexy, but Angel turns to Sadie with pleading eyes. Sadie allows her to at least try it on. Seeing the lovely top on her, Sadie pushes Michael to give his approval which he does because he trusts Sadie. Sadie also helps her pick out new underwear and a bra. Angel's are old and ratty and some are thongs which will disappear from the laundry thanks to Sadie.

"Okay, one last thing," Michael informs her, "You need a dress for church."

"I don't wear dresses," she contradicts.

"It won't kill you to wear a dress," Michael persists.

"Sadie," Angel again turns to her negotiator.

Sadie looks all around her, "How about one those black flare caprices with one of those tunics?"

Angel selects a tunic covered in black and blue shapes and swirls with a tie around the middle. Michael agrees with the compromise.

The next day, Angel heads for school feeling happy in her new jeans with a diamond threaded design up the side to her knees and her new favorite top

94

that Sadie had pushed the Reverend to allow her to buy. She wears her make up in the new light fashion the way Sadie taught her. Ronald Moore notices her walking in, thinking that the preacher is trying hard with this girl.

Cole Monroe, Rob's teenage son, also notices Angel entering the school, "Angel? Is that you?"

"Hey Cole," Angel smiles at him.

"Wow, you look great. I almost didn't recognize you," Cole compliments.

"So, you don't think I usually look great?" Angel jabs.

Cole laughs as he walks on without responding.

Angel turns bumping into Becky who is not impressed with the new look. She hates that her friend is changing. Becky likes things the way they were and she doesn't want her best friend turning into a dorky preacher's kid. She bursts Angel's bubble when she begins making fun of Angel's new look.

That night, Angel joins Sadie and her girls in the living room while the preacher works out in his garage office. Robin turns on an eighty's dance CD and begins to jump and dance around. She is quickly joined by her little sister who is adorable as she swings her hips back and forth. Sadie and Angel laugh. Soon, Sadie joins her daughters dancing around to the driving beat. Robin only coaxes Angel for a second before she too jumps up to dance as well. Just as the four of them are whipped up into a frenzy of movement, they notice Michael standing there watching them. It throws them into fits of giggles.

"Dance with us Darling," Sadie invites.

"I don't think so," Michael protests as he turns to leave and almost trips over Rachel.

Rachael reaches up for her daddy begging, "Dance with me Daddy, please."

Michael cocks his head and then scoops her up into his arms bouncing her around to the beat. Soon he is in the middle of the room surrounded by all of his girls. As he bounces Rachel, he reaches down to twirl Robin a few times and holds her hand while moving to the beat. Angel is surprised by how well he can move. Still holding Rachel, he leans in to dance in front of Sadie as they gaze lovingly into each other's eyes.

Michael hands Rachel to Sadie and without warning, grabs Angel's hand twirling her around. He then pulls her towards him spinning in one direction, straightens his arms forcing her away from him, and pulling her back to spin around the other way. Letting go of her hands, he scoops up Robin for a turn. While they both hold a daughter and right in front of Angel, Michael and Sadie lean in for a kiss.

Angel shakes her head, "I feel like I'm living with some TV family."

Sadie places her arm around Angel, "My dear, reality doesn't always have to suck."

Angel lies in bed awake late into the night with that phrase, "Reality doesn't always have to suck," stuck in her head. Sadie and Michael's life seems unrealistically happy and perfect, yet they had shown her physical scars from horrible times they had survived. She wonders if after living a life that had always sucked, if it is possible that there could be actual happiness in her future or will all of this simply evaporate like all of her other dreams have?

Saturday afternoon, Becky arrives at the parsonage with a big smile and asks the preacher in a silly voice, "Can Angel come out to play?"

Laughing, Michael invites her in and directs her to the basement stairs. Becky is impressed and also a little jealous of the new room. She and Angel lie around the room talking a mile a minute. Shortly, the friends run up to the living room where they find Sadie and Michael playing with Peter who is now almost two months old.

"Can we go to the mall, please? We want to go to the new store on the strip that opened this week," requests Angel.

"How are you going to get there?" Michael questions.

"Becky drives," Angel indicates her friend.

"I don't think so," Michael shakes his head.

"But Becky drives real well. It's the one thing she's actually good at. Come on, please, that's what teenagers do on a Saturday; hang at the mall," Angel pleads her case.

"Who all is going?" he interrogates.

"Just the two of us, I promise. We've hardly seen each other since I moved in here and we have some catching up to do. No David, no boys," she pledges crossing her heart.

"Okay, I'll let you go, but I get to look in your purses first," he bargains.

"Our purses are private. Girls have private things in their purses," Angel argues.

"I've seen a tampon. I'll let you girls go if I can check your purses first. Take it or leave it," he offers.

Angel, who is becoming accustom the preacher's ways, snatches Becky's purse and hands both to Michael who glances briefly in Angel's before handing it back. He then looks in Becky's removing a pack of cigarettes and her lighter.

"Do I get those back when we come home?" Becky checks.

"Yeah, right, it's almost one now. Be back no later than seven. That's more than enough time to be at the mall," pulling out his wallet, he hands Angel a twenty to her surprise. She had often taken money from her mother or grandmother's purse, but she is not accustomed to someone just assuming that she could use money.

Angel thanks him and the girls hurry off to the church parking lot where Becky's old clunker is parked. They run into Amber Monroe, Rob's daughter, who is in Angel's grade. They stop to talk for a moment. Angel brags that they are heading out to the new tattoo parlor at the mall. Amber is surprised, but Angel insists that the Reverend just gave her permission to go.

After Becky and Angel drive off, Rob, who has a group of kids playing soccer on one of the fields, sends Amber to the parsonage to borrow a set of church keys so that one of his kids can use the restroom.

As Michael hands her the keys, Amber comments, "I saw Angel. I'm surprised that you would let her go to that new tattoo parlor at the mall."

"What?"

"She said that you said she could go," Amber tattles.

Michael looks over his shoulder at Sadie before heading through the kitchen to grab his keys and head into the garage. As Michael makes the forty minute drive to the mall, he tries to remain calm knowing that he is only a couple minutes behind her.

Michael enters the tattoo parlor immediately spotting Angel and Becky with their backs to the door leaning on a counter studying drawings which cover the wall.

"Hey, check that one out," Angel points, "the one with the cross surrounded by roses. My name's Angel and I live with the Reverend. A cross would be perfect don't you think. The Reverend couldn't be that mad about a cross could he?"

"Want to make a bet?" Michael startles them.

"What are you doing here?" she asks.

"No, what are you doing here?" Michael shoots back his lips tight and his eyes revealing his anger.

Angel looks up at the wall of tattoos and then becomes a little panicked, "I wasn't going to get a tattoo. We were just looking, honest. I couldn't even get a tattoo without parental consent. We were just looking, honest."

Michael just glares, not believing a word of it. A rather large man with tattoos covering his arms and neck walks behind the counter addressing Angel, "So Angel, have you decided which one you want yet?"

Michael shakes his head, "Do you have any idea what honest means?"

Angel turns to the tattooed man, "Please tell him that I wasn't trying to get a tattoo."

The man backs her up, "She never asked for a tattoo. She was trying to decide between an eyebrow ring or a lip ring."

"I see," Michael takes her by the arm, "Come on, go get in the car."

As they reach the door, Michael stops and returns to pull out Becky as well. Once outside, Becky argues that they didn't do anything wrong and that she still wants to go to the mall to walk around. Michael insists that Angel leaves with him making Becky furious.

On the drive home, Michael adds rules to the list, "There will be no body piercing. The six earrings that you have in each ear are plenty. I trusted you, not only allowing you to go to the mall, but to also hang out with Becky and then you go to a tattoo parlor to have your face pierced?! Didn't you know that it would be a waste of money because I would have made you take it out the minute you came home?"

"I'm just not use to answering to anybody or having to ask permission to do anything let alone asking permission to do absolutely everything," Angel complains.

"I know this is hard for you, but you need to train yourself to make better decisions. Until you do, you are going to have to check with me or Sadie. You are a sophomore. In two and a half years, you will be out on your own and making all of your own decisions. I only have a short time to try to teach you to recognize right from wrong. It doesn't seem like anyone has ever really tried. It even says so in the Bible in Proverbs, *Teach your children to choose the right path and when they are older, they will remain upon it.*"

"You are such a preacher. It's going to be a long two years," she whines. "You know, Grams just wanted you to put a roof over my head. She didn't want you to change me."

"Oh yes she did. She feels guilty about how your mother's life turned out and she is very worried about you ending up in the same place. She most definitely wanted me to do exactly this and you know it. She said it clearly the day I offered to take you in," he states firmly.

"Don't talk about my mother!" Angel orders. "I don't do drugs. I will never do drugs."

Michael raises his voice as well, "You do everything else and at your age the things you are doing lead to drugs."

"I said I won't take drugs!" she repeats.

"Dealing drugs makes a lot of money. How are you planning to make enough money for a decent life if you don't study in school so you can have a career that will support you and that you can be proud of? What are you going to do, be a waitress who lives with some loser who will spend all your hard earned money on alcohol and then hit you for your trouble?" he challenges.

"Oh just shut up!" Angel snaps angrily.

"Don't talk to me that way little girl. What's wrong? Did you run out of answers?" Michael pushes.

Angel crosses her arms and stares out the window. Michael decides to leave her alone to think.

Chapter 14

Sunday morning, Sadie begins her new job as the church organist. She had practiced for several hours on Friday and Saturday. Not feeling comfortable in her new parish, Sadie feels very nervous this morning, especially because some people believe that she should be volunteering instead of being paid. She wants people to feel that she is worth the money.

Angel sits in the second pew in front of the organ next to Robin and Rachel with Peter strapped into a baby carrier. Many people immediately notice Angel's make-over with her new hairdo and new clothes. Most people are impressed that this young family would be willing to take in a girl in need, while others believe that it is down-right foolish.

Sadie begins with an impressive prelude on the gorgeous pipe organ. While there are mistakes, there are none that are noticeable. Michael smiles at her as he climbs into the pulpit for the greeting and morning announcements. He still feels awkward standing high up in the grand ornamental lectern. When he finishes, the congregation stands as Sadie leads them through the opening hymn.

The first part of the service goes very well. Sadie plays beautifully, the service flows well, and the children all behave. During the offertory, Peter begins to fuss. Angel sets Rachel off her lap, undoes the straps, and pulls him out to hold and cuddle. Michael takes a seat as the choir stands for the anthem. Sadie moves to the grand piano.

As the song begins, Angel stares down at the precious baby in her arms. She loves holding him. Preoccupied, she doesn't notice as Rachel climbs down off the pew and wanders away. Angel looks up in time to see Rachel toddling up the steps in front of the altar. Michael holds out his arms and she runs to him. Michael lifts her onto his lap where she curls up against him. He looks over at Angel who mouths the word "sorry", but the Reverend only smiles and winks at her.

When the anthem ends, Sadie goes to sit with the children during the sermon and immediately notices that Rachel is missing. Angel points up front. Sadie and Michael walk to each other so Sadie can take the girl as the congregation giggles. While most of the congregation enjoys this sweet, young family and their loving ways, there is a group within the church who are annoyed that the minister and his wife let their children have run of the sanctuary. After all there is a nursery!

Sadie allows Angel to continue holding Peter through the sermon while she cuddles Rachel and Robin leans against her mommy's arm.

Cole and Amber stare at Angel. They are surprised by the changes they see in Angel already in the short time that Angel has lived with the Reverend and Sadie. Cole also thinks for the first time that Angel is actually pretty.

That evening, Michael knocks on Angel's bedroom door, "Come on."

Angel opens the door, "Where to?"

"You're going to the Youth Group meeting," he informs her.

"Do I have to?" she whines.

"Yes you do and I expect you to behave yourself. Maybe you can make a new friend."

"But they're all geeks and nerds. I don't want to join that boring good-doer club."

"Why is doing something good a bad thing?" he questions.

"It's boring," she replies.

"Boredom never killed anyone," he cheerfully insists, "Let's go."

Michael walks her to the church with her muttering and shuffling her feet all of the way. She stomps into the room slamming down into an old armchair in the back corner. Jonel Monroe is the Youth Director with a group consisting of her two step children and five other teens. Michael pulls Jonel aside to let her know that he will be in his office during the entire meeting and to send for him if Angel causes any problems. Jonel nods happy to assist the Reverend and Sadie with their work with Angel in any way she can.

Angel sits quietly in the back of the room during the meeting portion making faces, rolling her eyes, and swatting at a window blind. The group opens with prayer and then discusses business. They chart out a calendar for the year consisting of their outings and fund raisers. The ski trip sounds like fun to Angel, but she pretends not to care. Jonel informs them that the new pastor is an excellent skier and will be going. He and her husband, Rob, will be able to take the dare devils on the more difficult runs.

Angel thinks to herself, "Great, he'll be there too. I'll never get away from him."

The group then begins to discuss their church project for the year which will be to create banners and wall hangings for the different liturgical times of the year. Jonel instructs the group to begin working on designs. Every now and then, she attempts to draw Angel in, but to no avail. Even when they eat a snack and drink pop while they visit, Angel hangs back by herself.

Cole decides to give it a try. Cole is tall with sandy blond hair and big dimples when he smiles. A varsity basketball player and track star, he is popular at school. He straddles a chair backwards by Angel, "So, the preacher made you come?" She nods without answering. He lowers his voice, "I know how you feel. Being that my step mom is the director, I don't have much choice either. If you relax, it's actually not all that bad."

Despite her best efforts, she is drawn into a conversation. Soon, his sister joins them. Angel jabs at her for getting her in trouble at the tattoo parlor with the Reverend, but Amber points out that she had been told that the preacher gave her his permission.

As the meeting ends, Jonel reports on Angel's behavior to Michael. He simply shakes his head. Jonel assures him that it is fine. She believes that the best thing to do is simply allow Angel to sit in the back until she voluntarily joins in even if it takes weeks. Michael is relieved that Jonel is so willing to patiently work with her.

The following week of school seems to go well. Angel appears to be adjusting to life in her new home. She calls her grandmother a couple times a week and Michael vows to get her to the nursing home for a visit at least once every two weeks if not more often.

October blows in. Sadie enjoys working with Michael as the church organist and works out at *Curves* three or four times a week. Peter is about two and a half months old. Robin enjoys kindergarten and is completely thrilled with her riding lessons. Rachel seems to have finally adjusted to their new home and cries for Ambrose less often. Michael keeps track of Angel's assignments online and to Angel's surprise, her grades begin to climb for the first time since fifth grade actually earning A's and B's.

Angel continues to date David, spending as much time at school with him as she can. She sneaks off under the guise of spending time with Becky to see him. Michael allows Angel to continue spending time with Becky against his better judgment.

Tuesday night Michael attends the Pastor/Parish committee meeting. He had come under attack a few times at these meetings during his first year in ministry, but it has been years since anything major had come up. Tonight's meeting takes him by surprise.

Ted Lawrence, the chairperson, begins, "We have some concerns Pastor."

"Is there a problem?" Michael leans forward.

"We know that you are new, but I guess we were use to a friendlier minister's family," Ted insults.

"What are you talking about?" Michael is taken aback.

"Well, since you moved in three months ago, you and your wife haven't invited anyone into your home for dinner so we can get to know you, nor have you had an open house at the parsonage," accuses Ted.

"Are you kidding me? You do know that my wife was eight months pregnant when we moved in and ended up giving birth to our child in the car? You also know that despite having three young children, we took in a teenager from your congregation.

"How can you label and insult my wife as being unfriendly? She has been working closely with the choir as the church organist and even though she is paid for that, she has also volunteered to be the Sunday School Superintendent when no one here stepped up to offer. Sadie is now working closely with the teachers and Jonel Monroe," he defends his wife.

"Yes, and when you needed help moving in and needed help with the baby after his birth, you ignored us and brought in your friends again from your last church instead of turning to your new congregation. We thought the church law prohibits visitation with former parishioners for the first year," Ted continues the attack.

"Those people were not just some parishioners. They are personal friends who are like family to us. They have nothing to do with the church, but with our personal life," Michael defends.

"I see. Another complaint is that you haven't been visiting the hospital enough when the papers in your file had very high marks consistently for calling on the sick," Ted charges.

"I have gone and I haven't missed a request, but I admit I haven't been going as much as I used to, but that will change with time. The hospital is far away and I haven't figured out a good schedule, especially since I'm so needed at home right now. Like you said earlier, I have only been here for three months. Give me time to get in step. I'm not use to this lifestyle. I have never lived in the country before," Michael admits.

"Are you saying that you don't like living here?" he interrogates insulted.

"No, of course not, I'm simply saying that I never lived in the country before. I haven't figured out a good schedule yet with the long drives. However, as I've said, I have gone to the hospital."

"We have all noticed that your family and friends come first. We think that you should leave your children in the nursery during the service," Ted coldly suggests. "And as for being needed at home, we all have families and family issues, but we go to work. You should be putting our church first."

Anger flashes through Michael causing his face muscles to twitch so that he sits completely still attempting to remain in control before answering, "I tore my family out of their home to come here putting my work first. Sadie lost her job as a first grade teacher putting this church first; Sadie almost lost our baby trying to pack to move here putting my career first. We brought the havoc of an angry young girl into our home with our family because we felt God pushing us to help her. Even with a tiny infant, Sadie has immersed herself into the ministry of this church with me. We may not be perfect, but we are trying and we are adjusting to everything in our lives being new and very different.

"And by the way, my children will always be welcomed in my church service. I also believe that it is good modeling for me as your pastor to show a man as a caring father and husband. I am not ashamed of being a good family man or for having good friends."

"Your whole argument just now centered on only you and your family. What about the other people in this church? Have you even made a friend within the walls of the church?" Ted interrogates.

"I spent the summer carpooling to swimming lessons with Rob Monroe. We are getting to know their family quite well and we very much like them. I am quite impressed with how Jonel runs the youth group and how hard Rob works in the church. Sadie often works out at *Curves* with Jonel and Kim Weaver," Michael offers.

"Sure you like him. He has a daughter for your girls to play with, he built your wife a dining room since our parsonage wasn't adequate, and he approved another bedroom built in the parsonage. You are still only talking about your family," Ted charges.

"That bedroom is for Angel and I turned to my parents for the money which I swore I would never do just so that it didn't cost the church anything. And all Sadie asked for was a decent carpet in one room. Rob did the rest on his own accord," Michael justifies.

Michael hadn't been this angry in a church meeting ever. He had heard stories from other ministers and from Sadie as a preacher's kid about nightmarish committee meetings, but this is the first one he ever experienced. No meeting at Ambrose rivals this one, not even the one when Mac demanded to know if he and Sadie were having premarital sex.

No one on the committee seemed to agree with him or feel the need to defend his family. He sits there staring back at their cold faces and for the first time ever inside the church building, he loses his cool, "Fine, you win. You want my undivided attention at church, you have it. If my daughters aren't welcomed in your church, that is fine with me, but Sadie will need to stay home with them. So you will need to get yourself a new organist and a new Sunday School Superintendent because I certainly wouldn't want to offend you with my unfriendly wife."

Michael stands up and storms out of the meeting. Once home, he rants and raves to Sadie with every detail. Sadie becomes furious about her children and husband being attacked. They both carry on blowing off steam.

"I promise you this. I am putting in for a move this year. Angel will be better off away from that school, her friend, and her boyfriend that she is dumb enough to think that I don't know she is still seeing. Our children and you will be better off out of this hateful church. And what good am I here as a minister when I feel no connection at all with my congregation? We need to grit our teeth and bare this the best we can, but come July, we are out of here."

Angel sits at the top of the stairs listening to every word, just as Sadie had listened to her parents. Angel had never heard the Reverend so angry. She had never known her church to be so cold. It angers her to think of this family being thought of as selfish. There is so much hate in this world, even in a church. She also caught that the Reverend knows that she is still with David.

Michael sits in his recliner rocking fast and hard stewing. Soon, Sadie calms down sitting on his lap, "You know the conference will never let you move after only one year even if the committee and you both request it. They will send in the District Superintendent to negotiate and they will come down hard on you for not working this out for yourself. I also know for a fact that phones all over are ringing off the hook tonight. News of that meeting will be known not just all over church, but all over town."

"Great," Michael nuzzles his face into Sadie's neck.

"Don't worry darling; we will survive this and things will get better. Come to bed and I will rub these tense muscles for you," she coaxes.

"Sunday, you stay home with the kids and I will run the service without the benefit of music," he declares.

"No you won't. You are the pastor. You have to be the bigger man. We will attend church just the same even, with our children in tow. You will apologize…"

"Apologize?!" Michael interrupts.

"Yes, apologize," Sadie continues, "but only for losing your temper. You will stick to your guns on the other issues. You answered well, but just too loudly."

Michael nods recognizing Sadie as the voice of reason. He wonders if he could have ever handled being a minister without her. He hugs her tighter and soon begins kissing her passionately.

Breathless, Sadie suggests, "With a small house full of children of all ages, I think we better continue this behind our locked bedroom door."

Michael stands lifting Sadie into his arms and carrying her to the bedroom. Angel becomes overwhelmed with temptation and curiosity.

Slowly, silently, she sneaks into the hall and sits close to the door listening to them make love. She has had sex several times with David, but she has never really enjoyed it. When she had sex, it never sounded like this. She knows she should leave, but she can't seem to force herself to go. They speak in low loving voices. Then Sadie giggles and Michael chuckles, after a bit, moaning and movement.

After a while, it becomes quiet. Angel, afraid of being caught, carefully crawls away. Taking her time, she descends into the basement quietly. Lying in bed, she thinks about how close their relationship is and how Sadie had gone from furious to comforting, to the voice of reason, to his stress reliever. Usually men she had seen that angry, take their anger out on the woman, sometimes even hitting her.

Chapter 15

Sunday morning, Angel watches as Michael paces around the kitchen nervously. He had always seemed so calm, cool, and in charge. It seems odd to her to see him this way. Sadie calmly prepares for church doing her best to calm him down despite the fact that she is uncomfortable about going herself knowing that people are judging her and her family so harshly. She knows from experience and keeps reminding her husband over and over that these are not the "church's" feelings, but a small group of noisemakers.

Sadie walks Robin over to Sunday school. This is the first week that Sadie begins an opening exercise program to teach children's Bible songs and open with a prayer before dismissing to their classes. The teachers, Jonel, Janey, and Ruthie, appear nervous, but are friendly. They have only had one meeting with Sadie, but they already like her. Jonel whispers supportive comments to Sadie.

Michael walks over with Angel, Rachel, and Peter in the baby carrier. People are walking around awkwardly. Some avoid looking at Michael directly.

Rob approaches his pastor, "Good morning Michael. I heard you had an interesting meeting this week."

Michael smiles at him, "Yeah, I lost my cool. I wasn't prepared to hear my family insulted. My last church adored Sadie before I was even appointed there."

"I don't think I could keep my cool if someone said mean things about Jonel or the kids. Michael, I know that the gossip is flying around, but you should know that there are a lot of people sticking up for you. Jonel and I are on your side in this. We are amazed by how much you have already done here in three months. Many people agree," Rob comforts.

"Thanks, that's nice to know."

Church begins as Sadie plays the prelude with Angel and their three children sitting in the second pew by the organ. Michael leads the service as if it were like any other Sunday until he comes to the sermon. Sadie leaves the organ to sit with her family and so Michael can easily look at her when he wishes.

Michael has always faced church problems head on. He would simply step up to the pulpit and openly address the issue. Today is no different as he mounts the high pulpit. He had worried that the attendance would be low this morning because of the argument, but quite to the contrary, the church is full. Michael knows that he has to handle this well or the congregation could easily shrink.

"Before I get into the sermon which takes a closer look at the Old Testament reading this morning, I feel I need to address events earlier in the week. For those of you who haven't heard the story yet, I will start at the beginning. We had a Pastor/Parish committee meeting this week in which the members had compiled a list of complaints about your new minister.

"At first, I thought I could handle it and discuss the issues. However, I was unprepared for how many of the complaints were about my family. I did allow my temper to get the best of me and for that I want to apologize. As your pastor, I'm sure you expected me to remain more professional and I will do my best to do better in the future.

"That said, I expect this church to be respectful to my family. The issue of whether or not a parent uses the nursery during church is a personal decision. My wife and I enjoy having the children in church with us in the hope that they will grow up feeling at home and understand the importance of attending church. Our children were wound up our first Sunday here and caused commotion, but since then, they have not been that disruptive. There have been incidents here and there, but I do not believe that it is that serious of a problem.

"Mark 10:13-16 reads *One day some parents brought their children to Jesus so He could touch them and bless them, but the disciples told them not to bother Him. But when Jesus saw what was happening, He was very displeased with his disciples. He said to them 'Let the children come to me. Don't stop them! For the Kingdom of God belongs to such as these. I assure you, anyone who doesn't have their kind of faith will never get into the Kingdom of God.' Then He took the children into his arms and placed his hands on their heads and blessed them.*"

"I, also, understand that the previous minister's wife here often had dinner parties and open houses. While that is very nice, that is not something that Sadie has done much of. However, Sadie is a different woman and this does not make her unfriendly. My wife always attends church services and church events. She has agreed to be the church organist when the job had been offered to her and has volunteered to be Sunday School Superintendent when after a month, Mrs. Heckathorn could not find a replacement. Sadie is a friendly, loving woman with a beautiful faith who has even opened our home to one of our parishioners.

"Again, I am heartfully sorry for losing my temper, but I will always defend my family. Some may say that I should put the church before my family, but I believe that being a good family man makes me a better minister and a better model for the men of the church. Also, my family is now members of this church and not a separate entity and I know for a fact that Sadie makes me a better minister."

Michael then turns to the Old Testament transitioning into his sermon. Angel is again impressed by him. The powerful love he has for his family is new to her. Her friends and family haven't had men like this in their lives.

Becky's father left them and she seldom sees him. David's father is a truck driver who is away for days or even weeks and pays little attention to David and Jerry when he is home. She often wonders who her father is and what he was like and how her life might have been different had she had him in her life. She wonders what is so awful about him that her mother and grandmother won't even tell her his name.

After church, many people make it a point to tell both Sadie and Michael that they had not agreed with these complaints. Many enjoy their daughters. Angel quietly slips away and sits in a corner.

Janey approaches Sadie where Angel can overhear the discussion, "Sadie, no one has planned the Sunday School Halloween Party. We have always had one in the past. The last minister's wife was always in charge of it, but no one thought about it this year. Do you think you can put something together? I'm not asking you because you are the new minister's wife, but because you are superintendent."

Sadie sighs, "I understand. We only have two weeks. I'll work on it this week so it can be announced by next weekend."

Sadie and Michael return home relieved that the morning is over and satisfied with the way it went. Angel is oddly moved by the whole week.

As they eat lunch Michael reminds Sadie, "Friday's your birthday. What would you like to do?"

"I want to go home," she quickly states without thought.

Michael leans toward her, "Darling, this is our home now."

"Whatever," Sadie returns to eating.

"If you want to go back to Ambrose to be with our friends for your birthday, I'll call Steve and see what I can arrange," he promises.

"You said that we would visit once a month and we have lived here for four months and we haven't been back once," Sadie complains.

"Sweetheart, we both have new jobs, new baby, and new teenager. Things will calm down and we will make it back more often. They've come here three times and we will take our turns. Do you remember your first birthday that we spent together at Duffy's? You were so drunk."

Angel looks up startled as Sadie smiles at her husband, "I wasn't that drunk. I used the fact that I was tipsy to get away with doing and saying things that I had not allowed myself to do before. I remember admitting for the first time that I really liked you and that my head and heart were having a fight and it was the first time that I told you that I thought that you are amazingly handsome. We had all those pictures taken."

"How old will you be?" Angel asks.

"Twenty-six," Sadie smiles.

"Careful sweetheart, you're going to be struck by lightning," Michael taunts.

"Okay, okay, I guess I'll be thirty-one years young."

Sadie leaves the room for a moment returning with a small photo album. She shows Angel pictures from her birthday party at the bar that her close friends, Steve and Brenda Duffy, own. Several were pictures of Sadie pretending to be a model with her friends, Colleen, Brenda, and Stephanie. The next pictures were the four women surrounding Michael with Sadie on his lap posing while Michael looked surprised and embarrassed. Then there is a picture of Sadie almost falling off his lap as he catches her smiling at each other. There is a beautiful picture of Michael standing behind Sadie with his chin almost on her shoulder. Then the last one of the whole group including Aidan and Steve, the three women, and Sadie with her arms wrapped around Michael's waist.

"You were already a minister and you hung out at a bar?" Angel asked.

"I was over twenty-one and I never got drunk, not once since I have been a minister. I do enjoy the occasional beer. My friend Steve owns that bar and Sadie and her friends hung out there. I really liked Steve and Aidan, but I was desperate to be near Sadie," Michael answers honestly to Angel's surprise.

That evening, Angel attends the youth meeting without complaining to Michael. She sits quietly in the back corner listening to the meeting portion of the evening. When Jonel asks if there is any new business, Angel speaks up to Jonel's surprise, "I have an idea."

Every head turns toward her in a stunned silence. She swallows and then talks in a rough voice, "No one has planned the Sunday School Halloween party this year and it was just dumped into Sadie's lap this morning to prepare on her own. It might be fun for us to throw the Halloween party."

Jonel smiles broadly as Angel shows concern for her new family, "I think that is a fantastic idea. We can all wear costumes and divide up all of the work."

The teens spend the rest of the meeting planning the party. Cole comes up with an idea for making a maze with the fellowship hall tables and chairs. Amber comes up with a few simple craft ideas. Jessica knows a couple of fun games that they can play, Ghost Golf, Pumpkin Roll, Freeze Dance, and Witch Balloon Bump. Jonel can read several stories. They all are to bring in decorations. They make a list of refreshments and divide up the list.

Angel runs home excitedly, "Sadie, Sadie, guess what!"

Michael and Sadie are sitting in the living room on the couch with Peter as they turn their attention to her.

Angel's face lights up, "At the meeting tonight, I suggested that we throw the Sunday School Halloween party. They really got into it."

Angel sits next to Sadie to share all of the plans that they came up with. Michael smiles warmly at the girl satisfied that they are seeing some success. She voluntarily works with the youth group already, demonstrates concern for Sadie, and has initiated a project for the church. Michael is proud of her.

Chapter 16

Tuesday night, Angel comes home with Becky in tow and finds Michael kneeling on the couch, looking behind it. Angel requests, "Hey Reverend, can Becky spend the night?"

Michael moves to the end of the couch looking under the end table, "It's a school night."

"I know," Angel acknowledges, "I promise we won't stay up late."

"I don't think it's a good idea. She can stay Friday night," Michael offers as he crosses the room, opens the coat closet and moves the coats around.

"Reverend, it's important," Angel begins, but Becky grabs her arm to stop her. "It's okay Beck. Ministers have heard it all."

Michael closes the closet door turning his full attention to the girls with his fist on his waist as Angel explains, "Becky's mom has been called into work tonight, and her little brother and sister are at their father's which leaves Becky home alone with Darrel and he's drinking."

"Who's Darrel?"

"Her mom's latest boyfriend and he gives both of us the creeps."

Michael shakes his head, "Why didn't you go to your father's with your brother and sister?"

Becky rolls her eyes and coldly answers, "Their dad ain't my dad."

"Okay, she can stay. Upstairs, the first cubby toward the front of the house has our camping stuff. You can find a sleeping bag and an air mat."

"Thanks."

Becky asks, "What are you looking for?"

"The girls begged for a round of hide-n-seek," he steps closer whispering, "Rachel is in her usual spot, but Robin is getting better at this. I can't find her. Did you give her a new spot?" Angel giggles. "Oh great, help me out here. Where should I look?" Angel shrugs with a smirk, "Gee, thanks."

Michael walks into the bathroom where he suddenly yanks the shower curtain open where Rachel is standing in the bathtub causing her to scream and giggle. Michael grabs and tickles her as he taunts, "Found you."

He then turns pleading eyes to Angel who subtly points toward Peter's room. Michael enters the nursery where Sadie sits in the rocking chair playing with Peter. Michael asks her if she has seen Robin to which she denies as she indicates the crib with her eyes. Michael drops to his knees lifting the dust ruffle. Robin begins screaming as Michael pulls her out by her legs to tickle her.

The teenage girls walk up the steps into the girls' toy cluttered yet cute bedroom. Angel crawls into the cubby looking for the sleeping bag and mat. Becky looks around the sweet room with pastel bedspreads covered with pictures of cute creatures to posters on the walls of puppy dogs, horses, and princesses. There is a small white bookcase filled with picture books. She notices on the wall above one of the beds a framed picture of a laughing Jesus surrounded by children while he holds one child on his lap. There is also a glow in the dark cross.

"Good Lord, this house is cutesy. How can you stand it here?" Becky asks.

"I'm kind of use to it," Angel bluffs not admitting that she actually likes it.

"So you play hide-n-seek? Do you also play with Barbie?" Becky teases.

Angel simply rolls her eyes as she picks up the bag and mat. Becky follows her down to the basement. They lie around watching a ghost story DVD and snacking on chips and pop. More than halfway through the movie, Michael knocks on the door and Angel pauses the movie and invites him in.

Michael leans in through the doorway, "Girls, you need to go to sleep. You have school in the morning."

"There's only about twenty minutes left in our movie," Angel begs.

Michael rolls his eyes, "Okay, finish the movie, but then straight to sleep. Goodnight." Michael closes the door.

Becky makes fun of her friend, "What the hell was that, a bed check or does he tuck you in?"

"Oh shut up," Angel hits her with a pillow.

Becky can't remember anyone worrying whether she is even home or not, let alone worrying about her bedtime. In the morning, Sadie makes scrambled eggs and toast for breakfast for her family and guest. Michael reminds Angel to bring her science book home because there is a test in two days and he wants to go over her algebra tonight. Becky, who usually grabs a Pop Tart for breakfast and never brings a book home, is still amazed by Angel's new life.

At lunch, Becky relays to David and Jerry all about life in the parsonage and they tease Angel for having parents who treat her like one of their little girls. David complains about not spending intimate time with her and warns that he is losing patience. She is his girlfriend and he needs time with her. She promises to sneak out and meet him in the pavilion at midnight.

That night, Angel quietly dresses and slowly climbs the stairs carefully, trying not to make a squeak. She tiptoes through the kitchen checking to see if anyone is up. The house is dark. Quietly and slowly, she unlocks the door leading into the garage. She sneaks to the door leading to the patio, but bangs into a red metal tricycle. Freezing for a moment, she continues to the door. As she unlocks it, the door to the office opens. Angel jumps, turning to discover Michael standing in the doorway.

"Angel? Where are you going?" Michael demands.

"I, um, I was just going to sit out on the patio. It is a warm night for October and I can't sleep," she lies.

"You're lying. How many times have you snuck out?" he interrogates.

"Never, this is the first time I tried and I got caught. You should be a prison guard," she sasses.

Michael smirks, "Go to your room and stay there."

"What are you doing out here anyway?" she asks.

"I'm writing my newsletter article. Go to bed and stay there," he orders.

Angel stomps all the way back to her room and slams her door leaving Michael with his hands on his hips. Michael returns to his computer. At twelve-thirty, he finishes his article. As he heads towards the kitchen, he hears noises out on the patio. Carefully, he walks to the patio door. Opening it, he discovers a shadow of someone on his hands and knees trying to look in a basement window.

Hearing the door open, he jumps up whispering, "Angel is that you?"

Michael answers in his deep voice, "No."

David startles, "Pastor?"

"Don't worry David. She tried to sneak out like you two planned. She didn't expect that I would be in the office. I sent her back down to her room."

"Figures."

"So what are you going to do about it? Are you going to hurt her again to get back at me?" Michael challenges.

"Why do you hate me so much? I have been friends with Angel since we were young kids and we have dated for over a year. She is special to me. Why won't you let me see her?"

"I found you practically sitting on her face. I found you drinking and on top of her with your hand up her shirt. The last time I made you mad, you gave her those terrible hickeys. I'm not unfairly judging you. I'm judging what I have seen and I haven't seen you treat her in a loving way once. Go home David."

David fumes and seethes with anger and hatred, "What right do you have to decide who she dates or loves? She is old enough to make these decisions for herself."

"She's just fifteen and I'm her guardian, so I'm guarding her. Go home David," Michael returns to the garage and carefully locks the door behind him. He then locks the kitchen door and heads down to Angel's room. He enters the room to find her sitting on the bed crying.

"Are you okay?" he gently checks on her.

"Go away and leave me alone," her voice trembles. Instead, he walks over to the bed to look out the window, but she assures him, "Don't worry. I saw him leave."

Michael sits next to her on the bed, "Angel, I'm sorry this is so hard for you. I know that I have turned your life upside down, but I don't want to be your jailer. How can I make you understand that a girl of fifteen should have rules and boundaries? She should not be sneaking out in the middle of the night to be with a boy, especially that boy."

"If you don't stop this, he's going to break up with me," she warns.

"That's kind of what I've been going for," he reminds her.

"Leave me alone," she whimpers.

Michael rubs her back for a moment before leaving the room. Just as he is about to drop into bed, he hears Peter fussing. He goes to change him and bring him to Sadie. As Sadie nurses, he recounts the events of the night. Sadie reminds him not to lose faith. Angel has come so far, but she will not nor cannot change her ways in such a short time. Sadie points out that she participated in the Youth Group, her grades are up, she sits with their children in church, and she has been helping with the cooking and laundry as well as helping with the girls and Peter. Michael knows that she is right, but can't stop worrying.

The next night, Angel sits quietly through dinner, after which Michael checks her algebra which is mostly correct. He then sends her downstairs to study her science. She pouts and says little all night.

Michael crawls in bed early with Sadie to watch a little TV. Suddenly, they hear high pitched screaming. Michael jumps up running to the basement with Sadie close behind him. The screaming continues. Michael throws Angel's door open to find Angel standing on her bed carrying on. Michael scans the room not seeing a problem.

"What is it? What's wrong?" Michael questions.

"There's a snake under my bed," Angel trembles.

Michael gives her a skeptical look. Shaking his head, he approaches the bed, drops to his knees, and lifts the blankets. He jumps back falling into a sitting position. He exclaims, "Damn, there is a large black snake under her bed. How did that get in here?"

"I was hot. I opened the window and a snake that was in the window well fell in," Angel explains jumping from one foot to the other.

Michael stands, "Okay, I'll figure out how to get it out of here before it gets lost in the house. You go up to our room."

Angel is too terrified to step on the floor shaking her head and whimpering. Michael reaches out for her hand, but the girl is petrified and shaken.

"Come on sweetheart. Go up to my room and get out of here. I'll take care of it. I don't know how, but I will take care of it," he coaxes.

Angel takes his hand tip toeing in baby steps across the bed. She can't quite get her herself to step off the bed onto the floor. Michael turns to look at Sadie when Angel suddenly jumps on his back. Michael catches her legs giving her a piggyback ride out of the room. He sets her down just outside of the door and she quickly sprints up the stairs.

To Michael's surprise, Sadie offers to stay and help. Michael locates a large box and an unused curtain rod. He instructs Sadie to reach between the wall and bed with the rod to scare the snake out from under the bed and he will drop the box down over snake when it slithers out. He comforts her that this is not a poisonous snake. Michael informs her that is about two feet long and a little more than an inch thick.

Michael gets down on his knees holding the box. Sadie pulls up the blankets and then lies on her stomach dragging the rod around until she feels it pushing on the snake. The snake slithers out faster than Michael expects, but he manages to get the box over most of the snake. He slides the box around until the snake is completely underneath. Sadie flattens another box which Michael carefully slides under the box and underneath the snake.

Michael carefully carries the box with the snake out into the field beyond the pavilion before letting it go. When he returns, Sadie and Angel are in bed watching TV. Michael slides in next to Sadie and they watch together for a while allowing the girl time to calm down. When the show ends, Michael suggests that Angel head down to bed, but she does not want to go back down tonight. She would rather sleep on the couch in the living room. Michael assures her that would be fine.

Friday morning, Angel begs to be left at home that night because she doesn't know anyone in Ambrose. Michael just doesn't quite trust Angel to be alone in the house all night. He mostly doesn't trust that she would stay alone. He tells her that Aidan has hired two teenagers to watch the kids tonight and that she can go too and he will pay her to play with the kids. Between the four couples, there are eight children and babies to care for under the age of five. Angel rolls her eyes, but she has learned that Michael is stubborn.

That afternoon, they load up the minivan and head back to Ambrose for the night to celebrate Sadie's birthday. They drive to Aidan and Colleen's split level house. They introduce Angel to their friends. Angel looks at the basement full of children and wishes she had been allowed to stay home. Colleen's children, Jordan and Autumn, are also five and three. Brenda's sons, Tyler and Dylan, are four and two. Stephanie's son, Korey, is one. Michael asks her to watch over Peter the most and let the other girls worry about the crowd. Sadie and Michael are having trouble leaving Peter. Michael tells her to have fun and that he counted the beers in the fridge.

The Donnelly's and their friends go to Duffy's like the old days when they were first dating. Sadie is excited to be with her friends for an evening at the bar. Michael shares the events of the night before with the snake. Aidan laughs commenting that these things only happen to them and that life is boring without them. They spend time discussing Angel.

Sadie and her friends leave the table to dance. They have always loved dancing since back in their college days. Brenda goes to the DJ equipment and plays old college day sexy song to which they do a provocative hip gyrating dance for their husbands' amusement.

The men join their wives for the next song. Michael pulls Sadie tightly up against him as their bodies move as one. Although they love their children, the couple enjoys the time by themselves. However, Peter is so small that Sadie calls to check on him every other hour promising Angel that she trusts her.

The children stretch out in sleeping bags all over the finished basement. Watching a movie, Angel lies on a couch next to Peter's Pack-n-Play. The other sitters went home once all of the children were asleep. Aidan, Colleen, Michael, and Sadie do not return home until after two since they closed up the bar. Michael had only had a couple beers over the course of the evening and Sadie only had one Margarita because she is still nursing. They check on the kids and thank Angel. Michael and Sadie camp-out on a pull out sofa on the main floor of the house.

Saturday morning, the family heads home. Sadie sleeps almost the whole way back. Michael informs Angel that later that evening they are going to go to the mall to buy Halloween costumes and a birthday present for Sadie. Angel asks if she can invite Becky to go with them. Michael agrees since Angel had been so good about being stuck with so many rug rats.

Later that day, Angel, Becky, and Robin climb in the back of the van behind the baby car seats for the ride to the mall. Michael informs the girls that he wants them to go to the Halloween store with them first because they need costumes for the church party. Then they can go off on their own.

At the store Robin chooses a cowgirl costume with a stuffed horse that she steps into and Rachael wants to be Dorothy from the Wizard of Oz. Sadie selects a Superman costume for Peter. The first costume Angel picks up is a French maid to which Michael only glares until she replaces it on the rack with a smirk. She had only selected it to get his goat. She likes a vampiress costume. Michael has never liked Halloween, but Sadie always enjoyed it. Michael has given up the fight against it, but he never dresses the children in any witch or monster costumes. He wants to say no, but Sadie approves it for her as he rolls his eyes and bites his tongue.

Michael pulls out his wallet handing Angel a twenty and instructs them to get something to eat at the eatery, to not get into trouble, not to be returned by a security guard, and not to pierce anything. The girls quickly disappear into the crowd.

As the girls eat their mall version of Chinese food, Cole and two of his friends with milkshakes pass by noticing Angel. Cole and his friends join them to Becky's surprise. Cole talks to Angel about the Halloween party next weekend and asks if she bought a costume. She answers that she had just purchased a vampiress costume. Cole laughs since he has a vampire costume. They will match. They smile at each other for a moment. Then he and his friends move on. Becky notices that Cole looks back over his shoulder as he leaves and Angel is still smiling even after he is gone.

"What the hell was that all about?" Becky snaps.

"What? I told you that I'm working on a Halloween party for Sadie," Angel reminds her.

"Babe, you two were flirting. God, David will kill both of you. What are you thinking? He's Mr. Popularity. Why would he hang out with someone grungy like you, unless he thinks you're an easy lay?" Becky accuses.

"You must be high. We weren't flirting. His step-mom's the Youth Group director and we've known each other because of church for like years. We're just old friends and nothing more so don't go stirring up trouble between David and me. The Reverend is doing more of that than I can handle," Angel defends herself.

"You know, you have to change things up," Becky warns. "I know that you have to please your new daddy and all, but you better please your man as well. What if you meet me in the restroom first thing in the morning at school? We could change your clothes and redo your make up and then at the end of the day, you can change back into the sweet preacher's kid."

Angel wants to say no, but she feels a strong pressure not to lose her group of friends who have for better or worse been like her family for the past couple years and Becky has been her best friend for as long as she can remember. David is really upset about the argument he had the other night with the Reverend. Maybe looking like his old girlfriend next week would go a long way with him.

Michael notices on the long drive home that Becky and Angel are rather quiet and wonders if something is wrong. He looks in the review mirror and can see that Robin has fallen asleep leaning against Angel's arm.

Chapter 17

Thursday morning Michael works in the office with Grace on a church calendar. He wants to print out a copy of scheduled events from November through Easter that had been discussed the night before at a planning session for publication in the newsletter. He also purchased a large calendar to hang on the wall in Grace's office like he had in Ambrose so that they can easily check it when scheduling other church events like weddings.

While double checking all of the dates his cell phone vibrates. It is the high school's vice principal, Glenn Foster, "Hello Reverend Donnelly. I have Angel in the office. She was caught cutting class to smoke in the girl's restroom. I'm afraid that we are going to have to suspend her for two days. We were wondering if you could come in."

Michael sighs, "Oh great! Yeah, I'll be right there."

Michael explains to Grace and then runs home to let Sadie know where he is going and to get the car. He feels very frustrated. Things had seemed to be going so well overall. Sadie warns him not to go too crazy and that there were bound to be setbacks. Michael drives to the school determined to remain calm and rational. He had told Sadie that what Angel needs is a good old fashioned spanking, but Sadie had responded that the last thing she needs is a man inflicting physical pain. He wishes he could have brought Sadie with him, but she has to take care of Rachel and Peter and it would be too chaotic to bring them to the school.

When Michael arrives at the school, Mr. Moore, the principal greets him. While the vice principal usually takes care of these matters, the principal invites Michael into his office because he has taken a personal interest in this case.

"Mr. Moore," Michael begins as he takes a seat across from the principal's desk.

"You can call me Ronald," he offers.

"Thank you, Ronald. First, I completely believe that she is guilty of this and that she should have harsh consequences. However, I have been working so hard to keep her in school and to help her keep her grades up, that I just hate to see her out of school for two days. I mean, we could easily do it. Sadie is home fulltime right now, but I'm not sure how being out of school for two days detours her from cutting one class. Is there some kind of in-school suspension or Saturday school or even a week of detentions? I would be willing to drive out here for however long it takes," Michael offers. "Plus, of course, there will be consequences at home as well, I assure you."

"You make a good point. Suspensions usually work because of the inconvenience to the parents to get them to care. You obviously already care, so I tend to agree with you. We do have an in-school suspension room, but again, she would be out of classes. I will give you your choice of in-school suspension for two days or a week of after school detentions here in the office where she can work on schoolwork or some days, we loan them to the cleaning staff to wash desks and scrape up old gum out from under desks, chairs, and the bleachers."

Michael smiles, "I think helping out some hard working people during detention is perfect. Plus, the first time I punished her, I had her scrub all of the pews in the sanctuary. The punishment will be consistent. She will either get her grades up for college or she'll be trained as a custodian."

"There is another problem that I'm not exactly sure that you are aware of. I stand out front every morning watching the students arrive at school and I have seen how you have been sending her for weeks, but this week things have changed again," he informs Michael.

"Changed how?"

Ronald picks up his phone and requests, "Oh Nancy, would you please send Angel in?"

The door opens and Angel shuffles in wearing a very mini, miniskirt, a tank top, thick black eyeliner, and blood red lipstick. The green streak hairclips are back in her hair. She appears surprised to see Michael as his eyes grow large and his lips pull tight with anger.

Michael demands, "Where exactly between home and school did half of your clothes fall off?" Angel stares at the floor not answering. Michael stands roaring, "Answer me."

"Becky started taking the bus with me in the morning," she mumbles.

Michael towers over her, "You have been changing your clothes on the bus in front of the other students?"

"Not exactly," she almost whispers. "Becky blocks the others' view and I had this on under my other clothes and I change back in the restroom at the end of the day before I get on the bus. I didn't have a mirror in the mornings, so Becky has been redoing my make-up."

"Sit down," he points at a chair, "How long has this been going on, this quick change act of yours?"

Angel slowly sits, "Just this week."

"Why? What's the point?"

"My friends didn't want me to change so much and Becky said I had to do something," she lamely responds.

"So what, you two hatched this plot at the mall Saturday night?" Michael shakes his head turning to Ronald, "Was Becky with her smoking in the restroom?" Ronald nods.

Michael pulls a chair in front of her and sits down, "Okay, this is how it's going to be. Number one, Mr. Moore has agreed not to suspend you. Instead, you will serve five detentions doing whatever they ask you to do without complaining or even rolling your eyes. Number two, Mr. Moore knows how I have been allowing you to dress and what I'm not allowing you to wear and he will e-mail or call me anytime you show up to school dressed inappropriately. Number three, you will write a two page, single spaced paper on the dangers of smoking and why you gave it up.

"Number four, and I mean it this time, you are done with Becky. You begged for another chance with her, and I gave it to you. I allowed her to stay in my house, I took her to the mall with us and we ignored all her dirty looks and snide remarks. She drove you to a tattoo parlor, encourages you to dress like a slut, and ditches classes with you to smoke. I'm not blaming her for your bad decisions, but the two of you don't make good decisions when you are together."

"I hate you!" Angel blows her temper.

"That's a shame," Michael scoffs.

"You don't have the right to decide who my best friend is or who my boyfriend is. You are so judgmental and full of yourself. I have tried so hard to please you and be who you want me to be, but nothing is good enough for you. Sorry to disappoint you, but in the end I am still me. I'm sorry you hate who I am, but that is who I am."

"What a load of crap. I am not being unreasonable. Every child in this school in every grade is expected to attend class, do their work, and not smoke. I am not making up rules to torture you. I am trying to get you to obey rules that have already existed for everyone," Michael defends himself.

"Fine," Angel defies, "But I will not give up Becky or David and I'm not writing some stupid paper about smoking and you can't make me."

"Want to make a bet?"

"I'm done doing back flips for you. Things are going to change to be fair toward me or else," Angel challenges.

"Or else what?"

"Or else I could tell someone that you act in inappropriate ways with me in the privacy of your home," she threatens.

Michael freezes for a moment and then anger washes over him. His eyes flash and his lips pull tight. He remains still and silent staring at her coldly. He waits to feel in control of his fury. She visibly shrinks back scared of his reaction. Shocked, Ronald waits for Michael to respond.

Finally, Michael takes a deep breath, "I can't believe that you would ever accuse me of that. I can't believe that you would endanger my ministry and be willing to hurt my family like that."

Angel looks down into her lap not responding. Tears brim in her eyes.

Michael smacks his legs standing up, "Well Angel, I'm sorry that this didn't work out. I really do care about you, but I can't allow you to destroy my life and hurt my family. So good luck and I'll miss you."

Angel looks up wide eyed and scared, "What are you saying?"

"I'm saying goodbye dear."

"But you promised me that you wouldn't threaten to throw me out to get your way," she reminds him with her lips trembling.

"I'm not trying to get my way! Believe me, this is not my way or what I wanted. You crossed a line and I can't let this happen," he turns to Ronald, "Please call Children's Services and have them pick her up. They can let me know where to send her things."

As Michael begins to leave, Angel bursts into tears, "Please don't leave me Reverend! I would never really do that, honest. I swear I'll never say anything like that again. Please don't leave me."

Michael turns back towards her, "You already did. You said that in front of your principal and you can't take it back. The mere suggestion of inappropriate behavior like that can ruin a teacher or minister. I care about you, but I'm not willing to let you destroy my life. Goodbye Angel. Take care of yourself."

As Michael reaches the door touching the doorknob, Angel throws herself at his feet wrapping her arms around his legs begging, "I'm sorry, Reverend. Please give me another chance, please. Mr. Moore didn't believe that you would do that. He knows that I was just being an ass. I swear, I swear that I would never hurt you like that. I promise. I love living with you and Sadie. I love your kids. Please take me home with you. I want to go home with you."

Michael firmly responds, "No."

Angel sobs causing her cheap eyeliner to run, "I'll do anything you want. I'll do anything you ask me to do. I'll write that paper. I'll go to class. I'll break up with David and Becky. I would rather live with you than be with them. I'm sorry. I'm so sorry."

Michael reaches down grabbing her arm and pulling her to her feet, "Don't you ever lie about me again." Angel nods frantically. He relents, "Okay, I'll take you home with me."

Angel wraps her arms around him burying her face in his chest. He holds her for a moment. Michael leads her to a chair and they sit back down.

"Do you really think that you can give up your old friends?"

"I'll do it. Becky will be hard, but I don't really care about David. I just didn't think I had a choice."

"That's what I have been trying to tell you. You always have a choice. It's your choice to stay with us. It's your choice whether you learn anything here or not. It's your choice of the type of people you spend time with. Your life has been undeniably hard, but the future is in your hands. Just because you have had a bad start doesn't mean that you can't find some happiness."

"Yes sir."

Ronald leans back in his chair relieved that the Reverend didn't leave her and wanting to help anyway he can.

"How far did you go with David? I know that you two made out heavily, but how far did you go?" Michael quietly asks.

Angel looks down in her lap, "We went all of the way. But I won't ever do it again. I never liked it anyway."

"Why not?"

"What do you mean?" Angel asks surprised by the question.

"Why didn't you like it?" he repeats.

"It's just weird and painful. Sex is just for men," Angel honestly answers.

Michael runs his hand over his face glancing at the principal who shrugs. "Angel, that's why you are too young to have sex. When you are not ready for something, it can be awful. If you didn't enjoy it, it is because you two didn't do it right."

"How do you do it right?" Angel questions.

Michael looks at the principal who just smirks and leans back before Michael turns back to Angel, "This is something that you and Sadie need to sit down and talk about. I think Sadie would do a much better job of discussing this in the privacy of your bedroom. I'm not sure why I just started this now."

"So you're saying that Sadie likes it?" she innocently questions.

Michael looks at the principal again who covers his mouth with his hand as Michael continues, "Yes, Sadie enjoys it, but you see I love Sadie. I love her deeply and I wouldn't do anything that she doesn't like or that would embarrass her or that would hurt her. David is too young to know what he is doing. He is too selfish to care how you were feeling. You need to back up and start over. You need to experience a more simple form of dating that does not include sex until you are ready for it. Sadie can be more specific later. Please, let's move on to other concerns."

Angel smiles shyly nodding her head.

"Angel, you need to make a new group of friends. You need to start developing a better transcript for college. Now a day, you can't make it without a college degree. You can choose what you want to study, but I expect you to go to college and find yourself a career that will fulfill you. You need to pick an extracurricular activity which will improve your transcript and introduce you to a new group of friends."

Angel shrugs, "Whatever you want."

Michael leans forward laying his hand on her arm, "No, what do you want? What would you find fun? Are you interested in the arts like choir, drama club, or band or would you be more interested in sports?"

Angel shrugs, "Sports I guess."

Michael turns to Ronald, "What kind of sports for girls have tryouts coming up?"

Ronald stands, "Wait here for a minute."

The principal hurries out of the office taking Mr. Foster with him down the hall to Daniel Haas's classroom, who is the sports director for the school. His class is quietly working on an assignment. Ronald leaves Mr. Foster with the biology class and requests that Dan come with him.

"Did you ever want to help a screwed up kid turn around with your sports program?" Mr. Moore asks.

"Of course, do you have someone in particular in mind?" Dan quizzes.

"Why, as a matter-of-fact, I do. Rev. Michael Donnelly is working his butt off with a foster child, Angel Heckathorn. He is interested in getting her involved in extracurricular activities and she said that sports interest her."

Dan follows Ronald into the office. Ronald introduces, "Rev. Donnelly, this is Dan Haas, our sports director."

Michael stands shaking hands. Dan looks down at Angel who is wearing the miniskirt and tank top and looks like raccoon with black smeared all over her cheeks. "I hear you are interested in trying out for a sports team."

"Yes sir," she nods.

"Well, it won't be easy. You have to keep your grades up and you will need to tryout. I won't bump someone more deserving if you are not prepared," Dan warns.

"Yes sir. My grades are better than they have been in years," she agrees.

"The next sport coming up is basketball. There will be tryouts in two weeks after school on Tuesday. Have you ever played basketball?" he questions.

"Only for fun, I've never been on a real team," she explains.

"Well you have two weeks. I suggest you practice and prepare for tryouts," Dan states.

"Yes sir."

Dan hands Michael a flier and paperwork. Michael extends his hand, "Thank you Mr. Haas." He then shakes hands with Mr. Moore, "Thank you for all of your help. I'm sorry that we took up the rest of your afternoon."

"I'm glad to help. I support what you are doing and will assist you anyway I can," Ronald promises.

"I know that school isn't over, but I would like to take her home with me now," Michael requests.

"That sounds like a good idea. We'll start fresh tomorrow," Ronald agrees.

On the way to the car, Angel quietly apologizes, "I'm sorry that I caused you so many problems. Thank you for taking me home with you."

Michael places his arm around her shoulders, "I don't expect you to be perfect, just don't hurt us on purpose. I just want you to try. When you make your next mistake, and you will, I want you to know that you can always come to me or Sadie."

"Yes sir... Reverend, I know that I don't have the right to ask for anything."

"What do you want?"

"I need to talk to Becky and explain why I can't hang out with her anymore. I probably should officially break up with David too."

"You're right. I don't care if you talk with Becky, but I'm afraid of David's reaction. I would prefer that you break up with David over the phone," Michael suggests. Angel nods.

They drive home to go over the events of the afternoon with Sadie who blows up when she hears the threat that Angel had made against her husband. Michael assures her that he has taken care of it, but Sadie takes a turn lecturing Angel for a long time on the horrible mistake that would be.

Later that evening, once Sadie calms down, she goes down to the basement where Angel sits on her bed staring at the wall. Sadie calmly sits on the bed beside her and has a surprisingly candid talk about sex. At first Angel is reluctant to talk, but Sadie is able to put her at ease. No adult has ever discussed this topic so openly, so freely. Sadie figures the girl already knows so much and that it is crucial to answer all of her questions. Soon, Angel begins asking questions and hanging on Sadie's every word.

Once in bed with Michael, Sadie gives him an idea of what the two had discussed to which he responds that he is relieved that he isn't a single parent who would be forced to have that discussion. Sadie laughs and then teases asking if he has any questions that he would like her to answer or demonstrate for him to which he responds that a refresher course couldn't hurt.

Chapter 18

The next evening, Angel calls David, "Hi David, it's me. Look, I almost got myself thrown out of the preacher's house yesterday. I know that you don't understand this, but I need to make it work here. I want to live here. When I was begging for him to keep me, I promised to break up with you."

"So?"

"So I'm gonna really break up with you. I'm not gonna sneak around anymore. I think I'm on my last chance here."

"Fine," David hangs up on her.

Angel sits quietly with her heart pounding and yet feeling somewhat relieved. Sadie enters her room and sits beside Angel on her bed. Sadie holds out her arms invitingly. Angel slides over allowing Sadie to hold her for awhile. She doesn't remember her mother sitting and holding her in her arms. Maybe she did when Angel was little, but not for a very long time.

After hearing from David about the phone call, Becky shows up to talk things over with Angel. The friends go out to the patio. Becky is completely unprepared for what Angel has to say. She yells and then cries with disbelief. Michael stands in the kitchen wondering if he is doing the right thing.

Soon Angel runs back into the kitchen and into Michael's arms. Once she calms down, Michael suggests a jog.

"Exercise helps with stress and you're now in training for the tryouts. Lucky for you, when I moved to Ambrose, my friends, Aidan and Steve, taught me to play basketball and I played with them for the last six years on and off. So, I know some and there are hoops out back."

Angel agrees running downstairs to change. Michael changes as well meeting Angel outside. They begin to jog. He slowly jogs beside her, but she has a cramp in her side and keeps stopping breathlessly.

"Okay sweetheart, stop. Let's start simply walking today and tomorrow speed walking. Then we can start walking two minutes, jogging two minutes alternating. We can build you up," Michael suggests.

He takes her on the paths through the cemetery. Angel tells him that as she was growing up, she always spent time here. She finds it peaceful and spooky. When her Mom would get high, she would come here to hide, play, or read. Angel stops by a large statue of an angel with the arms extended lovingly. The beautiful large wings spread open as if she is about to take off. Michael responds that since he has lived here, he jogs here and has always liked this statue as well. As their walk continues, Angel points out interesting tombstones that she has discovered over the years. They enjoy their time together.

When they return to the garage, Michael grabs a basketball and leads her to the court behind the parking lot. As they shoot baskets, Sadie and the children appear with Peter in the stroller and are on their way to the playground. Michael and Angel, both a sweaty mess, go and play with the girls before going in to take turns showering. Michael allows her to go first, sacrificing most of the hot water.

Saturday morning, when Michael asks if Angel is ready to jog, Angel informs him that Sadie invited her to go to *Curves* with her as a guest. As Angel enters *Curves* she looks around rolling her eyes. Sadie greets several women of various ages. Angel finds an open area to begin the circuit. Sadie carefully shows and explains how to use each machine and then what to do on the recovery squares. Angel whines that this is lame, but Sadie just keeps encouraging her to work out all her muscles. Sadie barks at Angel that she is only working on the machines with careless and little effort. A person only gets out what they put into it. Sadie pushes her teasing her for being wimpy. By the second time around the circuit, Angel actually gets into it and attempts to keep up with Sadie's energy.

On the recovery squares, Sadie begins to dance to the seventies dance music. Several of the other women do the same and soon everyone is laughing and having a good time. Angel simply steps back and forth to the side. She seems as if she thinks the whole thing is dumb. After a few machines, Angel gives in and actually joins in dancing. As they are halfway around the circuit for the second time, Jonel and Kim enter surprised to find their minister's wife and Angel dancing around. Angel gives her all on each machine. Jonel and Kim begin their circuit right behind Sadie to join in the fun.

Once they finish their workout, they go to the back corner to do their cool down stretches. While Angel won't admit it to Sadie, she is surprised how much fun she actually had. However, Sadie can tell.

Sunday before church, Angel asks Sadie for a favor and they disappear into Sadie's room. Michael fixes the girls their breakfast while they wait. As they eat, Michael looks up in time to see Angel enter the kitchen wearing a light blue short sleeved blouse with a darker blue skirt and white sandals. He boasts that she looks beautiful. He recognizes that it is one of Sadie's old outfits that she can't fit into anymore since having three babies.

Many people at church notice that Angel wears a skirt for the first time. She feels shy and a little embarrassed by the compliments. Even Cole stops to smile at her thinking that she looks pretty. Cole is impressed. He has been watching her transformation over the past two months.

After church the youth group sets up for the children's Halloween party. Cole hangs around Angel. They joke around and laugh as they decorate. She helps him and his friends set up a maze with tables, blankets and chairs. Angel figures out how to use some blankets to create a tunnel which the children will need to crawl under a table where she hangs black construction paper spiders with yarn legs that she and Amber made.

Michael helps out trying to give Angel her space, yet watching her. She has loosened up with the other seven teens in the group as she gets into making decorations. She and Amber bring in a basketball and a white table cloth to create a flying ghost in the corner with rope and string. Angel appears prettier than ever with her face relaxed and laughing, the usual hard bitter expression missing.

The three boys stay at church to change into their costumes, but Angel invites the four girls over to the parsonage to change down in her room. Michael and Sadie sit in the kitchen listening to the four girls laughing and carrying on as they talk very fast and loudly. To them, this is how a teenage girl should act. They emerge from the basement dressed as a witch, a zombie bride, some kind of girl covered in cobwebs, a pale ghost in a ragged, yet once formal gown, and last, but not least, the vampiress. Michael has to admit that Sadie had been right about allowing Angel to buy her costume, because she definitely fits in.

Michael and Sadie take their three children to the party. Cole flies Peter around the basement reciting Superman dialogue. Robin spends the party playing with Cassie and Rachel follows Angel around. Rachel loves Angel. Having the teens run the party was an excellent idea. They are old enough to do the work, but young enough to really get down and play with the children. The teens have as much fun as the kids. The attendance is better than usual.

As he watches Angel laughing and helping a group of kids with a craft, Michael feels relieved that he hadn't left Angel for Children Services to pick up. He can't believe the difference in her this week has brought and prays that it lasts.

The following week goes very well. Michael and Angel jog and play basketball. Thursday night, Sadie stays home with Peter to pass out Halloween candy while Michael and Angel take the girls trick-or-treating.

Saturday, Michael has a big surprise for Angel. For November, the weather is beautiful, still in the mid sixties. He and his family take Angel out to the parking lot where she finds several cars unloading. The Donnellys' friends from Ambrose pour into the parking lot.

"I don't want to appear rude, but how are your friends a surprise for me?" Angel questions.

Michael props his elbows up on Aidan and Steve's shoulders, "These two were on their high school basketball teams. They are here to coach and drill you today. Graham is here because he is one of us, but don't watch him, he's bad."

"Hey," Graham acts insulted.

"The rest are here for the girls and Sadie," Michael explains.

The loud happy group takes to the field. The children storm the playground while the women talk like rapid gunfire. The men take Angel to the basketball court to drill and coach her. Michael has done a pretty good job working with her, but Aidan and Steve know how to fine tune and what the coach will be looking for.

After a couple hours, the ladies set up a picnic lunch in the pavilion. When lunch is ready, Sadie arms the children with small water guns. The ladies sneak the kids up close to the basketball court and then sic them on the players to open fire. The men pretend to be upset and run around, yet stay in range of the children. Michael slowly runs backward while his giggling daughters shoot him.

The children scream and the men yell playfully. Sadie saunters up to Angel holding up the biggest water gun, "Go get him."

Angel shakes her head shyly, but Sadie coaxes her, "Think about how hard he has ridden you over the past few months."

A smile slowly crosses her face as she grabs the gun and runs after him opening fire. Michael is surprised when he is hit in the back. He turns to see Angel coming after him. He laughs and dodges her, but she chases him. Finally he spins around and manages to get behind her. Wrapping his arms around her waist, he lifts her off the ground to swing her to and fro.

Once the water guns have been confiscated, they walk to the pavilion for a nice luncheon. The one cooler is full of water bottles, pop, and juice boxes. Another cooler has beer and wine coolers. The guys sit on a table grabbing a beer. Sadie and her friends make up plates for the children first. Angel sneaks behind the men and quietly takes a beer. As she casually walks around the table, Michael senses her guilt. Looking over his shoulder, he notices the beer cooler. He looks back at Angel who has one hand hidden from him.

Michael stands. Walking up behind her, he wraps one arm around her waist and pulls up her hidden hand with the other discovering the stolen beer.

He takes it away, "Angel, go get a pop."

"Oh come on. You guys are enjoying a cold beer after that hard work out," she reasons, but Michael simply keeps his steady gaze on her. "Okay, okay, I'll get a pop."

Michael rejoins his friends shaking his head and Sadie hits her on the head with a paper plate. After lunch, they announce that it is time to return to the court, but she sighs and rolls her eyes. They promise to play a game this time instead of just drilling her.

Before they begin their game, a car pulls up in the parking lot by the court. Rob, Cole, and Amber climb out.

"Hey Reverend, what are you guys up to?" Rob greets them.

"Angel is trying out for the basketball team on Tuesday, so we're helping her practice," Michael informs them.

"Amber's trying out too, so Cole and I came to work her out," Rob claps her on the back.

"Well, join us," Michael invites, "These are my friends, Aidan, Steve, and Graham. This is my friend Rob and his kids, Cole and Amber."

They divide up into teams to scrimmage. Cole is on the opposing team from Angel and makes it a point to guard her which Michael notices. Cole is impressed with Angel's game. Rob easily fits in with Michael's friends and has a great time. Aidan stops a few times to give both Amber and Angel pointers. Cole, who is on the varsity team, also has helpful hints for his sister and friend.

The ladies and kids come to watch the game and cheer the game on. Angel has a great day. She had never been at a family picnic, let alone one that had been organized for her benefit. Once everyone heads home, Angel walks down to her room overwhelmed by the day. The Reverend had been fun. Everyone was backing her and Cole even gave her suggestions and played with her.

Overcome with emotion, she lies on her bed sobbing. Michael heads for the garage office to print the outline he made for the next morning's sermon, hears her, and goes to her room. Knocking on her door, she yells to go away, but he enters anyway and sits on the edge of her bed.

"Why are you crying?"

"I don't know."

"How can you not know?"

"I don't know."

"Well, what are you thinking about?"

"The day."

"Didn't you have fun? Am I putting too much pressure on you? You know that if you don't make the team that's okay. I have enjoyed jogging with you and playing ball. If you don't make the team, you can find something else to do. I'm proud of you already for just how hard you have worked," he assures her.

"It's not that," she sits up, "I don't know how to explain it. I've never been to a picnic like that and I never had so many people rooting for me, even people who don't even know me. I don't know why that makes me cry. I'm just being stupid."

Michael smiles warmly at Angel pulling a handkerchief out of his pocket for her to wipe her face, "That's okay and you're not stupid. You don't have to understand. Sadie has been trying to explain to me for years that sometimes a girl just needs a good cry. Men don't really understand this, but I believe Sadie." He rubs her back for a moment before he stands, "Sadie is in Peter's room if you want to talk to her. She may be better at this than me."

"No, I'm okay. I'm exhausted. I think I'll just watch a little TV and then go to sleep."

"Okay, goodnight," he kisses her on top of her head and leaves.

The next day, the family heads for church. This morning, Michael is beginning a children's sermon between the readings and the offertory. His father-in-law suggested having the children bring in anything they want in a brown lunch bag and then he randomly picks a bag and gives a children's moment off the top of his head. Michael didn't think this sounded like a good idea, but Martin goaded him into it calling him a coward and daring him to try it.

Sadie encourages Michael to give it a try. She insists that it could be fun. She tells him that when she was in high school, she and her brother attended a special youth conference in Erieton. At one point the bishop came to speak the teens. Of all of the bishops she had seen over the years, this one had always been her favorite. He was a tall, thin black man with graying hair at the temples. He was a gentleman who exuded an air of spirituality.

The bishop announced that he knew the Bible so well, they could give him any word and he could recite an appropriate Bible verse. Teens began to raise their hands to challenge him. Two boys sitting in the front row huddled up and began laughing. The bishop kept a close watch on the boys and when they sat up with their hands stretched up high, the bishop called on them.

"Constipation!" they challenged.

The room filled with laughter as the bishop rubbed his chin thoughtfully with a smirk. When the room quieted, the bishop lifted his pointer finger and spoke, "And God said to Moses, take two tablets and go into the wilderness."

The room erupted with laughter.

Michael laughs at Sadie's story and wonders if he could be that witty. He also wonders if he will be able to relate whatever a child thinks to place in a bag to a Bible story, but Michael, who has always been an athlete and competitor, thrives on challenges, even in his ministry.

So, last week, he announced that the children could bring in the bags for the next week's service. Once the readings are finished, Michael sits on the steps inviting the young ones to join him and eight kids between the ages of three and seven run up the aisle to sit around him including his daughters and Cassie. Sadie sits at the organ and smiles thinking that Michael looks sweet surrounded by the children.

Only two actually remembered to bring in brown paper bags, Robin and Cassie. So he announces that he will open both of them this week so not to disappoint either or to appear to play favorites. First, he opens Robin's and pulls out a stuffed animal, Piglet, from the Winnie the Pooh books. He holds it up for everyone to see. Then he opens Cassie's bag and pulls out a plastic police car.

Michael sits up front with a pig in one hand and a police car in the other. The room goes silent and Michael's eyes connect with his friend, Officer Rob as he and Jonel struggle to keep from bursting into laughter. Sadie covers her mouth with her hand.

Michael looks at the two toys and begins, "Well, this is Piglet and as we all know, Piglet is a very good friend of Winnie the Pooh and Christopher Robin. This is a police car and I hope that all of you kids realize that the police are your friends and are there to protect and help you. If you are ever in trouble or lost, you should trust and go to a police officer.

"Jesus wants to be your friend too. He wants to love you, guide you, and comfort you. There is a wonderful song called, '*What a Friend We Have in Jesus.*' Now, let's see if I can remember; it goes something like, '*What a friend we have in Jesus, all our sins and grief to bear! What a privilege to carry everything to God in prayer!*'

"What this means is that whether you are having good times or bad, you are to remember to include Jesus by praying to Him and He will always be there for you. Let's pray."

Michael concludes with a prayer and sends the children skipping back to their seats. As he stands, he locks eyes with Rob again who smiles and nods approvingly. After church, many comment positively about the adorable and clever children's sermon. Once home, Michael calls Martin to relay the story to which his father-in-law laughs heartedly.

Chapter 19

Tuesday after school, Angel stays for the girls Junior Varsity tryouts since she is a sophomore. Michael arrives at school to pick her up and waits outside the gym for her with the other parents who are gathering. He visits with Rob while they wait. Mr. Moore sees the Reverend as he walks by signaling to him.

"I called your house and your wife said that you were on your way," Ronald begins.

"Why? Is there a problem?"

"Yes, but I'm not sure how serious it is. I can't quite tell. After Angel's lunch period, I saw her coming up from the basement. I asked where she had been. She said that she was just eating lunch and reading a book. I smelled her and she didn't smell like smoke or anything. I took a look around the basement and I didn't see anything out of place. I told her that we have to know where our students are at all times and that she has to go to the cafeteria when she is supposed to. She nodded, but never really answered me about why she was eating down there."

Soon, the gym empties. Amber reports to Michael that Angel was fabulous and that there is no way that she'll be cut. Amber also tells them that for some reason, Mr. Haas had sat in on the tryouts. There will be a list posted on the athletics' room door in the morning.

Michael tells Angel that he is proud of how hard she had worked. On the way home, Michael questions Angel about eating in the basement. She rolls her eyes and then stares out the window stating that she didn't do anything wrong. Gently Michael encourages her to explain what is going on.

"I can't sit with my old friends and everyone else already has their groups. It's awkward and embarrassing to eat by myself and just sit there staring off. So, for the past several weeks I've been packing my lunch and eating by myself and reading a book in the basement. I've kinda like the quiet alone time," she explains.

"I see. I'm sorry things are hard for you. What about someone from youth group? Maybe you could ask if you could sit with one of them," he suggests.

"They are friendly at church, but at school, they ignore me. I have a bad reputation and I don't think that they want their friends to think that we are friends."

Michael wishes he knew what to say. He forgets how hard what he is asking of her actually is.

The next day, when Angel arrives home from school, she runs into the house shouting that she had made the team. Michael lifts her off the floor swinging her around. To celebrate, the family walks down the street to The Hungry Wolf for supper with ice cream for dessert.

Practices are scheduled to start after Thanksgiving and go through December. Their first game is scheduled for January. For Thanksgiving, the Donnellys' go to Michael's parents' house first and then to Sadie's parents' house on Saturday. Angel can't believe her eyes when they drive up to the mansion where Michael had been raised.

Sophia is pleasantly surprised to see how Angel looks now compared to their first meeting in September. She had worried about her son taking in this stray, but like always, Michael's decisions seem to work out for him. She wishes that she shared Sadie's faith in Michael's relationship with God. Michael definitely needs a wife like Sadie to do what he does.

Angel is quiet as she stares around one elegant room after another and observes, "Reverend, you went from living here to living in our tiny house? Our whole downstairs would fit in this living room."

Michael and his family laughs. Michael's sister, Carol, and her husband, Drew, arrive with their two year old daughter, Tiffany.

"Don't you have any family or friends with a child older than five?" Angel asks.

"Sorry dear, but no."

Angel is even more surprised when Michael's brother, Sean, arrives with his partner, Jeremy. Michael hadn't warned her that his brother is openly gay. Sean walks in carrying a tiny baby.

"Hey, look who I brought," Sean beams happily. "Three days ago, we were given our first foster baby."

Everyone cheers and gathers around to meet the new arrival. Sophia gasps, "Oh my, that is the smallest baby I have ever seen."

The family looks down at a teeny tiny black baby boy who begins to tremble and cry surprisingly loud for his size. Everyone takes a seat in the living room while Sean fills them in on the details.

"This is Astro," Sean introduces.

"Astro?" Sophia snaps.

"We didn't name him. Anyway, Astro only weighs five pounds six ounces. This poor little guy was born addicted to cocaine. He's already a month old. He was four pounds five ounces at birth. He's going through withdrawal. He cries at a gentle touch or sound. He's jittery and has trouble both sleeping and eating. We're really struggling to feed the little guy. He will most likely have trouble bonding, so one of us is almost always holding him even though it brings him little comfort. He doesn't respond to our faces and voices like most babies do. He has poor reflexes and is in serious danger of SIDS, mental retardation, cerebral palsy, visual and hearing impairments.

"Jeremy gave up his job to stay home fulltime to care for him and I go home as soon as possible to take my turn and give Jeremy as many breaks as I can."

Sophia stares at her son in disbelief, "Why would you take something like this on by choice? Why would you do this to yourself on purpose?"

With a warm smile, Sean responds, "Because he needs someone to care. What would happen to him if no one was willing to take care of him? Besides, look at those big eyes. We don't mind holding and rocking him day and night."

James looks at his sons from Sean holding the painfully tiny baby to Michael sitting beside Angel, "My sons have more in common than I ever realized."

Michael and Sean smile at each other, but Angel huffs, "Oh great, now I'm being compared to a crack baby."

Michael laughs patting her knee, "No way, not even close. My dad just means that we are willing to open our homes to a child in need. You're way easier to care for than that."

Sophia looks around the room at her family shaking her head, while her gay son holds a black crack baby and her minister son sits by a troubled teenager and sighs, "I'm just not open-minded enough for my own family."

James smiles at his wife, "Don't worry dear, our children are teaching us as we go along."

"We may not stay for dinner," Jeremy speaks up.

"Not stay for Thanksgiving dinner? Why?" Sophia demands.

"Astro cries constantly and spits up often. He may get on everyone's nerves and ruin your day," Jeremy explains.

Everyone promises that they can take the crying and want them to stay. Then they turn to Sophia who sits quietly for moment before caving into the pressure and insisting that she is fine with them staying for dinner with their baby boy.

Angel is impressed with the wonderful food which is served. She has never seen a place setting with so many pieces of silverware which is apparently actually silver. Her ice water is in real crystal stemware. Angel is almost afraid to eat off the shiny white plates with gold trim for fear of breaking something. The napkins are green cloth embossed with a rose pattern.

Jeremy and Sean take turns leaving the room to walk Astro when he cries. During a moment of quiet, all sit at the table together. Sadie sits at the end of the table beside James who sits at the head of the table with an extra chair sitting close by with the baby carrier holding Peter. Sadie pulls Peter out and holds him on her lap as they eat. Rachel sits beside Michael who encourages and practically forces her to eat even though this is not food that she is used to eating. Carol fights the same struggle with her two year old, Tiffany.

Sean looks down into Astro's big eyes, "Oh Mikey, I wish we could have you baptize Astro. He could use the blessing and prayers for his health. However, he is just our foster baby and we can't do something like that."

Angel giggles, "Mikey?"

"Shut up," Michael teases, "You know Sean, I may not be able to baptize the little guy, but that doesn't mean that I can't bless him and pray for his special needs and to pray for you two."

After supper, the family gathers in the living room and stands in a circle. Michael takes Astro into his arms cooing and comforting him, "Wow, compared to Peter, I feel like I'm holding a small throw pillow. It's kind of like holding a ragdoll. Let us pray."

Michael places his hand on the baby's forehead giving him a blessing and praying for God's healing power. He prays for Sean and Jeremy's strength, wisdom, and guidance. The family responds in unison, "Amen."

Angel walks over to the carrier, gazing down at the baby and gently strokes his arms and chest softly talking to him unaware that she has caught everyone's attention. Her words brings a silence to the room and tears to several eyes, "I'm sorry that you are going through this. I probably get you better than anyone in this room. Listen to me, just because your mom has a terrible problem and she makes really bad decisions, doesn't mean that she doesn't love you. She loves you, but you are lucky that someone else is taking care of you and loves you like Grams always took care of me."

Embarrassed, Angel suddenly becomes aware that everyone is listening and quickly moves away from the baby. Soon, Sean and Carol's family leave for the night.

The guestroom that Angel is given just for her is huge and beautiful. She is surprised that she doesn't have to share a room with the little ones. The queen size bed is stacked with a half dozen pillows and the thickest, most plush comforter she ever felt. The sheets are satin and luxurious. There are also beautiful bouquets of silk flowers placed throughout the room.

When Sadie had suggested that Angel pack a swimsuit in November, Angel had assumed that they might go to the country club. It never occurred to her that the Donnellys would have a full size indoor swimming pool complete with a diving board. Glass French style doors lead to a family room. The room with the pool has changing areas, several white metal round tables with matching chairs and a Tiki bar.

Angel discovers another room, which they refer to as the library. It is full of bookshelves, a huge ornate desk, and a comfortable oxblood leather couch and chairs. On the one wall, shelves are full of for trophies, plaques, and ribbons that their children had won. Paintings, pencil sketches, and chalk drawings sport ribbons earned by Sean. There are pictures of a young Carol winning a couple local beauty contests with a few tiaras setting in front of the pictures. She also won trophies for swimming meets and diving competitions.

There is a large collection of tennis trophies and tennis awards that Michael won, as well as, trophies and awards in track. There are pictures of Michael on swim teams, on golf leagues, riding a horse, and in track. There is a picture of Michael after winning a large tennis competition with his beautiful, young partner perched on his shoulder.

Michael walks in behind Angel and looks over her shoulder at what she is looking at, "That's Barbara. She was my first fiancée."

"You were with someone before Sadie? Wow, I can't picture you with anyone but Sadie."

"Me either. Barbara was with me in college when I was planning to attend Harvard with my close friends, Graham and Colby, to be a lawyer. We were going to start our own law firm, Worthington, Donnelly, and Stark. When I decided to go to a seminary to be a minister, they weren't just surprised, they were furious. Barbara left me. Graham and I made up eventually, but Colby and I have drifted apart. Graham has become a prestigious defense attorney, but Colby didn't do as well as Graham. He's a divorce lawyer. And Barbara, she would have never made it in my current lifestyle.

"I thought I loved her, but I didn't know real love until I met Sadie, but at first Sadie didn't want to be with me. It took me five months to get her to admit that she even liked me and to admit that we were dating. I can be stubborn too. You see, she didn't trust men after Troy had almost killed her, plus she was a minister's kid and she didn't want to give up her job to follow me around from one parsonage to another."

"So what happened to Barbara?"

"She was married, but according to Graham, Colby is handling her divorce. Barbara blames me for her problems because I left her, but she couldn't have handled being a minister's wife. She would have divorced me the by now and if not, she would have left the day I brought you home," he teases.

Angel playfully punches his arm, "So why did you leave all of this to be a minister?"

"I received what is referred to as a calling. God wants me to do this."

"How do you receive a calling? When God talks to you, do you literally hear a voice in your head?"

"No, it sort of varies. Sometimes you can become plagued with a thought or sometimes it's a strong feeling. Sometimes when I pray I will have a sick feeling in the pit of my stomach letting me know that I'm not doing the right thing or I'll pray about a decision and have a calm or good feeling about it.

"I went for a walk the weekend before my fall semester as a sophomore at college began and passed this little brick church with a sign out front that listed the service times. The next morning I woke up with the picture of that sign in my head, so out of curiosity, I attended the service. I thought about it and started going every week. The minister had a feeling about me and started pulling me aside to talk. After awhile, he talked me into being a lector and participating in various ways in the service. Before I knew it, I started thinking about being a minister but tried to ignore it for two years.

"I couldn't actually visualize myself as a lawyer, but I could picture myself as a minister. Even though Barbara left me, my friends and parents were angry with me, and Sadie wouldn't date me, I never doubted that I was supposed to be a minister."

Angel requests, "Would you pray and find out what I am supposed to do?"

"Sweetheart, I have been praying for you since I met you. I'm not sure I'm always doing the right thing, but I pray and, of course, I go to Sadie. Right now, my goal is to make sure that you are safe, that you are healthy, and to prepare you over the next two and a half years for college. What you will study there and what career path you will follow, you have to choose and pray about for yourself. My father was convinced that I should be a lawyer and pushed me hard in that direction, but he was wrong. Your parents can't choose your career. My mother didn't want me to date or marry Sadie, but I knew better."

Michael shows her his awards and shares some of his favorite memories. Then he asks her if she has ever played pool to which she responds never. He offers to teach her inviting her to the billiards room. She stares at him in disbelief that his childhood home has a billiards room and agrees to play pool. On their way, they stop at the top of the stairs hearing Sadie playing the grand piano in the living room beautifully. Angel has never seen a house like this and it doesn't feel real.

The next day, they pack up to leave to go visit Sadie's family who is celebrating Thanksgiving on Saturday, so that all four of their children were free to visit their new families and everyone could make it together. The family is so big now and their parsonage is only a small ranch house that they plan to have their dinner in Martin's church fellowship hall.

While they are saying their goodbyes, Michael notices his dad closely examining the minivan again, "Dad, our van is fine."

"It doesn't have very many options and it's beginning to rust in several places. What year is this?" his dad questions.

"Goodbye Dad, it was nice seeing you. Don't worry about us. We are doing great," Michael assures his father. He hurries his family into the van declaring that they had to get going.

Chapter 20

December passes by quickly. Sadie decorates the house beautifully with the kids and Angel. The kids are excited about Santa and Christmas lists. There are several special parties and events at church for the season which includes a Youth Group trip to a special lighting display, as well as, Christmas caroling at Grams's nursing home.

Robin and Rachel are in the Christmas pageant starring Peter as the baby Jesus. Robin and Cassie play angels and Rachel is one of the sheep. Sadie and Jonel co-direct. The pageant takes place on the fourth Sunday of Advent in place of Michael's sermon. The children are adorable. Two sixth graders play Mary and Joseph because they are old enough to handle Peter. Angel and Amber help dress the children and send them out on their cues.

The five teenage girls in the youth group sing a beautiful contemporary Christmas song, *"Mary, Did You Know?"* during the pageant that is very impressive. Michael and Sadie discover that Angel has a lovely alto voice.

At school, Angel's grades are all A's and B's, her basketball practices are going well, and she continues to sneak away from the lunchroom. Several times a week, Angel notices David and/or Becky glaring at her. The last day of school before Christmas, David and Becky approach Angel to let her know that she is welcomed back with them whenever she wants or when she gets tired of being daddy's good little girl. Angel is lonely and misses her friends, especially Becky.

Angel spends her own money on gifts for her new family. She buys a play dough vet kit for Rachel, a kit with colored pencils, crayons, markers, and water colors for Robin, a toy boat for bath time for Peter, a music box shaped like an organ being played by an angel with the tune, *Amazing Grace* for Sadie and a statue of Jesus playing basketball with a girl and a boy for the Reverend.

Christmas morning, Robin and Rachel run into the basement jumping on Angel, "Wake up, wake up! Santa came!"

Laughing, Angel follows the girls upstairs to watch as the little girls jump up and down on their parents. Michael pretends to be too tired to wake up as the girls pull and push on him begging him to wake up. Finally, he climbs out of bed and picks up six month old Peter who can now sit up on his own. Running into the living room with the excited little girls, Angel enjoys the best Christmas morning she ever had.

One of Angel's gifts is a large fluffy, blue and yellow duck which lies flat and is meant to be placed on a bed. Angel hates to admit it, but she actually likes the goofy thing. Sometimes it almost seems as if Sadie knows Angel better than she knows herself. She also likes the clothes that Sadie picked out for her. Sadie has definitely figured out Angel's taste. Her new family also gives her a book, CDs, and a hand held video game.

Angel curls up in the corner of the couch watching the picturesque family sitting on the floor amongst a mess of wrapping paper and bows. Michael sits on the floor leaning on the couch struggling to free toys and dolls which are tied with strings and plastic to the boxes as anxious daughters sit on their knees bouncing up and down with anticipation. Sadie plays with Peter who is laughing hard with the cutest little baby laugh which causes everyone in the room to laugh and giggle.

Angel's mind drifts back to her childhood. For the first ten years of her life Grams had been healthy and her grandfather, Gramps, had been alive. Her childhood had been fairly normal and her grandparents loved her. Her mother was nothing but a visitor, feeling more like a favorite aunt than a mother. When her mother left the hospital with her new little baby girl, she went straight to her parents, handed over the baby, and ran like hell. Back then her Christmases had been fun although not quite as magical as the one with the Donnellys. She would get up and open some presents and then play by herself for most of the day. Grams would make an okay dinner. Most of the time, her mom would show up for the holidays with a gift or two. Sometimes she wouldn't show up at all.

Her Gramps always called her his special Christmas Angel, but at ten years old, right after Christmas, on January 10, her Gramps died suddenly of a massive heart attack in the house right in front of Grams and Angel. Garnet ran to the phone to call for help and Angel threw herself on her grandfather sobbing and begging him not to die, but he was already dead. Garnet was never quite the same after losing her beloved husband. It was the beginning of the shift in the course of Angel's life.

When Angel was twelve, her mom came home for the holidays. On Christmas Eve, Tara got drunk, wasted, scaring her daughter. The next morning, while Angel opened her Christmas morning gifts, her mom sat on the couch, crabby with a horrendous hangover. It made Grams angry.

Then, in November, when Angel was thirteen, Angel had been home alone with her mom one night while Grams was at a women's meeting at the church, when the door had been broken down and the house filled with police officers. The raid discovered drugs hidden all over the house. Her mother was arrested and Angel was taken away by Children's Services.

It took two days for Grams to beg Children Services to give Angel back to her. Angel hasn't seen her mother since that night refusing to go to court or even visit her in jail. However, Tara and Angel do write to each other all of the time and Angel sends her mom photos.

That summer when Angel was fourteen, her mother was sentenced to five years in prison. It broke both Grams and Angel's hearts. Grams was left angry, frustrated, and difficult to live with. Angel, filled with anger and disappointment, couldn't take it anymore and ran away from home. As she walked down the highway alone, she had no idea where she was going. She became more and more frightened and regretted her decision to leave.

Then David, who had been an acquaintance for years, a friend even, pulled up beside Angel in his jalopy of a car. She was so relieved to see him. He climbed out of the car, touched her arm, and asked if she was okay. Breaking down into tears, she could barely talk. David wrapped his arms around her comforting her the best he could. They sat in the car for a long time talking. David leaned over and kissed her. Angel wasn't sure if she liked it, but after feeling so alone in the world, she enjoyed the attention, the feeling that someone loved her, wanted her. She soon became David's girl and she felt as if she belonged to someone who wanted her. Her mother didn't want her. Her father didn't want her, but David wanted her.

David always made out too heavily with her and sex soon followed. She had hedged and suggested waiting, but he had insisted and had been pushy. He practically forced her. She hated it. The first time hurt so badly, but he refused to stop…

Sadie crawls across the floor through the wrapping paper and toys to her husband to give him a kiss. She then turns leaning back on his chest while he wraps his arms around her resting his chin on her shoulder as they watch their children play. The girls play with toys while Peter plays with the ripped up colorful paper and boxes.

Michael reminisces about the Christmas morning he and Sadie had sat alone by the tree and Michael began day dreaming about watching children play under the Christmas tree. Suddenly, Michael had taken Sadie by surprise by proposing for the first time. Sadie, after some discussion, had answered, "Not yet."

Now the couple enjoys their family and Angel enjoys being part of it even if it still doesn't seem real to her. Part of her wonders how long all of this will even last before she has to start over somewhere else. She just can't trust this to last.

The next day, the family returns to the Donnelly mansion to celebrate the holiday with Michael's family. Michael pulls the van up in the driveway, stops, and turns off the engine, but just sits there, not moving.

"Is something wrong?" Sadie asks.

"Look over there," Michael indicates a shiny new red minivan. "Now who do you suppose would be here that drives a minivan? My brother and sister don't drive minivans."

They enter the house to hugs and kisses. They take their suitcases upstairs and then sit around the family room visiting by a ten foot elegantly decorated Christmas tree with strictly gold and silver bulbs and formal bows with a string of white, glittering lights.

Michael can't wait, "Dad, who owns that red minivan in your driveway?"

James and Sophia exchange glances, before James responds, "Merry Christmas son, the minivan is yours and Sadie's Christmas present."

Michael jumps up, "No, we cannot accept that kind of gift."

James jumps up as well, "Why the hell not?"

"We are not accepting a gift that is that expensive. Dad, just because we asked for help with a room and accepted riding lessons for Robin, doesn't mean that I want you to begin subsidizing my salary. I am perfectly capable of taking care of my family," Michael declares.

"Sadie made more than you so you have lost more than half your income and you have added two more people to your family. So what if I want to help you a little? Sadie, help me out here," James turns to Sadie and Michael turns to face her as well.

"Girls, let's go with Grandma to the library and let Daddy and Grandpa talk," Sadie shoos the girls out and Sophia quickly follows.

Before Sadie reaches the door, James tries one more time to solicit her help because he knows that she is the one person Michael listens to, "Sadie, don't you have an opinion on this one? The minivan is for you too."

"Nope, no opinion here. Good luck, gotta go," Sadie hurries from the room.

"Son, I respect that you are a good father and husband and that you can take care of your family on your own, but try to look at it from my point of view. I'm your father and I want to help you. You are my son and I love you and Sadie and my beautiful grandchildren. The new van has many safety options like antilock brakes and traction control for country driving in the snow with your family in the car. It also has some nice things for my grandchildren like a DVD player," his father debates.

"If I take this, what are you going to give me next without asking? You knew that I didn't want help with a vehicle. You didn't respect my wishes. I know that you struggle with the fact that I became a minister and you hate the way I live but…"

"That's not true! Well, that's not true anymore. I fought you hard at first, but I can see what good you have done. Sadie was the first to force me to look at what you were doing when she called inviting us to your first Christmas Eve service and started telling stories about the people you had helped. Michael, I have been paying attention to what you are doing and I am proud of you.

"You are doing so great. You have a beautiful family and they are happy, loved, and well cared for. You are more hands on than I ever was changing diapers, helping in the kitchen, running errands. The difference that you are making in Angel's life is amazing. Opening your home to a girl like that just because you had the feeling that God wanted you to do this? Your mother and I were worried, but it seems to be going well.

"All I want to do is help out here and there in small ways. It's just a vehicle and it is safer especially on snow covered country roads. Can't you just understand that I love you and say thank you?"

"Fine, thank you," Michael huffs.

"Now that wasn't so hard, was it?" James smirks.

"I love you, but you drive me crazy," Michael sighs.

"I bet you drive Angel crazy. That's what fathers do," James jabs.

Michael attempts to hide a smile knowing that he has done nothing but drive that child crazy.

Soon the others arrive. Sean and Jeremy enter with their tiny Astro. Sean brags to Michael using a baby talk tone, "He has gained two whole pounds. Yes he has and is beginning to eat better. While his reflexes are still slow, he is beginning to respond to Jeremy and my voice sometimes. Don't you? Yes you do. Yes you do. And he doesn't cry as much, but still cries quite a bit. He still can't make it through the night, can you my sweet little boy."

"Whoa Sean, you are spending too much time with the baby. Switch to your adult voice, please," Michael jokes.

"Sorry," Sean laughs placing Astro up on his shoulder.

Sadie brought the smallest clothes that she could find that Peter once wore and some extra baby supplies for Astro.

Sean spreads out an adorable pastel baby blanket with teddy bears all over it. He lies Astro down and then sets a state of the art baby gym over him with sounds and blinking lights to rouse and stimulate the baby. They don't need Sadie's hand-me-downs. Jeremy and Sean spare no expense on their young ward. They have even already had professional pictures taken, but not wanting to expose him to all the germs at a mall, they paid a photographer to come to their home.

The pair does not use store bought baby food like Sadie, but instead pay their chef extra to purée a specific doctor suggested diet. The nursery is the size of the Donnellys' living room with an air purifier. Sean purchased a special monitor to use at night which has an alarm that sounds if the baby stops breathing to fight Sudden Infant Death Syndrome. They pay a nurse to stop by each morning to weigh him and take his vitals.

Instead of a simple rocking chair in the nursery, Jeremy purchased a comfortable rocking recliner since there is no telling how long it will be before Astro actually sleeps through the night. They play Mozart softly in the nursery and read Dickens and poetry to the baby. Sean and Jeremy dote on the baby giving him their hearts even though he is unable to return their affection. Sean and Jeremy work hard to bond with the boy in the hopes that he can learn to love and trust. While they are aware that they cannot fix this broken child, they attempt to give him every advantage to help him be the best he can be.

Astro's case worker who had been slow to give a child to a gay couple is overwhelmed by the men's dedication and the home they are providing, promising to provide them with more children. They request time to learn how to do this with Astro first, not wanting to divide their time just yet with other children, but are thrilled to have the approval.

The family enjoys their Christmas dinner together. Robin makes several comments that she wishes she lived in a house like this. Angel agrees in her head.

The next day, Michael and his family drive away with a car full of gifts in the new bright red minivan. Angel can't believe that James and Sophia bought her an IPod. Sadie smiles at Michael as she climbs into his father's gift, but he simply warns her not to say anything.

Once back home, Sadie prepares Peter for his six month portrait. She instructs Angel to dress in a completely white shirt and blue jeans. When Angel comes upstairs, she finds everyone dressed in a white top and jeans. Sadie explains that for Christmas at the women's church group, the Rebecca Circle, she received a gift certificate for a 10x12 family portrait and two sheets of wallets as her exchange present. After Peter finishes his sitting, they are all going to have a family picture taken.

"You want me in your family portrait?" Angel asks with disbelief.

"Of course," Sadie responds.

They drive out to the mall. Sadie does not want a normal, formal portrait. They have a creamy drapery back drop. Michael lies on his side propped up on his elbow. Sadie sits behind Michael with her hand on his arm looking over him. Angel lies in front of Michael in the same direction as Michael with her head in front of his stomach also propped up on her elbow. Robin lies in front of Angel in the same position. Rachel sits with her back against the arm Michael has propped up and Peter sits in front of Michael's arm.

Afterwards, Michael takes them to the eatery for supper. Angel loves the portrait and that they included her. She feels comfortable living with them now and asks if she can have one of the wallet sized pictures when they come in, to which they respond, "Of course."

Chapter 21

The first Tuesday evening in January, Angel's basketball team plays their first game. As the girls warm up, Angel notices Amber's family including Cole in the stands. She also sees Michael and Sadie with the kids. Then to her and Michael's surprise, Aidan and Steve show up to watch her first game. The girl's junior varsity team does not bring in a crowd, but instead tends to simply bring in the girls' families.

To Angel's embarrassment, Michael, Steve, and Aidan yell and cheer at a game that is usually quiet except for clapping after a score. Angel gives them several "be quiet" looks and waves to no avail. Rob and Cole join Michael to share in the fun and become rather rowdy too. Angel runs down the court, Gina passes her the ball, and Angel shoots scoring the first points of the evening. Her fan club goes wild. She turns to them waving at them to shut up. Sadie and Jonel pull the men down shushing the guys.

A minute later, Amber manages a three pointer to which the group of men goes wild again. Other men who are usually bored at these games, begin to get worked up along with Amber and Angel's cheerleaders. By halftime, the Logan River Muskrats are ahead by eight points with Angel and Amber the leading scorers. Their coach is completely amused by the unusually rowdy crowd spurring the girls on.

During the halftime break, Michael and Rob take Rachel, Robin, and Cassie to the concession area to load up with popcorn, nachos with cheese and pop. While in line, Dan Haas approaches Michael. "Angel is a real scrapper. I went to the tryouts to be sure that she would make the team, but there was no problem. She was by far one of the best girls there and it shows tonight. I think that Angel, Amber, and Katie have scored all of the points out there. Between you and me, I have no idea what the hell Nicole is doing. Oh, excuse me Reverend."

"Oh, I understand. I was pretty much wondering the same thing. She looks at the ceiling when she shoots as if she is afraid that her chin is in the way," Michael agrees.

"We are all proud of the progress Angel has made in such a short time. I checked all of the girls' grades and wow, the jump in Angel's grades are amazing."

"Well, Angel has always been smart. She's just actually turning in her work now."

Dan laughs clapping Michael on the arm. Michael and the little girls return to the stands.

Just as the third period is about to start, Angel slips across the court motioning for Michael, so he climbs down to her, "Reverend, would you please do me a favor? You are being a tad bit too noisy. Could you just watch the game, please?"

"Sure honey, no problem," Michael promises heading back to his seat relaying her request to which Sadie nods in agreement. Less than two minutes into the period, Angel scores again and the group of men goes wild. Angel smacks herself in the forehead and her coach laughs. Cole thinks this is the most fun he has had at a girls' game which is usually so sedate.

During the last period, Angel is fouled and receives two shots from the free throw line. The men become dead silent. Before she shoots, she glares at them. Then she concentrates for a moment before shooting. She scores. The guys clap, but quickly get quiet again. She shoots again. The ball hits the rim and rolls around as if it is about to fall, but then falls into the hoop scoring again. The men jump up cheering again.

By the end of the evening, The Logan River Muskrats win by twelve points. Angel meets her new family in the lobby where Michael gives her a hug and Aidan and Steve rave over her performance.

"Thanks," she mumbles shyly, "But you're not all coming again next time are you?"

"Well, it's an hour and forty minute drive, but we might try to come to a few," Aidan offers.

"Reverend, you don't have to come to every game," she informs him.

"Don't worry Darling," Michael smirks placing his arm around her shoulders knowing that he embarrassed her a little, "I will be at every single game. I promise."

She rolls her eyes and Sadie laughs.

The next day at school, Angel takes her lunch and begins to sneak off to the basement stairs where she has been going for over a month when Amber and Katie run into her excited about their first game. Angel is swept up with them and actually follows them into the cafeteria where she sits with four other girls from the team who are all wound up, laughing and chatting loudly.

Angel sits with her new friends thinking to herself, "Damn, the Reverend was right. Joining an activity at school did bring her into a new group of friends, friends who are pulling in good grades and other kids in the school respect." No one is pointing at them and laughing. It is all over school that the junior varsity girls rock.

"Hey Angel," Nicole shouts to her, "Your Pastor is one rowdy dude."

Angel laughs covering her face.

Cole and three of his varsity friends come noisily by, "Well if it isn't Katie, Amber, and Angel, the scoring trio. You guys played your asses off last night. I swear these guys are coming with me to your game Saturday." Cole sets his foot on the bench beside Angel leaning his elbow on his knee, "So are you ladies coming to our game Friday?"

Angel smiles shyly at him, "I'll have to ask the Reverend, but I bet he'll let me come. Would you like him to come and cheer for you?" she teases.

"Hell yes. We want the crowd to go wild. Why do you think Dad and I wanted to sit with them? We had a blast. You don't know it, but we actually helped you out. There was high energy in the room."

"Well, well, well, look who's hanging with the cool crowd?" David jeers as he walks up with Becky and Jerry. "So what, now you're a great jock? I bet your new Daddy is proud as can be. Who knew that you would make such a sweet little preacher's kid?"

Cole stands up straight, "Aw, what's the matter Davey? Don't like someone who excels? Does her success make you feel like an even bigger loser?"

David walks up nose to nose with Cole to intimidate him, but Cole returns the glare not backing down.

"You want to swallow your front teeth pretty boy?" David threatens.

Cole's three friends step up closer to back their teammate. Angel jumps up pushing between them, "Stop it David."

David shoves her back down, "Don't talk to me like you're still my girlfriend. I'm done with you."

Cole shoves David, "Don't be pushing girls around."

David draws his fist back, but Becky grabs it warning, "Cool it. Foster just came in down there."

David steps back glaring hatefully down at Angel, "You think you are so much better than us now? Well, I can take you back down easily. You ain't actually a preacher's kid you know. You're the daughter of jailbird who is such a whore that you don't even know who your real daddy is, but trust me, he ain't no preacher."

David, Becky, and Jerry saunter off. Angel jumps up and runs out of the cafeteria. Once out of sight, she bursts into tears, completely humiliated by what David said in front of Cole and her team.

"Don't let him get to you," Cole startles her.

"Go away and leave me alone," she wipes at her eyes using her old harsh tone.

"Angel," he comforts.

"Cole," she faces him, "What David just said about who I am and who my mom really is, is true."

"Who cares who your mom really is? Do you know why my Dad left my mom? He was the cop called to an accident scene to find that my mom seriously injured a young college man because she was drinking and driving. My mom is an alcoholic. Jonel isn't really my mom, but I love living with her," he comforts. "It's not about who your mom is; it's about who you are and what you do."

Angel grins, "You sound like the Reverend."

Cole grins back.

Thursday morning, Sadie and Michael work in the church office while Rachel colors at the conference table interrupting them every couple minutes and Peter plays in a bouncy seat play saucer. They are two days behind preparing the information for the bulletin. Grace waits impatiently while Sadie and Michael choose hymns which coordinate with the readings.

Once Grace has what she needs to finish the bulletin and begins running them, Sadie and Michael look at the calendar for the next several weeks so that they get ahead. Sadie suggests allowing the children in Sunday school to sing during the service one of the songs that Sadie has been teaching during the opening exercises like a children's choir.

Michael's cell phone buzzes.

"Reverend Donnelly," Mr. Moore sounds serious, "Angel's in the office and this time it's serious."

"What happened?"

"We found drugs in her locker, marijuana. The police have been called."

"Oh you have got to be kidding me," Michael has a sinking feeling in the pit of his stomach. "I'm on my way."

Michael runs to his car disappointed and angry. He had been dumb enough to think that he had reached her and that things were going to continue to run smoothly. This will ruin everything. She will be out of basketball. This will take her reputation right back with the stoners. He wonders if she has been lying to him and she is still hanging out with David and Becky. He thinks maybe they have been meeting in the basement and he believed her sob story about not having anyone to sit with at lunch.

Michael enters the office attempting to remain calm. Mr. Moore greets him leading him into his office where the sheriff and Rob are standing. Angel is sitting in a chair and notices right away the anger on Michael's face.

"Reverend," she calls to him.

"Not now," he snaps wanting to talk with the principal and sheriff first.

"But Reverend," she pleads.

"Be quiet Angel," he orders.

The sheriff introduces himself as Sheriff Marsh, "Rev. Donnelly, this is very serious. She doesn't just have drugs on her; she has eight baggies full meaning that I am charging her with intent to distribute."

Michael's eyes widen, "You're charging her as a dealer?"

Rob looks away as the sheriff holds up a tin box opening the lid exposing baggies full of pot, "This was found in her locker."

"Damn it," Michael cusses shocking everyone in the room.

"We are taking her to the station for the night. Tomorrow there will be a preliminary hearing and then she will probably be moved to a detention center," he explains.

A cold chill runs through Michael. He looks over at Angel who is staring into her lap wringing her hands and trembling.

The sheriff comments, "I guess the acorn doesn't fall from the tree."

Ronald, Rob, and Michael's heads all snap up surprised by the heartless comment. Angel covers her face and cries. Michael has the urge to walk out of the office and simply go home, but he walks over looking down at her.

Angel looks up with pleading eyes, "Reverend, I didn't do this. I swear I didn't do this."

Michael looks away shaking his head, but Angel tugs on his hand, "Please listen to me."

Michael sits beside her leaning his elbows on his knees and cocking his head to look at her. She continues sitting on the edge of her seat, "You asked me how far I went with David and I told you that I had sex. I admitted to smoking and drinking. I'm telling you I didn't do this, not drugs, never drugs. I honestly don't know how that box got into my locker. It wasn't there this morning when I put in my coat and got my books."

Michael stares intently into her eyes. He almost believes her. He wants to believe her, but is not sure what to do. The sheriff walks in front of them ordering her to stand. Michael stands with her as the sheriff pulls out handcuffs. Angel throws her arms around Michael and he holds her leaning down kissing the top of her head.

The sheriff announces that it is time to go and to hold her arms out. Trembling, Angel faces the gruff officer holding up her hands as he handcuffs her.

"Is this really necessary?" Michael asks.

"It's procedure. I will call you with the information for the hearing tomorrow."

Michael looks at Rob who watches on helplessly. Rob and Marsh lead her out into the halls which are full of students with Michael and Ronald following. The students stop to stare. Angel keeps glancing over her shoulder at Michael who feels helpless and has a knot in the pit of his stomach. He notices David, Jerry, and Becky standing in a corner coldly watching. The knot in his stomach tightens painfully.

Cole runs to his dad, "What's going on?"

"Not now son," Rob shuts him down.

Michael watches Angel crying as she is put into the police cruiser with no idea of what he should do. Ronald claps him on the back before returning to the school. Michael drives home with his heart aching and feeling sick all over.

Sadie cries as he recounts what has happened. Sadie does not believe it for a minute. Michael looks down at the kitchen table where the family portrait lays out waiting to be framed. Michael paces around the house restlessly. Then he lies on the couch with his arm covering his eyes. Someone pounds loudly on the front door. Michael opens it to find a frantic Cole and Amber. He invites them in.

"Reverend, my dad won't talk to me about what's happening, but I'm telling you, Angel didn't do this," Cole practically yells.

"I don't think she did either son, but I don't know what to do about it."

"The stupid sheriff won't listen to me, but David threatened to bring her down yesterday. He said he could do it. He did this because he's jealous and hateful," Cole charges.

"What?!" Michael sits on the edge of the couch as Amber and Cole give every detail about lunch the preceding day. Cole tells Michael that three boy varsity players and four junior varsity girls, plus countless students at surrounding tables, witnessed the whole thing, but the sheriff won't listen to a word of it. Sadie stands in the doorway listening.

Michael smacks his legs standing up, "Thank you for coming over. I appreciate it more than I can say. Sadie, I'm going to the sheriff's office." Michael storms out of the house.

Angel sits in a small cell around the corner from the Sheriff Marsh's desk believing that she will be spending the rest of her high school career in the detention center. The thought of no longer living with the Donnelly's leaves a desperate hollow feeling inside her chest. She will be branded a drug dealer like her mother. Once again, all of her happiness and hopes dissolve before her eyes. The fact that the Reverend doesn't believe her cuts her deeply.

Suddenly, she hears Michael thunder into the office, "Sheriff, I want to see my girl."

"You can see her in the morning," he detours him.

"No, I will see her now. I have a few questions for you too. How exactly were those drugs discovered? Why was her locker searched?" he interrogates.

"Someone called in an anonymous tip."

"Are you kidding me? What evidence do you have that the drugs are Angel's besides the fact that you found them in her locker?" he demands.

"That's enough," the sheriff answers cockily.

"The hell it is," Michael counters. Angel's heart beats wildly. He's fighting for her.

"You watch yourself or I will arrest you for disorderly conduct," Marsh threatens.

"Angel denies ever seeing that box. Did you find her fingerprints on it?" he quizzes.

"I am not going over the evidence with you," Marsh arrogantly snipes.

"That's because you didn't bother to look for any. Are you telling me that you can't even prove that she ever touched the box?"

"No, I did not dust for fingerprints," Marsh admits.

"Witnesses came in and you refused to take their statements. Why?" Michael accuses. Angel listens intently, tearing up to hear that he is defending her. He believes her.

"I didn't feel that their information is pertinent to this case," Marsh scoffs.

Shaking his head, Michael continues, "I want you to release her to my custody until the hearing tomorrow. I don't want her spending the night in a cell."

"I believe that she was in your custody when she got herself into this trouble Pastor. Look, I'm sorry that you are upset, but there is nothing you can do here tonight. Go home," Marsh orders.

Michael paces trying to think of what to do. He pulls out his cell phone walking to the opposite side of the room to make a call, "Graham, I need your help."

Graham Worthington leaves his office to head to court for an important case for which he is the lead chair when his cell phone vibrates. With no intention of answering it, he glances down check his caller ID. Seeing Michael's name, he answers it planning a quick conversation on his way to the car.

"Graham, I need your help."

Graham stops walking for a moment. Being lifelong friends, Michael has never said that to him, "What's wrong Mike?"

As Graham heads toward his car, Michael fills him in on what is happening and that he is afraid that Angel will end up in a detention home and he will not be allowed to be her guardian. Graham continues the conversation as he drives to court.

"Mike, I have to go. I will call you back tonight. I can't come tomorrow because of my case, but I will send one of my associates. Don't worry; I can get one of them to come. Are you standing in the sheriff's office right now?"

"Yes."

"Let me talk with him," Graham orders.

Michael hands the phone to Marsh, "My lawyer wants to talk to you."

The sheriff looks skeptically as he takes the phone, "Yes?"

"My name is Graham Worthington and I am representing Miss Angel Heckathorn. You are not to question her in anyway tonight. Also, you either release Miss Heckathorn into Rev. Donnelly's care or you give me the phone number and name of the family court judge in charge of this case so I can immediately petition the court for her release. Now, I have to go into court on another matter, so which will it be?"

"I will release her into his care," Marsh crabs.

Graham shuts off his phone and runs up the stairs hurrying to his other case.

Marsh shoves back from his desk annoyed, handing Michael his phone and then walking around the corner to release Angel. Angel runs around the corner into Michael's arms. Glaring at Marsh, Michael turns leading Angel out of the building.

Before they reach the car, Angel stops, peering up at Michael, "Do you really believe me?"

"Yes, I believe you," Michael assures her which causes her to cry again.

"Thank you."

Chapter 22

Friday morning, Michael and Sadie drop their little ones off at Jonel's house and then take Angel to court. Angel wears Sadie's old the light blue blouse with the darker blue skirt. Michael dresses in his black suit with his clerical shirt and collar and Sadie wears a tope skirt suit. They sit in the hall at the family courthouse nervously waiting.

A lawyer approaches them with his hand extended, "I assume you are Rev. Donnelly. I'm John Sudosky. I've been assigned to this case by the family court."

Michael glances at Sadie and then back at John, "You weren't sent by Graham Worthington?"

"No."

"Thank you, but we have obtained private counsel," Michael informs him.

"Really, well, good luck," John leaves and Michael and Sadie nervously continue their wait.

Soon, the elevator opens and out walks Graham himself with his wife, Stephanie. Michael and Sadie hug their dear friends.

"I thought you were sending an associate," Michael reminds him.

"My other case is in recess for two days for a judicial conflict that came up, so I came out myself."

Graham sits down pulling out a legal pad on which he already has written notes last night and begins questioning Angel and Michael. They see Marsh and Rob arrive. Rob approaches them shaking Michael's hand whispering, "I'm on your side here. My children are furious with me for taking her out in handcuffs, but the sheriff is in charge."

Soon, they are called into court. Stephanie and Sadie sit in the front row and Michael sits at the defendant's table with Angel and Graham. Mr. Moore, Sheriff Marsh, and Rob Monroe are also present. Donna Richardson is prosecuting this case.

Judge Howard Henderson, a rather large, distinguished looking man with graying hair at the temples, presides. He calls the court to order referring to Donna for the charges.

Donna stands, "Your honor, a tin box containing eight baggies of marijuana was discovered in the locker of Angel Heckathorn in Logan River High School yesterday, Wednesday, January fifth at nine-thirty a.m. The court is charging Miss Heckathorn with possession with intent to distribute."

Donna takes her seat as Graham stands, "Hello your honor, I'm Graham Worthington representing Miss Heckathorn in this matter."

The judge and Donna are visibly surprised that a man with Graham's reputation from Columbus is in their court.

Graham continues, "I only arrived in town a few minutes ago and I respectfully request that Ms. Richardson would please finish disclosing the evidence that she has against my client."

The judge turns back to Donna who stands, "The tin box found in her locker is the evidence that we have against her."

Graham stands, "Your honor, Angel Heckathorn has been a poor student who earned poor grades and caused trouble in school for years. She hung out with, if you will, a group of trouble makers. Then in September of this school year, Rev. Michael Donnelly assumed guardianship of Miss Heckathorn with the support of his wife, Sadie Donnelly. Since this time, Angel now dresses appropriately for school, her grades are straight A's and B's. She now belongs to the church's youth group and plays on the girls' junior varsity basketball team for Logan River High.

"I submit to you, that on the day prior to the drugs being discovered in her locker, Angel was sitting at a table in the school's cafeteria with a group of her teammates and with a group of boys from the varsity basketball team having a goodtime, when her ex-boyfriend, David Salisbury, and her ex-best friend, Becky Kolinsky, whom Angel had been forbidden to see by Rev. Donnelly, approached Angel. They were both angry and jealous. They went on to tell Angel off accusing her of thinking that she is now better than them and also taunting and accusing her of being a goody, goody preacher's kid. David Salisbury loudly threatened my client, bragging that he could easily bring her down. He did this in front of no less than seven reliable, respectful student witnesses whom Sheriff Marsh refused to take statements from when the students voluntarily came forward.

"The very next day, the principal receives an anonymous tip that there are drugs in Miss Heckathorn's locker of which Angel insists that she has never even seen. Rev. Donnelly requested that the box be dusted for fingerprints to obtain evidence of whether or not my client had ever even touched the box. This request was denied and now the box has been handled by the police, the principal, the vice principal and the prosecutor contaminating any prints that could have been found. I also submit that no drug tests have been performed on Miss Heckathorn including hair analysis or a simple urine test.

"I would also like to point out that my client states that she, her now ex-best friend, Becky Kolinsky, and now ex-boyfriend, David Salisbury, all exchanged locker combinations at the beginning of the year before she cut off relations with them which can be proven by the fact that Angel can in fact open both David Salisbury and Becky Kolinsky's lockers. David threatened Miss Heckathorn and has access to her locker.

"Also, the first time David learned that Rev. Donnelly was forbidding Angel from dating him, David grabbed her in the school halls dragging her to the boiler room in the basement where he pinned her down inflicting four large, painful hickeys on her neck. This event is well documented with the boy having been suspended from school for ten days. This event demonstrates prior bad acts toward my client.

"The evidence, I acknowledge, does not prove that Mr. Salisbury or Miss Kolinsky committed this crime, but I believe that it casts more than a reasonable doubt about my client's guilt. This case could ruin Angel's life by taking her from a loving home where she is demonstrating amazing progress and placing her in a detention center based on two simple facts. Number one, an anonymous tip led authorities to find drugs in Miss Heckathorn's locker and number two, that her mother is serving time in prison for dealing drugs. The sheriff made no attempt whatsoever to investigate this charge in anyway shape or form.

"If this goes to trial, there will be a thorough investigation including a hair analyst and many, many witness statements. I plan to call no less than twenty witnesses to testify in this matter. I submit that there is not adequate evidence to prosecute this young lady. I therefore request that the charges against Miss Angel Heckathorn be immediately dismissed and that she be reinstated to her school."

Michael looks over his shoulder at Sadie who mouths the word, "Wow." Michael then reaches over taking Angel's hand.

Judge Henderson turns to Donna, "Your honor, in an attempt to battle drugs in the schools, the administrators rely on their tip line. This is however the extent of our evidence."

"In that case, the charges against Angel Heckathorn are dismissed."

Michael and Angel embrace. Before they disperse, the Judge interrupts the celebration, "Excuse me, just out of curiosity for my own benefit, may I ask how a foster teenage girl living with a country minister manages to obtain a first rate defense attorney from Columbus?"

Graham and Michael chuckle, before Graham explains, "Your honor, Michael Donnelly and I were raised together. We were even college roommates. As a matter of fact, Michael was actually accepted into Harvard Law School with me. Imagine my surprise when he chose to attend a seminary instead. I believe that you know his father, James Harris Donnelly."

"What? This is James's boy, Michael?" the Judge appears surprised turning to Michael, "Are you the son that played tennis back in high school?"

"Yes sir," Michael answers.

"You used to play my son, Emmet," Henderson reminisces.

"I remember Emmet," Michael affirms.

Sheriff Marsh leaves obviously annoyed that Michael has connections to a powerful attorney and was just insulted him in open court. He is angry that Michael has connections to the judge. Marsh asks Donna if it is inappropriate that the judge knows Michael, but Donna points out that the judge didn't recognize Michael and didn't ask any questions until after the ruling had been made. She then reprimands him for embarrassing her in court having not disclosed that he had refused to check for fingerprints and for not listening to the students who came forward or telling her about potential witnesses. Marsh insists that the kids' statements are irrelevant to which she points out that they lost the case based on those witnesses.

Michael shakes hands with Ronald Moore asking if there will be any problems with Angel returning to school or with her playing in the game tomorrow. Ronald assures him that he believes Angel and that with a popular group backing her, she should be fine with the other students. However, Michael informs Ronald that he is still concerned about protecting Angel from David and Becky. Ronald promises to do the best he can and to provide her with a new locker.

Michael and Sadie thank Graham and Stephanie for coming and saving their girl. Graham is happy to be able to help and thought it was fun to wipe up the floor with the prosecution's case. He wishes that his other case was this easy, but he needs to hurry back to continue working on that one.

Once at home, Amber calls to congratulate Angel having heard from her father that the charges had been dropped and invites her to go to Cole's game that night. Michael quickly gives permission and life seems to be back on track.

Chapter 23

By the end of January, Angel is considered a basketball star as she, Amber, and Katie remain the high scorers winning most of their games. Michael notices that Cole, along with groups of his friends, attends the girls' games. Rob enjoys having Michael to sit with at these games and Michael also goes to several of Cole's games with Rob. Angel attends all of Cole's games.

There is a group of students who believe that Angel had been guilty, but most believe that the lowlife David and Becky were the culprits. David is angrier than ever, but Becky is hurt. Becky misses her best friend and is jealous seeing Angel laughing and hanging out with her new friends, appearing happier than she has ever been.

One night, Michael locks up the church after a long drawn out finance committee meeting and heads home across the parking lot. Strong winds blow, freezing him to the bone. Snow whips around him stacking deeply. Michael prays that the roads are not too bad for the committee members heading home on these country roads.

As Michael reaches his patio, he notices a shadow of someone sitting on the glider in the cold. Michael cautiously walks up to discover Becky.

"What are you doing here out in this cold?" Michael questions.

She shrugs.

Michael unlocks the door to the garage door inviting Becky to follow him inside. Michael leads her into the garage office to talk. The house heat does a poor job of heating this additional room, so Michael has a space heater out there which takes awhile to warm the room up, and then only a little. It is a cold room to work in during the winter.

"So why are you sitting on my patio? What do you want Becky?"

"You know exactly what I want," Becky blurts out.

"I know that you must miss Angel. Give it some time and maybe we can try again, but I don't know. Becky, the tip about the drugs in Angel's locker came from a girl. Was it you? Did you do that to her on purpose?" Becky glares at him saying nothing, "Becky, Angel could have ended up in a detention home. Do you realize how much that would have hurt her? You almost wrecked her life."

Becky stands and stomps out of the office. Michael chases her out onto the patio, "Becky, wait," he catches her by the arm, "Becky, the snow is coming down hard and you're upset. Why don't you leave your car in the parking lot tonight and let me drive you home?"

"Like you care!"

"Of course I care. Becky, I don't trust you right now. You will have to work to build up trust with me. I'm not sure how, but what are you willing to do?" he challenges.

"I'm not willing to turn into some sweetsy church going girl to please you like Angel did. I am true to myself," she declares proudly.

"So being true to yourself includes smoking, drinking, and not learning anything at school?"

"Go to hell."

"I am not the one heading in that direction."

Becky disappears into the snowstorm. Michael says a quick prayer that she makes it home safely. Michael enters the house. He finds Angel watching television in the living room with Sadie. Michael asks her how she feels about Becky now and how much does she miss her.

"I don't know. I thought we were good friends, but now I'm not so sure. Becky was always telling me what to do and making fun of me. Amber's different. She likes to laugh and she just takes it easy. I never hung out with anyone who laughs so much. She's always saying nice things to me like she loves my hair or I have the prettiest eyes. And when she flirts with the boys, it is cute and kind of funny. It's not like Becky who almost seemed like she was offering to please them. Amber flirts like, I'm pretty and you don't have a chance."

Michael and Sadie laugh. Michael teases, "Hey, that's how Sadie flirted. Hi, your handsome, but fat chance."

Angel laughs and then becomes serious, "Hanging out with Becky would cause my new friends to avoid me and I don't want that to happen. I like having fun with them. Does that make me selfish?"

"No, of course not. There's nothing wrong with wanting to have fun in high school. Besides, I'm the one who wanted you to make new friends to hang out with, remember?" Michael assures her.

The three of them watch a practical joke TV show and enjoy laughing together.

Saturday, Angel and Amber help Sadie in the kitchen to prepare food for tomorrow's celebration of Peter's baptism. They have a large group of friends and family heading this way and Michael and Sadie keep teasing that this church is going to be jealous despite the fact that the church is invited to join them. As they work, Michael appears in his black clerical suit.

"Can Amber spend the night?" Angel asks.

"Sure," Sadie warns, "But you make sure that your room stays clean. I want this house perfect for tomorrow."

"Can you girls babysit for us tonight?" Michael requests.

"Why?" Sadie sounds surprised. "I'm not going anywhere with everyone coming tomorrow."

"Relax, the house is perfect and your food will be ready. Come on, come to the wedding reception with me," he begs.

"No."

Michael comes up behind Sadie wrapping his arms around her and nuzzling her neck, "Come on sweetheart. It's a beautiful dinner and dance. Romance is in the air." He sways her to imaginary music. "Besides, this isn't just one of my weddings. This one is a parishioner. You don't want to be considered unfriendly."

Sadie shoves both her elbows back into his stomach to which he moans, "Oof, I don't know why anyone would call you unfriendly."

Sadie spins around slapping his arms. Laughing, Michael grabs her wrists and wrestling around with her, he pins her to the refrigerator, "So are you coming with me or not? It's no fun at these things without my date."

"Fine, if I finish the food in time I'll think about going with you."

"Gee, thanks a lot," he kisses her and heads out to be sure the church is ready for the wedding. He calls over his shoulder to the girls as he leaves, "You girls help her get this done."

Amber remarks to Angel, "I wouldn't have expected a minister to be so flirty."

"You have no idea," Angel thinks back to the night she sat outside their bedroom door.

Laura and Keith look like a Barbie and a Ken doll. They are a beautiful couple and will undoubtedly be a beautiful bride and groom. Laura's family has been members of Grace church for over thirty years. Liza Piazza is the bride's mother.

Angel and Amber take a short break just before the wedding starts. The girls sneak in an unused door with a key Angel took from the parsonage. They carefully sneak as if they are secret agents up a back staircase. Once at the top of the stairs, they army crawl across the floor of the balcony. Slowly getting up on their knees, they peek over the banister down to the sanctuary which is covered with flowers and candles.

The wedding begins. The men are wearing charcoal tuxedoes with tails. The girls are wearing beautiful, long, hunter green, lace covered gowns; each carries a single long stem rose. The bride dons a body hugging, off the shoulder gown with a long train. Her veil brushes the top of her shoulders and is covered with cubic zirconium diamonds which catch the light from the candles.

Michael wears his white robe that Sadie gave him for their first Easter together with a white stole covered with gold trim and stitching and wears a large gold cross hanging on a thick gold chain. Sadie is not playing the organ for this wedding because the bride's cousin plays and her aunt has an amazing voice. The whole wedding party is gorgeous. Once the procession ends, Michael spreads his arms and begins the service with his strong deep voice.

"Dearly beloved, we are gathered on this most special day to share in the joy, love, and celebration as Laura and Keith vow to share their lives together here in the presence of God, their family, and friends..."

The girls drop down and army crawl back to the stairs where they secret agent sneak back out of the church running to the parsonage. After the service ends and all the pictures have been taken Michael returns home.

"So Sadie, we have two hours before we need to leave for the reception. How are we doing here?"

"I'm trying," she promises.

Michael places an arm around each girl's shoulder, "So how did you girls like the wedding procession? It was beautiful, wasn't it?"

The girls exchange quick glances. Angel nervously asks, "Are you angry?"

"No, you two didn't do anything to cause a disruption and I believe that I'm the only one who noticed. However, don't make it a habit."

Half an hour before time to leave, Michael returns to the kitchen twirling Sadie around, pulling her close, and swaying her to the imaginary music again. Sadie shakes her head, "I have two more things I want to finish."

"Oh just go with him," Angel prompts. "We'll finish these last two things and babysit because, as it turns out, we are the best behaved teens for miles."

"Okay, I'll go get dressed," Sadie rushes off.

Michael kisses Angel on top of the head and slips each girl a twenty. Angel's new goal in life is to find someone as wonderful as the Reverend to marry. After six and a half years of marriage, three children and a foster child, Michael and Sadie still look as if they just fell in love. Nothing seems old. Michael honestly wants to be with her. Angel never wants to date someone who treats her the way David did ever again. She wants someone who feels like he can't live without her instead of someone who thinks he owns her.

Chapter 24

The next morning, Sadie dresses Peter in the cutest little white satin suit with a tie and suspenders. She poses him all over the living room with a white blanket for pictures. The girls wear their prettiest little dresses. Angel wears a pretty dress that Amber loaned her.

The church is crowded first with the regular crowd plus people who came for the baptism. Sadie's parents, Martin and Joy Stevens, her two sisters, and her brother with their spouses arrive as well as Michael's parents, his sister with her husband and daughter, and brother with his partner and tiny Astro. Their friends come, Graham, Stephanie, Aidan, Colleen, Steve, and Brenda with their brood of young children all of whom Michael has baptized.

Aidan and Colleen are the Godparents for Robin, Graham and Stephanie are Rachel's, and now Steve and Brenda will be the Godparents for Peter James. The service is beautiful. When the time comes for the baptism, Angel is moved that they invite her to stand up front with the family and Godparents. Michael peers down lovingly at his son holding him over the baptismal font as he pours three handfuls of water over his head, blessing, "Peter James, I baptize you in the name of the Father, the Son, and the Holy Spirit."

Peter screams and cries with his hands trembling. Michael laughs rocking him back and forth and kissing the top of his head. After church Sadie teases that it is not a good sign that the blessed water appeared to burn. Many pictures are taken before they head down to the fellowship hall for a luncheon.

Angel feels as if she belongs. Michael's old friends get along with his new friend Rob and Cole and Amber hang around Angel. Peter is at a cute age, smiling and babbling. Cole and Angel each hold one of Rachel's hands as she lifts her legs to be swung about. Amber begs until Sean gives

174

in and allows her to hold tiny Astro. Michael thinks to himself just how much healthier Astro looks than the first day he saw the little guy. Although, compared to Peter, Astro still appears sickly.

Michael notices Ernestine Smith approaching him and cringes. "This is a very nice party Pastor. I was wondering, however, why it is that you and your wife never entertain at the parsonage?"

Michael cocks his head, "Mrs. Smith, the six of us barely squeeze around the table, how would we squeeze all of these people into that house?"

"That house is plenty big enough for a family and I don't think it is right that you complain about a free house," she snipes.

"Again, the house is not free. It is part of my salary and I was not complaining. The fact is this large group of people wouldn't fit in our house."

"Well, when my friends used this hall for a party, the church charged them rent. Are you paying rent?"

Exasperated, Michael rolls his eyes, "Your friends are not members, so they paid rent. Any member of this congregation can request to use this hall without being charged just like Laura wasn't charged to have her bridal shower here. Mrs. Smith, why do you dislike me so much? What is it that I did to upset you?"

Ernestine appears surprised, "I never said that I didn't like you. Why would you ask me that?"

"This is my son's baptism party and you are asking me questions as if I am doing something wrong and as if you are angry with me. The truth of the matter is, the parsonage is cute, well kept, and cozy, but there are six of us squeezed in there with one bathroom. Also, I am the pastor of this church and there is nothing wrong with me using the fellowship hall for a reception for my son."

Mrs. Smith shrugs, "Sorry, I didn't know you're so sensitive."

She saunters off leaving Michael shaking his head. Soon, most of the church members head home, but their friends and family stay visiting into the evening, not quite able to get enough of each other. They play cards and visit. They bring toys down from the nursery for all of the kids. Rob's family stays with the group which makes Angel happy because she now has some teenagers to hang out with. Amber, Cole, and Angel have a great time playing Uno.

Colleen asks Sadie, "So, do you miss working?"

"Oh, I don't have time to teach anymore. With six people in the house and one who pees and pukes on himself and everyone else, I spend most of my time just doing laundry and dishes. Plus I'm the organist, the Superintendent, and a member of the Rebecca Circle. I go to Curves several times a week. I help Angel study and since there is no preschool for three year olds around here, I try to do crafts, read, and go over basic preschool workbooks with animals, shapes, and colors for Rachel.

"Our biggest problem right now is lack of money. Michael's sister gave us a check to cover the expenses for this party and his parents are paying for Robin's riding lessons. We're receiving child support for Angel. I'll keep my teaching license current, but I don't think I'm going to go back to work for a while," Sadie shares.

Eventually, Sean offers to pay for pizzas for everyone and orders delivery. Michael points out that there aren't any pizza parlors that deliver to this area, but Sean is able to bribe one to deliver.

They finally all leave and Sadie is very happy having seen everyone, but also exhausted.

Thursday evening, Michael receives a frantic call from Sean. He was just notified that there is a hearing in the morning with Astro's mother. She wants her baby back. Apparently, she has been fighting to get him back all along. Sean can't imagine that the courts would give this tiny, sick, helpless baby back to the woman who purposefully made the baby sick. How could the courts believe that Astro would be better off with a drug addict who lives in a poor neighborhood in a cruddy little apartment? Can't the court see that the baby is so much better off with them in their upper class suburban home? Astro is thriving because of the constant attention he is given here and because they can afford to take care of all of his special needs. That woman can barely take care of herself. Even if she is sober and off the drugs, everyone has to know that it won't last. She is bound to start using again and Astro is difficult to take care of. Astro is a full time job.

Michael rubs his forehead, "Sean, the court's goal is to keep families together. You had to know that foster parents are the equivalent of full time, long term baby sitters. Astro was bound to leave for a new home or be returned to his family. You had to know that going in?"

"But we are better equipped to take care of him. Jeremy thinks that there is nothing we can do, but I'm going to fight this!" Sean declares.

"Brother, I understand your pain. If Tara would suddenly be released on parole, I would have a terrible time letting Angel go, especially to a place where I don't think she would be safe, but you can't fight it. Foster parents don't have any kind of standing in the courts. You wouldn't just lose; you wouldn't even be heard," Michael reasons.

"I have another plan. Jeremy doesn't think I should try, but I know in my heart it will work," Sean stammers sounding crazy.

"Sean, don't do anything crazy. If you don't handle this the correct way, they won't allow you to take in other children and there are so many children who need a wonderful foster home like the one you provide," Michael coaxes.

"But I know a way that we can keep Astro," Sean insists.

Michael hears Jeremy in the background, "Mike! Talk him out of it!"

"Sean, tell me what you are planning to do," he orders.

"That woman is a junky and poor. Dope means more to her than her son. All I have to do is offer her enough money, and she will leave Astro with us," Sean schemes.

"Sean, don't do that. You are talking about bribery. You're talking about buying a baby. That's illegal. You could end up in jail. If the courts give Astro back to his mother that means that she did everything the courts told her to do. She apparently loves him if she is fighting to get him back. Sean, you have to let him go."

"But he was making progress here. We were making him healthier. If he goes home with her, he could die. Do you realize that three different nights the alarm went off that he stopped breathing? We had to run in and pick him up to bring him around before he died. He won't have the healthy food and good care that we can provide. Why can't the courts think of what is best for the baby instead of what is the best thing for the parents?"

"Many, many parents have asked that question. The courts aren't perfect, but it's the best we have right now. Even though it hurts, hurts like hell, you have to abide by their decision. You have to."

Michael hears a click and knows that his brother just hung up on him.

Friday morning, Sean stays home from work pacing the floor to take turns with Jeremy holding Astro as they wait to hear the court's decision, praying that Astro won't be taken, when they hear a knock on the door. Nervously, Jeremy answers the door to find Michael standing there. He came to wait with them and to help in case they have to hand over the baby. Sean and his brother stare at each other for a minute, before Sean walks over hugging his brother and thanking him for coming.

The agonizing wait continues endlessly. Finally, the phone rings. Jeremy turns white as he listens and looks away from Sean. Sean knows that it is over. They have to give Astro back. An hour later, the social worker arrives at the house to pick up Astro. Jeremy shows her a notebook which explains the care that has been helping him, including directions for using the monitor at night. Jeremy explains that Astro has stopped breathing in the night three times and that this monitor saved his life. Jeremy gives her the monitor, a suitcase full of his clothes, and a box with homemade food for him.

Michael, Jeremy, and Sean each kiss the baby goodbye and watch as he disappears with the social worker. Michael sits quietly by wishing he had some magical words as Jeremy and Sean embrace and cry.

Suddenly Sean declares, "That's it! I can't go through this again. I'm done with being a foster parent. I don't need this. I thought it would fill a need that I had, but this hurts so much worse. I'm not doing this again."

Jeremy shakes his head, "What about me? I stayed home to take care of him. Maybe I want to help another baby."

Sean turns his back looking out the window. Michael walks up to his brother, "Taking Astro in wasn't just about filling your need; it was about filling Astro's need. I saw you with him and I saw the room and care you provided. You are doing God's work here and I will let you in on a little secret. When you work for God, you get hurt. God asks you to do the right thing even though it is hard and even though you get hurt."

"Bullshit," Sean mumbles.

"Do you know how much it hurt Sadie and the girls to leave Ambrose? They left their best friends, their school, and Sadie gave up her job, a career that she loved and was very good at doing. Sadie didn't want to bring Angel into our home because she was afraid of ruining our happy, loving home life. But, God kept bothering her because Angel needs us.

"Look in the Bible. John the Baptist was beheaded, Stephan was stoned, Job was tortured, Moses went from living in the palace to living in the desert herding sheep, and look at everything that Jesus went through. God's path is never easy. But if you choose to take it, He will get you through it. You will find peace and happiness, but there will definitely be more pain. With or without God, there is always pain. However, you will get through the pain better, if you go with God," Michael preaches.

"God? I'm gay. God's book says that my very existence is a sin. I was born like this and if I accept who I am, then I'm sinning. We don't even feel comfortable belonging to a church because we are constantly judged. You are the one who told me that," Sean challenges.

"I'm sorry. I'm so sorry, not my best hour. I'm the one who sinned that day treating you that way. I wish I understood or could explain the whole homosexuality versus Christianity issue. But if it was easy and people could explain it, then it wouldn't be such a nonstop debate. I do know for a fact that you and Jeremy are good people, good, loving people. I know that what I saw happen in this house was God's work. I'm sorry that you don't feel comfortable in church, but that doesn't have to stop you from praying. Give yourself some time to heal from the pain of losing Astro, but don't shut your heart to the others out there that could benefit from the amazing capacity that you and Jeremy have to love and care. The problem is, love and care also hurts; hurts bad. Everything usually turns out to be a double edged sword."

Sean thanks Michael for coming and being here for them, but Jeremy and he now need some quiet time for themselves. Michael embraces them both and says his goodbyes. Michael prays for them and for Astro on his way home. He wishes he knew more ways to help, to explain, to make it easier in some way.

Monday after school, Angel arrives home to find Michael and Sadie waiting for her with serious expressions, "Is something wrong?"

"Come sit down," Michael pats the couch. "Angel, sweetheart, I'm sorry to have to tell you this, but the nursing home called today. Your grandma has been moved to hospice. The doctor and she have decided not to continue treatments any longer and just make her comfortable. It could be weeks or maybe months. Would you like to go see her now? I'll take you."

Angel nods tearing up. As they bundle up for the winter weather, Angel begins to cry. Michael holds her for a little bit rocking her slightly. They drive out to the nursing home to see Garnet who is happy to see them.

Angel sits on the bed hugging her grandmother. Garnet comforts her, "Don't cry baby. It's just my time. I actually feel ready to go. I used to think that I was going to hell because of everything that happened with your mother and then I didn't think that I did right by you. I started praying harder than I had ever prayed in my life that He would save you and then Rev. Donnelly and his family moved in.

"I believe that I have made my peace with God. Look at you. You are beautiful and your grades are high and you are on a high school team. I am so proud of you."

"Thanks Grams. I love you. You never did badly by me. I always knew that you loved me. I'm sorry that I gave you a hard time. Here, I brought you this," Angel hands her one of the wallets from the family portrait she had taken with the Donnellys'. Garnet loves it and thanks Rev. Donnelly for everything that he has done for her, especially keeping her out of the detention center.

Chapter 25

Friday, February 13, after school, Angel sits on the couch looking rather sad. Michael asks, "Is something wrong?"

"No, I'm just tired. Can I just stay home tonight? I don't want to go," she requests.

"No, I want you to come with us. You might find it interesting. Why don't you go put on a nice pair of jeans and your favorite top that Sadie let you buy? You may feel better if you look pretty and fix your hair and make-up," he instructs.

"What is this thing again?" she whines.

"He is a missionary from India and he has also been to the Holy Land. There will be a potluck supper and then he has a power point presentation, followed by a slide show of Jerusalem," Michael lists the itinerary.

Angel folds her hands pleading, "Please, don't make me go."

Michael laughs, "Come on. Hey, you want to go for a long ride? Sadie wants me to pick up some food she ordered for tonight and I could use the help. Come on, change your clothes and help me out. I don't want to drive out there and back all by myself."

"Why do I have to get dressed up? If he's a missionary then he is used to seeing people in rags with bloated stomachs," she reasons.

"Ha, ha, very funny, now go get dressed like I told you to," Michael orders.

"Why?" she whines.

"Because I said so."

Angel rolls her eyes and shuffles out of the room. Michael stands on the small landing by the door to the garage and calls down the stairs to rush Angel. Angel finally comes up and they head out in Michael's car. Angel sits staring out the window quietly.

"Other than not wanting to hear a missionary speak about the poor people of India is there something else bothering you?" Angel shrugs not looking at him. "Well, if you want to talk, I'll listen."

They arrive at the grocery store where Michael picks up a huge submarine sandwich shaped in a ring, a huge bag of salad, and a variety of chips and pop. Once back in the car, Angel sighs and leans her face against the window as they drive.

"Angel, you can trust me. Tell me what's bothering you," he persuades.

"Okay, well, it's really no big deal. I shouldn't even say anything, but today's my birthday," Angel informs him.

Michael lifts his eyebrows shocked, "Angel, why didn't you tell us? We would have done something for you. Wow, you are sixteen! That's a big one, your sweet sixteen. I'm so sorry sweetheart. We should have asked when your birthday is. Well, I'll tell you what. We have to do this church thing tonight, but tomorrow we will do something just for you. You and the girls can have some fun making a cake and then we can drive out to the mall to buy you a present and you can choose any restaurant you like."

"You don't have to do anything," Angel denies shyly.

"Sure we do. Hey, before the missionary starts his presentation, I could have the congregation sing happy birthday to you," he offers.

Angel sits bolt upright, "Don't you dare! I swear I will hurt you. Please don't. I'm sorry I told you," she moans.

Michael laughs, "Alright, alright, take it easy. Take it easy. I won't do anything tonight. But tomorrow, we will and maybe we can even pick up your driver's permit. I can teach you how to drive. Boy, it would be nice next year if you could drive yourself home from basketball practice."

Happy that she told him, Angel's mood changes and they cheerfully chat the rest of the way home. The parking lot has several cars already parked as they reach the church. Michael parks in the lot close to the door to the fellowship hall. As they climb out, Michael and Angel pick up a bunch of the groceries. They enter the church through a side door and head for the basement. Sadie and Jonel meet them at the bottom of the stairs taking the groceries in the kitchen. Michael and Angel take off their coats and winter gear and hang them up.

Michael tells her to go on in. Angel shuffles to the doors to the fellowship hall which are closed. As she opens the door and steps in, there is an explosion of noise, "Surprise!"

The room is decorated with streamers and balloons and is full of teenagers and children. Angel's heart jumps into her throat, pounding wildly. Embarrassment washes over her. Quickly, she turns running past Michael and back up the stairs.

Michael leans in the room, "We'll be right back."

He chases her up the stairs in time to see her duck into the sanctuary. Following her in, he finds her agitated, pacing up and down the center aisle. She runs at him pounding his chest with her fists.

"How could you do that to me?"

Michael wraps his arms around her holding her tightly to stop her attack, "Oh great, you hit like Sadie. Oh by the way, I did know it's your birthday. With all the court forms and school forms to fill out, how could I not know when your birthday is?"

Angel pushes away from him, "Go tell them all to go away."

"Why? Sweetheart, that's your sweet sixteen party. I thought you would love it."

"I hate it. This is messed up. I'm not going back down there," she insists.

"Why?"

"I don't know. This is so messed up. I'm just so embarrassed," she attempts to explain.

"It will be fine. We invited the youth group and your basketball team. We let Cole and Amber invite some more boys and there you have a party. My friends from Ambrose are here too. After the party starts, the ladies are going to take the children over to our house to play and watch movies and most of the adults are going up to my office, but I will check in on you. My friend Steve brought DJ equipment from his bar, and he's going to play music. Come on, they're waiting for you."

Michael places his arm around her shoulders leading her back to the party. She snips at him, "I hate you."

Leaning down, he kisses the top of her head, "I love you too."

She smiles. She thinks to herself that this is the first time he actually said that to her. He had always said that he cared about her, but this is the first time he said love. She enters the room shyly. A group of girls snatch her away teasing that they never saw anyone that surprised at a surprise party. Sadie had invited everyone to start eating while they waited for her to return. The children are allowed to stay to eat and watch Angel open presents before they lead them away. Once Angel seems relaxed, Sadie lights the candles on a cake and everyone sings to her as she blushes and hides her face. She blows out the candles with the encouragement of her friends. She quietly whispers to Sadie that this is her first real birthday party ever.

Sadie kisses her cheek, "I love you."

This is the first time Sadie had said it as well. Shyly, she begins opening a ton of presents. There is a large box from the Reverend, Sadie, and the girls. She opens the card to find a coupon book for driving lessons. Then she unwraps the box discovering a bigger, better TV for her bedroom.

The Donnelly's friends went in together to buy her a new Wii System. She opens presents from her friends consisting of clothes, purses, games, jewelry, a photo album, a stuffed brown horse, and a diary that comes with a lock and key.

Angel picks up a small square box with a card signed "from Cole." She opens the box to find a silver heart shaped locket necklace. All of their friends howl, "Oooooo…"

Angel blushes and Cole smirks shyly, punching a friend beside him in the arm. Sadie and Michael lock eyes for a moment.

Michael claps his hands, "Okay, I want to thank you all for coming and for the presents. There is plenty of food and drinks. Mr. Duffy here is going to start the dance. All children under the age of six line up at the door. Some of the ladies are taking you over to our house for movies. Now listen up, Mr. Monroe, a group of other adults and I are going upstairs. You will never know when one of us will pop in to check on you. Have fun."

Steve begins the music and Colleen and Stephanie head over to the house with the little ones. The rest hang around the food watching the group of teens mill around not dancing. Sadie grabs Jonel and Brenda and dances to the center of the dance floor beginning to feel the beat. Soon, Sadie grabs Angel and Jonel snatches Amber and Jessica, one of her youth group members. The girls act embarrassed at first, but begin to dance. Sadie and Jonel continue to pull out Katie, Gina, and Nicole. The girls begin to dance, but the boys shy away.

As the next song starts, Angel yells out, "You should see the Reverend dance!"

The kids call for Michael, but he shakes his head and backs away. Sadie goes to him whispering, "Come on. The boys aren't dancing. Show them how it's done."

Giving her a dirty look, he allows her to pull him to the dance floor. The truth is that he had been raised going to the country club with his parents and he is a great dancer. He starts slowly, but then catches the beat. Soon, he and Sadie are showing off. A circle forms around them. Rob and Jonel, who also can cut a rug, join them. The kids clap their hands and cheer.

Michael moves to the edge of the circle taking Angel's hand. He drags her into the middle and begins twirling her around. He then moves in a more modern style. The kids cheer Angel and she finally loosens up and dances. Michael watches her and follows her style.

Jonel moves to the edge of the circle grabbing Cole and dragging him in with her and his dad. Cole begins to dance and Amber and Jessica join in. Michael works his way back to Sadie allowing Cole and Angel to dance near each other with Amber. As the kids slowly join their friends, the adults fade out to the side.

Steve strategically plays a popular line dance and the kids form three lines performing the routine while the adults watch. Brenda moves to Steve to help with the music. Sadie and Jonel check the food supply and then head over to the parsonage to help with the children and babies as well as visit with Colleen and Stephanie. Sadie plans to run back and forth.

Michael, Aidan, Graham, and Rob head upstairs to Michael's office. At the conference table, Aidan pulls out cards and poker chips. Michael strongly objects, "Hey, you can't be playing poker in the church. That being said, deal me in." He takes his seat.

Rob jokes, "You know, if Ernestine Smith walked into her minister's office and found us playing poker with the minister, she would probably keel over with a heart attack."

"Hey, let's call her," Michael suggests.

"Problems with Ernie?" Aidan inquires.

Rob leans back, "Ernestine is a tough duck. Her husband treated her so badly for so many years, that she is just such a bitter old woman. While I think that there was some physical abuse, I think mostly there had been verbal abuse. Even though he has been dead for almost twenty years, she is still bitter and I think she is painfully lonely. Her sons have little to do with her and they learned how to treat her from their father."

Michael shakes his head, "That does explain so much. You know, Sadie always said that her students that were the hardest to love were the ones who needed her the most. I never thought about it, but I guess that applies to my congregation. The ones who are so hard to deal with are probably the ones who need me the most."

The kids dance, mill around visiting, and frequent the food tables. Angel pours herself a drink, when Cole walks to the door and motions to her with his head to follow him into the hall. She follows him and they lean awkwardly on a wall.

"Thank you for the necklace. It's really pretty," she thanks him.

"You're welcome. This is a nice party. The Reverend and Sadie are the coolest preacher and wife that I've ever met."

"They can be strict, but I have to admit that they're a lot of fun. I never saw this coming. I didn't even know that they knew it was my birthday. I never had a birthday party before, at least not one with streamers and balloons and the whole bit."

Cole moves in front of her, "Happy birthday Angel."

He leans in and gently kisses her on the lips. Looking into her eyes, he softly kisses her again only a little longer this time. Angel's heart jumps and she feels butterflies in her stomach. She never had this reaction to a kiss before. Michael comes around the corner to check in on the party. Seeing Cole kissing Angel, he slips back around the corner smiling to himself. He quietly heads back up the stairs.

In a way, Angel seems like a little girl to him, but then he remembers that Barbara had only been sixteen the first time he had kissed her. She had been a junior in high school and he had been a freshman in college. He laughs to himself as he realizes that he would not like it if a college student was kissing Angel. Then again, Angel is a sophomore and Cole is a senior. It is the same age difference as between Barbara and him.

Michael rejoins the poker game. Rob asks how the party's going.

"I don't know," Michael remarks, "I never made it to the door. When I came around the corner your son was kissing my girl and I didn't want to bother them."

Rob looks up surprised and then laughs shaking his head, "I wondered about those two when he came home with that necklace."

"Aw, they've been flirting and smiling at each other for a while now," Michael comments.

Angel leans on the wall as Cole stands in front of her smiling. Suddenly, Angel has a sinking feeling in her stomach. She becomes nervous pulling away.

"Cole, I... I don't know how to ask this," she stutters.

"Ask what? It's okay. You can ask me anything," he encourages.

"I know that I have a reputation for certain things and I want you to know that things have kind of..."

"Angel," Cole interrupts, "I have known you for years. I've watched you slowly change since you moved in with the Reverend. I'm really impressed by how you have been willing to work with the Reverend and Sadie. A lot of people said that you wouldn't make it; that they would either give up or you would run away. But ever since the first night that you were dropped off at Youth Group, I've been rooting for you. You changed so quickly that it's my guess that this is who you have truly been all along and you just needed a chance to get away from the group you were hanging with."

Angel leans in softly kissing him lightly setting her hands on his shoulders. To her, this almost feels like her first real kiss, true kiss. This is a kiss that makes her happy in a way that she has never felt. He just spoke to her as if he knows her and as if he actually cares for her.

Not wanting to ruin this feeling by going too far, she steps back, "You want to dance with me?"

"Sure, it's your birthday," Cole takes her hand returning to the party.

Brenda notices them walking in holding hands and encourages Steve that he needs to play a nice slow song for them. Steve quickly finds one before the current song finishes. The next song played is slow and Cole dances with Angel.

Michael and Rob peek in to make sure that the two didn't get carried away. They are both aware of Angel's past and worry a little. They are relieved that the two had already rejoined the group. Steve waves and the two head back to the poker game snagging a bowl of chips and several pops.

The music's pace picks up and Cole dances with Angel while several of his friends join them to show off. Just as most of them are dancing, Amber stops and stares. Angel and Cole turn to see what she is looking at. There in the doorway stand David, Becky, and Jerry. Angel thinks that they look grungy compared to the teens at her party. She feels almost ashamed to think that was what people had seen when she entered a room.

Angel crosses the room to her old friends hoping that they don't ruin her party. Jessica quietly slides out through the kitchen. Cole and Amber follow Angel.

"Gee Angel, we thought that you might want to do something special for your birthday," Becky mocks, "But it already looks like you are doing something special. Wow, this is some party and you didn't even invite your best friend."

Amber attempts to help, "Actually, this is a surprise party. She had no idea. She had nothing to do with the guest list."

"I wasn't talking to you," Becky snaps.

"Don't talk to her that way," Angel defends her new friend. "You're always looking for a fight. That's why the Reverend didn't invite you. She was just trying to be nice. She is always nice."

"So what, she's your new best friend?" Becky challenges.

"All I know is that she doesn't boss me around or make fun of me. She just laughs all of the time and wants to have fun," Angel speaks up to them for the very first time.

Becky snorts angrily, "Fine, have your sweet sixteen party. After all, you are such a sweet little preacher's kid now. Did you pray before you ate?"

"Go home Becky. I don't need you crapping all over me like you always do anymore."

Becky looks genuinely hurt to have her best friend honestly wanting her to leave, not because the preacher doesn't want her here, but because her friend doesn't want her here. "I see Cole standing behind you. You know David, I saw them flirting with each other way back in October at the mall. Angel insisted that they weren't, but here he is with her at her big party and we saw you dancing when we came in."

David angrily demands, "Were you cheating on me before we broke up?"

"No. We weren't flirting that night," Angel defends.

"Liar, I have been watching you two flirt at school for months. You go to each others' games to cheer each other on. You two are such a sweet couple. I bet you'll be king and queen of the prom," David mocks hatefully.

Michael hears someone coming and grabs Rob's jacket tossing it over the poker game. Jessica runs into his office, "Angel's old friends just crashed the party."

The men immediately jump up and rush to the party. As Angel confronts her old friends with her new friends behind her, Steve notices and hurries over.

"Is there a problem here?"

"No, there's no problem sir," David assures him. "We have been Angel's friends for years and I'm sure that she wouldn't want us to miss this lovely party."

Michael, Rob, Graham, and Aidan walk up behind the group, "Hello David." David and Becky roll their eyes when they see the preacher and his friend, the cop. Michael gently lays his hand on Becky's shoulder, "I'm sorry, but this is a private party. You need to leave."

Becky jerks her shoulder away shooting daggers with her eyes. David steps up to stare Michael down, but Michael simply glares back.

Rob, using his police voice, orders, "Step back David. You three need to leave, now."

David smirks at Angel, "Enjoy your party sweetie-pie."

Becky barks hatefully, "Happy birthday."

Jerry simply salutes and the three saunter out. Rob whispers to Michael that he is going to get his coat and patrol outside to watch out for vandalism. Aidan offers to go with him. Michael checks that everyone is okay and then pulls Angel aside.

"Are you okay, sweetheart?" he worries.

Angel holds her head high, "I'm great. I stuck up for Amber, I stuck up for myself, and for the first time ever, I didn't just stand there and take their crap. I told them to leave. They didn't actually go until you showed up, but I said it. Tonight, I wasn't with them, not because you said so, but because I said so. Don't let this go to your head, but you were right about me getting involved in something at school giving me new friends."

Michael smiles warmly down at her, "I'm proud of you. Go enjoy your party."

Michael and Graham hang around the party for the rest of the evening. Angel returns to the party feeling stronger and more confident than ever which puts her friends at ease. They all return to the party gossiping as if that short argument was something exciting to see.

Rob and Aidan walk around in the bitter cold to protect the church and the cars in the parking lot from the angry kids. Once all of the kids are picked up, Michael decides that they will clean up in the morning instead of tonight. He, Rob, and the kids quickly put things in the refrigerator and leave the rest. Once home, all of the small children have been bedded down in the girls' room or Peter's room. Sadie and Colleen sleep on camping mats in sleeping bags on Angel's floor. Brenda and Stephanie sleep in Sadie's bed. Graham sleeps on the couch. Steve sleeps in the recliner, while Michael and Aidan stretch out on the living room floor.

Michael remarks, "I hope there isn't a fire here tonight. Although, the scariest part is that there is only one bathroom." They laugh as they attempt to fall asleep.

In the morning, the men take a group of kids and head to the church to use the restrooms over there. Eventually, they all end up over there passing around doughnuts, bagels, juice, and coffee for breakfast. The large group cleans up from the party and packs up Steve's DJ equipment. They all help carry Angel's presents home and then they put the tables back. Once finished, they all hug each other goodbye with thank yous and promises of seeing each other again soon and jokes about not having any hotels nearby to help with a crowd.

Once alone in the house, Angel stutters around, "I don't know how to thank you for last night. I never had anything like that before. I think that was the best night of my life. I don't know how to thank you for letting me live here. I just don't know how to thank you."

Sadie hugs her, "You just did and that was more than enough. We had fun too."

Michael hugs her, "We love you Angel."

"How did you afford all of that?" Angel worries.

"The hall was free, but don't tell Mrs. Smith. Steve didn't charge to be your DJ and we took most of it from your child support checks that we had been saving, so in a way, the party was from your Grams as well."

Angel nods hugging a stuffed horse that Jessica bought her.

Chapter 26

Sunday morning Sadie bundles up Robin to walk over to Sunday school while Michael finishes feeding Peter his oatmeal, trying desperately not to get any food on his black suit. Angel and Rachel also sit at the table eating cereal. Sadie gives Michael a kiss and heads out through the garage to the patio.

Michael hears Sadie from outside yelling, "Michael! Michael!"

He jumps up running outside to discover that the patio has been sprayed all over with black and blue spray paint. The spray swirls around the siding, their glider, their picnic table, and the cement floor. There are large words across the siding just below the kitchen windows, "Fuck you."

Michael wipes his face with his hands. Running back into the house, he grabs his coat and then walks around the house to look for further damage. Angel joins Sadie to see what happened.

Michael completes his circle around the house, "There is no more damage to the house, but the side of my car reads 'asshole'."

"I'm so sorry," Angel sighs.

"Don't apologize. This is not your fault," Michael announces firmly. "Sadie, go ahead to Sunday school. I'll call Rob. He's not only a police officer, but he's the head of the trustees. Angel, go finish feeding Peter and watch Rachel."

Angel hurries back into the house filled with a sick feeling in the pit of her stomach. Sadie takes hold of Robin's hand and trudges across the frozen parking lot. Michael sits down on the picnic bench staring at the back of his house, attempting to keep control of his emotions.

"Michael! Michael!" he hears Sadie from across the parking lot.

"Oh shit," he mumbles to himself as he springs to his feet running to Sadie.

The back of the church is covered with graffiti and profanity as well. Michael's eyes flash with anger. Michael takes a jog circling the church to check for further damage discovering that the sign out front with the service times had also been vandalized. People begin arriving for Sunday school. Jonel drives up with Cassie and quickly pulls out her cell phone calling Rob.

Michael slowly walks toward the corner where there is a huge picture of a stick figure with large wings and a halo hanging with a noose around the neck and the eyes are X's. A cold chill runs up and down his spine as he stands unable to move his eyes from the painting.

"Michael?" Sadie steps up beside him. "What do you make of that?"

"It's a death threat."

Michael instructs Sadie to open the church and begin Sunday school and encourages people to move into the church. Rob soon arrives with Cole and Amber. The teens run to the parsonage as Michael and Rob speak. Rob makes an official report. He and Michael circle the church and then move to the parsonage patio and his car. Rob doesn't think that the buildings can be power washed to remove the paint while the temperature is below freezing.

Rob meets with the sheriff in the parking lot to report on the events of the morning. Michael walks into the church to robe up for the service terribly distracted. He remembers sitting in the finance committee meeting when Brenda had burst in to tell him that Troy had shot Sadie. He remembers spending all night in a waiting room praying until his head throbbed.

Michael remembers being attacked in his house and tied to the chair. Troy told him that he planned to rape and kill Sadie in front of him. He remembers the helpless feeling of not being able to move while he watched Sadie being attacked. The terror, that had filled him, easily returns to his chest at the mere thought of that afternoon. Sadie had been pregnant with Robin during the attack, although he didn't know that yet. Shots were fired and fear for Sadie gripped his soul. Luckily, Sadie had managed to pull out a gun and shoot Troy in the leg. God was with her. She caught Troy by surprise and he didn't even get off one shot.

Then Michael's mind shifts to the first January as a minister when at almost midnight he had been called to the hospital because a car load of four young teenage girls had dodged an animal in the road and caused a terrible accident. Michael sat with the frantic parents all night. First, he went to a consultation room with parents of a fifteen year old girl, Jeannie, and witnessed the doctor telling them that she had died. Two hours later, he returned to that same room with his parishioners to watch as they were told that their fifteen year old daughter, Breanna, had also died.

Then he accompanied the broken-hearted parents as they were taken to their child's broken body for a final good-bye. He prayed over her. The vision of that the dead child sticks in his head. He now fears for Angel and the safety of his other children, as well as, Cole and Amber. He sits at his desk deep in prayer when he hears a knock at the door and Sadie pops in her head.

"Sweetheart, the service should have started ten minutes ago. People are just sitting there quietly waiting," she calmly prompts him.

"I'm scared Sadie. I'm scared that they are going to hurt her. I'm scared of who else could be hurt," he confides.

Sadie closes the door and goes to her husband, "I know dear, but the people of your congregation are waiting for you. Fight this evil with prayer. Go comfort your flock and then enlist them in helping you pray. I may have been attacked three different times, but I'm still here. Pray for the protection of your church and family. We may have scars, but we also have each other and we have been blessed with our four children. God gave us Angel to take care of her, so trust that He will help us."

Michael stands pulling Sadie into his arms and holding her tightly. Taking her hand, he walks with her to the sanctuary. He does not release her hand, but instead they walk to the front of the church together. Once up front, Sadie goes to the organ and Michael mounts the tall pulpit. He notices Jonel, Cassie, Cole, and Amber crammed into the second pew with his children.

"Good morning," the congregation responds and Michael continues, "I apologize for the late start of the service. As most of you noticed as you entered our church this morning, that we have had unexpected troubles. I have to admit to you that this incident has me very shaken. I am concerned that this is not the end of the violence. I am concerned for the safety of some of the youth in our congregation. I am fully aware that the police won't want me saying this, because we have no direct proof of who did this. However, I know in my heart exactly who I believe did this.

"So, this is what we are going to do. We will pray that today's damage is the end of it. We will pray for the culprits' troubled souls and we will pray for the protection for the people of our congregation, especially our youth group. We are going to now begin our worship service and not allow anything or anyone to stop what we do here each Sunday. Please turn in your hymnals to page 145, *Morning has Broken* and let's sing with gusto. Sadie…"

Sadie plays the introduction as the congregation stands. At first the singing begins quietly, but the song builds. By the second verse the congregation sings at full intensity. Rob and Sheriff Marsh enter the back as the congregation shakes the building with their voices celebrating their Lord.

Michael forces his focus on his service, the readings, the prayers, and even his sermon. He found it most difficult to focus on his sermon, but he pulls it off. During the church prayer he adds prayers for the angry teens who are obviously in pain and striking out, as well as, prayers for the safety of the people in this congregation, especially the youth group, without mentioning any specific names although in his heart he names Angel, Amber, and Cole.

Church ends and Michael spends time with Sheriff Marsh. Marsh reprimands him for publicly accusing someone of a crime without any proof and that his gut feeling isn't enough. Michael defends himself by pointing out that he never named names. However, the sheriff has no intention of questioning the kids that both Rob and Michael suspect and they will have to wait for a warm up in the weather to even attempt a cleanup. Then they will have to file with the church's insurance company.

Rob reports to Marsh that these teens are not just upset with Angel, but they have a grudge against Amber and Cole. Rob wants to question them, but Marsh cautions him that they have no real evidence. Michael asks about the death threat to Angel, but Marsh insists that Michael is reading too much into it. He said that the angel could simply be a disrespectful symbol of the church. Rob appears as frustrated as Michael.

Michael returns to the parsonage furious and dislikes Marsh even more than he already did. He informs Angel that for the next week or two that he will be driving her to and from school. He also plans to call Ronald Moore and provide him with a report of the events of the weekend.

Monday night, the trustees hold an emergency meeting to discuss the damage and to start looking into how to clean up the mess and how much it will cost. Rob had done research online and has some information. The tension in the meeting runs high and Michael still acts on edge. Rob comforts Michael that the kids had struck at night under the cover of darkness while no one was around. He agrees that that the painting of the hanging angel is meant to scare and intimidate Angel, but they probably won't actually hurt her.

Michael, however, has the image of the hickeys the boy inflicted on her while she begged him to stop. The first time he ever saw David, he had Angel pinned to a table practically sitting on her face. That same night he used his fingers to pretend to shoot Michael. He remembers telling Sadie that he could feel evil dripping off that boy.

Michael heads home through the bone chilling wind. He cringes as he once again passes the graffiti to enter his home. The house is quiet and chilly. He hangs his coat in the closet. The living room is dark. The kitchen only has on the small light above the kitchen sink which had been left on for his benefit. Michael descends the stairs to check on Angel, but she is not in her room making him nervous.

Michael hurries to look for Sadie. As he turns the corner stepping into his bedroom where he discovers Sadie and all four of his children cuddled up in bed watching TV. He exhales, relief washing over him.

"Hello darling. The house is cold tonight, so we decided to curl up in here under the covers instead of sitting in the living room," Sadie explains with a smile.

"Why is it so cold in here, Daddy?" Robin whines.

Michael reaches out touching an outside wall, "I don't think these walls are insulated or at least not insulted well."

Michael crosses to his closet to grab his sweatpants and sweatshirt. Going to the bathroom, he prepares for bed before returning to his room. They are lined up across the bed Angel, Robin, Sadie with Peter on her lap and Rachel. Michael walks around the bed. Lifting Rachel, he crawls in bed beside Sadie setting Rachel on his lap. They all giggle and squish together making room for him teasing Angel to be careful not to fall off. Robin crawls up on Angel's lap to make room.

Michael thinks that they must have gathered pillows from all over the house to prop themselves up. The bed is cozy and warm. Michael relaxes placing his arm around Sadie while she attempts to hang on to a wiggling Peter. Rachel cuddles up on her daddy's lap bringing him a warm feeling. The family enjoys snuggling together in a family bed.

Soon, the news is on and the three little ones are asleep. Michael carries Rachel up to her bed tucking her in with several blankets as Sadie places Peter in his crib. Michael returns lifting Robin in his arms to tuck her in warmly as well. When they return to the bedroom, Angel requests to use the sleeping bag on the floor by the dresser that was not yet put away since her birthday party. She wants to sleep on the couch in the living room because the basement is so cold. They approve and say goodnight.

Michael wraps himself around Sadie holding her tightly. He discloses, "I have a bad feeling darling. Do you think that we should bring a gun back into the house again for a while? I know that I don't really know how to use one, but you are pretty good with one."

Sadie rolls over startled, "You're that worried? Oh Michael, I would be scared of a gun in the house with such little curious kids. By the time we lock it up good enough unloaded, I couldn't get it fast enough to be helpful."

"You're probably right, but I just keep thinking that if you didn't have Steve's gun that night, Troy would have killed you."

"Michael, we don't know that. If I hadn't had that gun, I might have escaped another way. Besides, we are talking about kids. I don't think I could bring myself to shoot a kid. It was surprisingly easy to shoot Troy, but then, I didn't kill him."

"I know you're right. I can't shake that old helpless feeling again."

Sadie kisses his forehead snuggling up tightly. Michael props himself up on an elbow, gazing down on the love of his life. He traces her face with his finger and then leans down kissing her. He begins to undress her.

"Hey, it's cold," she complains.

"Don't worry. I'll warm you up," Michael promises as he climbs on top of her.

"You are one horny minister," Sadie giggles using her old phrase that she hadn't said in years which causes him to laugh and attack her even more.

ANITA WOLFE

For the next two days, the schools declare snow days and the family enjoys their time at home together. They play games, read books, bake cookies, and watch movies. Michael and Sadie hope that this gives David and Becky time to cool off and for things to blow over before returning to school.

Michael and Sadie bundle up the girls to take them to church with them during office hours. Since Grace can't make it in to work, Sadie helps Michael in the office. Angel stays home with Peter and the girls want to play in the nursery. Robin brought three dolls to play with and Rachel brought two.

Sadie takes a quick walk down to the nursery to check on the girls and discovers they are missing. She and Michael begin looking through the building for them. Hearing their voices coming from the sanctuary, Sadie and Michael quietly sneak up peeking quietly through the doorway.

Robin and Rachel are standing up front with the baptismal font opened. They are preaching and praying loudly. The girls are baptizing the five dolls they brought to church with them. Michael wraps his arms around Sadie's waist laying his cheek against her head as they quietly watch their precious daughters.

Once each doll has been baptized, they turn raising their arms up and repeating the type of Benedictions that Michael gives at the end of the service. The girls use strong booming voices causing Michael to laugh. The girls then sing a Bible song that Sadie taught in Sunday school as a closing hymn.

Half way through the second verse, Robin spots her parents in the back of the church and stops, laughing with embarrassment. The girls are worried that they are in trouble for playing in the sanctuary, but Michael and Sadie hug them having enjoyed watching the girls play church.

Finishing up in the office, they all return home for a hot soup for lunch.

By Thursday, the schools reopen and Angel and Robin head off for class. Part of Sadie misses teaching and wishes she could go too, but then she picks up Peter and is grateful for the opportunity to stay home during these crucial and short term years. Giving him a hug, she explains that they are in for a fun filled day of laundry.

As Michael prepares to drive out to the hospital, the phone rings, "Hey Sean. What's happening?"

"Well, I guess I'm diving back in," Sean announces.

198

"You're taking in another baby?"

"Oh, wait until you hear this one. Our case worker didn't like us when she met us. She didn't want to leave children with a gay couple, but when she was desperate to place Astro, she gave us a try. She was really impressed with the way we cared for Astro. I wasn't sure I can handle being a foster parent, but Jeremy told me to suck it up.

"Well, this morning, she called. A young single mother has been killed in a car accident leaving three little ones behind. It is difficult to place siblings together and they will probably be split up. She wondered if we are willing to take three. Jeremy said yes without even asking me. I started to complain, but he told me to suck it up. They lost their mother and it would be a crime for them to lose each other."

Michael agrees, "I've always liked Jeremy. He's right. They need you and you need to do the right thing."

"To tell you the truth, I'm kind of excited about the whole thing. There's a ten year old boy, a six year old girl, and a six month baby boy. Their names are Donzel, Carletta, and Anton Mezera," Sean informs.

Michael wishes him well and promises prayers. They talk for awhile before Michael leaves for the hospital and Sean hurries to help Jeremy prepare for three new children. While they are healthy children, they are also from a rough neighborhood and in mourning.

Chapter 27

Thursday night, Angel plays in yet another game and this one is a nail biter. Every time one team scores the other team scores as well. It is nip and tuck the whole game. Michael, Sadie, Rob, Jonel, Cole, and two of Cole's friends are going crazy. The game has forty seconds on the clock and the opposing team is ahead by only one point. Angel steals the ball from the other team and charges down the court as her friends and family jump to their feet. Angel stops passing to Amber who quickly passes to Katie. Katie takes the shot. The ball bounces off the rim. Amber catches the rebound, shoots and scores. The crowd goes wild and the Logan River Muskrats win.

Rob and Michael take their families out for ice cream which thrills Robin and Rachel. They rehash the game and enjoy being out together. While the families load up their vans, Rob looks over Michael's new minivan very impressed. The van even has an automatic sliding door. Michael is a little embarrassed as he admits that his father gave it to him. Cole and Angel slip around to the other side of Rob's minivan to sneak a kiss before heading home.

The family is wound up and has difficulty getting to bed on time. After Michael and Sadie finally manage to tuck Robin, Rachel, and Peter into bed, Michael runs down to check in on Angel. He finds her standing on her bed staring out the window with tears in her eyes.

"How are you doing?"

"I'm okay," she drops down to a sitting position. "Can I ask you a question?"

Michael walks in sitting on the edge of her bed, "Shoot."

"My whole life my mom and Grams have tried to protect me from the truth, but I'm old enough to know the truth. I promise I can handle it. What I can't handle is not knowing anymore," Angle works at convincing him.

"What do you want to know?"

"I want to know who my dad is and if mom doesn't know, surely she knows who could possibly be my dad. I don't know why they would keep this from me. He's my dad and I have a right to know what happened. How did I get here?" she pleads.

Michael leans forward resting his elbows on his knees attempting to decide how to handle this. He is not sure if he has the right to tell her, yet she is obviously suffering from not knowing.

"You know something. I can tell. Please tell me," she begs.

"I'm not sure I have the right," Michael admits.

"This is messed up. Don't I have the right to know? You are my guardian now. You are the one who is supposed to make these decisions. Grams is dying and I don't trust my mom to tell me the truth. I trust you. Reverend, please tell me. I'd rather hurt over the truth than trying to figure it out all of the time. Not knowing drives me crazy," Angel continues pleading.

"Okay, your grandma did tell me something and I believed her. Apparently your mother was taking drugs back in high school. One night, she went to a party where she was high, wasted. Apparently, the boys at the party began to… to have their way with her. There were rumors that a line formed. Your mother doesn't remember who or even how many. I'm sorry Angel."

Angel stares at him for a moment calmly before responding, "Thank you. Now I know and I can give it up now that I know it's hopeless. Thanks, goodnight."

Angel lifts her covers climbing into bed.

Michael tries to comfort her, "Grams also told me that even though it was extremely hard on your mother, she never took drugs while she was pregnant for you. She may be messed up, but she has always loved you. When you picture little Astro, your mother suffered and purposely didn't allow that to happen to you."

Angel fakes a smile, "Thanks. I know my mother loves me. She tells me in every letter. When I looked down at that pathetic baby, I thought to myself, thanks Mom. Goodnight. I'll see you in the morning."

"Are you sure you're okay?" Michael checks not wanting to leave yet.

"I'm fine, but I'm tired," she lies.

"Okay," Michael leaves the room, "Come find me if you change your mind," he closes the door behind him.

Tears begin to flow. Soon, she is sobbing and trembling. She sobs so hard that she has trouble catching her breath. The door opens again. Michael enters having not been able to leave. He sits back on the edge of the bed reaching out to touch her shoulder. She sits up wrapping her arms around him and he holds her tightly allowing her to cry out her sorrow.

As she catches her breath, she bawls, "David was right. He said that my mother was such a whore that she didn't even know who my father is."

"Shhh, it's okay. Your mother was not a whore. She didn't do this on purpose. She was messed up on drugs. Drugs destroy lives, but your mother tried hard for you. She stayed off drugs while she was pregnant and she took you home for Grams to take care of you. She couldn't get off the drugs, but that doesn't mean that she doesn't love you," he comforts.

Angel nods, but her crying escalates again. She wails, "Once Grams dies, I'm all alone!'

"No you're not. No you're not," Michael pulls her back to look at her face, "Angel, you belong here with us. We want you. When you graduate from high school, you will still be ours. I am going to help you get through college and when you are out on your own, you will always come back to us just like we go to my parents' and we go to Sadie's. This is not temporary, Angel. You are ours now."

Angel hugs him tightly burying her face in his shoulder. Michael looks up to see Sadie standing in the doorway watching with tears in her eyes. She joins them rubbing Angel's back.

Saturday, Michael takes Angel to visit her grandma who appears even weaker. Angel never mentions knowing about her father, but she comforts her Grams by telling her all that the Reverend had promised her last night. Grams reaches for Michael's hand to thank him.

Angel lightens the mood by sharing details about the games she has been winning. Grams smiles, but has little energy. Angel knows that the end is near. She kisses her goodbye promising to work hard in high school to make it into college to make something of herself. She promises that she will never take drugs and that she won't even smoke.

Grams worries about the money to attend college. The nursing home will take her house for payment and she is not leaving much to Angel, but Michael touches her arm comforting that he will be able to take care of all college expenses because he has special funding saved to take care of college for all of his kids.

While they had visited in the nursing home, snow had fallen harder and harder. By the time they reach the van, Michael has to brush off all the windows and scrape the windshield. The roads in town are not bad, but as they head for home, the rural state route is so covered with snow that Michael has difficulty seeing the edge lines on the road. He carefully slows worried of accidently driving into a ditch.

Suddenly, Michael hits a patch of black ice. The van begins to slide, but the traction control kicks in. He is surprised at how well this works pulling the vehicle back in control. He looks over at Angel who had been holding her breath. He thinks to himself, "Damn, Dad was right about needing a good vehicle for the country roads," and he smiles to himself.

Once they reach Shermanfield, Michael asks, "How are you doing today, Angel?"

"I'm okay. It's hard to see Grams like that, but I'm glad I went. It was hard finding out about my dad last night, but I'm glad to know. It's easier not wondering all of the time."

Michael is relieved to arrive home and put the minivan in the garage. His other car has been taken to a garage to take care of the paint damage. He just can't drive around town with a huge cuss word on the side.

Angel runs in the house as Michael exits out the backdoor to the patio heading for the church. Passing the damaged patio causes him to cringe each time and even angers him. The snow pelts his face as he hurries to the church for a men's group meeting for which he is late. As he passes the hung stick figure angel, he stops. He always stops. It has been a week and nothing else further has happened. He prays that Rob had been right about the picture only being meant to intimidate.

After supper, Michael sits in his recliner relaxing with his family in the living room watching a movie about a girl and her dog on TV while the wind howls all around outside. The little house feels cold. Peter wears pajamas with feet. Everyone wraps up in blankets and afghans. Rachel curls up on Angel's lap on the loveseat cuddling under a large, colorful, fleece blanket.

Robin enjoys the movie in a sleeping bag stretched out on the floor. During a commercial, Robin sits up turning toward Michael, "Daddy, can we get a dog?"

"No Robin, we can't get a dog," Michael sighs having been asked this often.

"Why?" she whines.

"Mommy and I don't want to take care of a dog," Michael attempts to explain.

Robin promises, "I would take care of it."

Her dad laughs, "No you wouldn't. You're too young." The little girl opens her mouth to continue the argument, but he interrupts, "I said no. Now, do you want to watch the end of this movie or do you want sent to bed?"

Undaunted, Robin persists, "Mommy, wouldn't you like a dog?"

"No. First of all, Daddy said no. Secondly, I don't want the dirt and fur in my house and I don't want to clean dog poop up out of the yard. I have enough to do and take care of right now, thank you. Thirdly, when Daddy tells you no, you don't ask someone else," Sadie reprimands.

Robin crosses her arms frustrated, "Maybe I'll ask Grandma and Grandpa. They'd get me a dog."

Sadie watches the anger flash in Michael's eyes, "Come here Robin." Robin sits still scared by the tone in his voice so he repeats, "I said come here."

Robin crawls out of the sleeping bag shuffling over to the recliner. He pulls her up on his lap questioning, "Is that how you think about your grandparents? They'll just give you whatever you want?"

Robin shrugs without answering.

"Don't you think what you just said sounds selfish?"

Robin shrugs.

"Mommy and I make the decisions in this house and if we say no, we mean no and you don't turn to anyone else. This has nothing to do with money. We don't want a dog. You are not going to get your way every time little girl. Do you understand me?"

"Yes Daddy."

"Why would you talk like that about your grandparents?" he demands.

"I don't know. They have so much and I don't get why we don't. You said I couldn't have riding lessons, but Grandma let me have them and you told Grandpa that you didn't want the van but you took it," Robin defends herself.

"Your Grandpa owns his own company and that is why he has so much. Your Daddy is a minister and we don't have as much, but that is okay with Mommy and me because we don't care as much about things people own. We have everything we need. We decided that you could take riding lessons since your Grandma had so lovingly offered and Grandpa really wanted me to take that van and he is my Daddy. But in the end, Mommy and I made all of the decisions. Now, go tell Mommy you're sorry for talking back to her and then go straight to bed," he orders.

Robin tears up as she hugs Sadie telling her that she is sorry and then runs pounding her feet up the stairs. Michael rolls his head looking over at Sadie.

"Growing up, I was happy with my life most of the time, but there were times when I didn't understand why I didn't have the stuff that my friends and cousins had. It will probably be a little harder for our kids with visiting your family and seeing how they live which, I have to admit, looks pretty good," Sadie sympathizes.

"Great," Michael bemoans, "first my parents and friends gave me a hard time about deciding to live like this, you didn't want to date me, and now my own children are going to resent it."

He stands walking out to the garage office. Sadie heads upstairs to her daughter who is pouting in her bed.

"You know you just hurt your Daddy's feelings. He loves you and he is always there for you. He spends time with you and takes care of you. You heard him stand up in church for us and demand that the people in his church are to treat you the right way.

"Your Daddy is such a good man that God called him to work for Him and Daddy said yes even though it meant sacrificing the way he had always lived. Most people in this world don't have the money that Grandpa has. We have more than a lot of people and we have everything that we need as well as a lot of things just for fun. We should be thankful for what we have and not be jealous about what other people have. Now, if you will excuse me, I have to try to leave this room without tripping on all of your toys," Sadie guilts her daughter the way her Mom had taught her.

Sadie returns to the living room with Angel, Rachel, and Peter. After about five minutes, Robin comes back down into the living room not saying a word. Sadie doesn't even look at her, but simply states that he is in his office. Robin quietly walks through the kitchen and out into the frigid garage and into the cold office where Michael is fiddling around on his computer.

Michael looks up surprised to see her, "What are you doing out here?"

"I'm sorry Daddy. I love you," Robin crawls up into his lap. He holds her thinking to himself that Sadie did something.

"I love you too Cupcake. Come on, it's too cold out here for you. Back to bed."

"Do I still have to go to bed now?"

"Yes you do."

Michael carries her back to bed tucks her in staying with her to talk for a few minutes. Picking up a book off the floor, he reads her a story. He then returns to the living room and smirks at Sadie.

Once the children are tucked in and they crawl into bed, Michael asks, "Sadie, if you had married someone like Graham, you would have so much more. Do you ever wish I had gone to law school like my dad wanted me too?"

"Michael, I didn't fall in love with a lawyer. I fell in love with a minister," she coos.

"But you always said that you never wanted to live out in the country or be a minister's wife," he reminds her.

"I would live anywhere as long as I live with you," she curls up against him. "Oh, but don't forget, at our wedding rehearsal you vowed not to become interested in the mission field and drag me off to Africa."

Michael laughs wrapping himself around his wife.

"You know sweetheart," Sadie muses, "Had you gone to law school, you wouldn't have met me and you would probably have married Barbara. You would have been miserable and unfulfilled."

"You mean because I wouldn't have been a minister fulfilling my calling?" Michael teases.

"No, because you wouldn't have been married to me," she kisses him.

Chapter 28

The following Saturday more snow falls. Angel walks into the living room finding Michael watching a skiing competition and accuses this of being completely boring. Michael informs her that he loves skiing even though he doesn't have a chance to ski often anymore. Angel slumps down on the couch to watch the ski jumpers as they are rated after each jump 6.1, 6.6, 6.2 etc. Angel stays in the room watching the competition with him.

Sunday morning Michael climbs up into the pulpit for announcements and notices that seven of the Youth Group members are sitting across the front up in the balcony. They look giddy as if they are up to something causing him to worry a little bit. Finishing the announcements, the service continues. The kids seem to be behaving and by the sermon, Michael relaxes. He is surprised by how attentive they seem to be.

As he finishes his sermon, each youth group member holds up a sign with large black numbers 6.1, 6.5, 6.4, 6.6, 5.7, 6.2, and 6.5. Michael glances up, does a double take, and then bursts into laughter. The choir and Sadie, who are the only other people who can see the kids in the balcony, begin laughing too.

Once they calm down, Michael leans on the pulpit, "I'm sorry about the laughter. You can't see what happened." Michael explains the Youth Group's joke and the congregation laughs. Before Sadie begins the closing hymn, Michael turns back to the kids calling, "Hey, which one of you gave me the 5.7?" The teens can be heard laughing.

After the benediction, Michael walks to the back of the church, but instead of standing by the door, he stands with his arms crossed by the stairs leading down from the balcony. He can hear the kids loudly stomping down the stairs. Jessica is the first to appear around the corner and loudly screams when she runs into Michael. Because of the sudden halt, the rest pile up as they each run into Jessica.

Amber yells to retreat. The kids turn and begin to run back up the stairs, but Michael calls in a firm voice, "Get back down here!"

The kids slowly walk back down forming a line in front of their pastor who still has his arms crossed.

Cole acts as the spokesman, "So, just how mad are you?"

"I'm trying to real hard to be angry and stern with all of you, but can't do it. It was too funny. Get out of here," he smirks.

The group immediately takes off as they giggle and chuckle. Rob and Ted walk up beside Michael and he explains, "I know Angel was behind that. We were watching skiing yesterday."

Ernestine Smith suddenly appears in front of Michael. He can't stop himself from jumping from being startled. She demands in a snide tone, "Well Reverend, what do you plan on doing about that?"

"About what?"

"About what? Certainly you don't condone that kind of behavior from the youth in this church."

Michael smiles warmly, "They didn't interrupt a prayer or the sermon. We were about to sing the closing hymn and it was funny. Kids will be kids. Besides, it was really my fault. If I hadn't laughed so hard, there would not have been such a disturbance. No one could see the kids except me and the choir. I'm sorry if it bothered you."

Ernestine simply looks as if she had been sucking on a lemon as usual as she gives up on her pastor's help and leaves with her chin held high. Ted heads off as well, leaving Rob and Michael alone.

Rob leans toward Michael, "Do you know what the best part about it is? Angel knew exactly how to make you laugh without getting you angry. She has only lived with you since, when? August? Seven months? So many of us thought that it wouldn't work. We thought she would drive you crazy and run away. Instead, she is actually hanging with the Youth Group and looking happy. I mean, she looks happier than I can ever remember. She usually would saunter in here with her grandmother dressed inappropriately looking disgusted and bored. You and Sadie have worked miracles with that girl. I can't wait to see what you do next in our church.

"You and Sadie bring an energy and excitement with you. I also love that you seem so at home in church. If your child runs up during a service, there is no awkward moment. You simply scoop her up. Sadie finishes at the organ and fetches her daughter so you can preach. You two are special."

"Do you want some kind of really big favor?" Michael jokes.

"I was that obvious huh? Seriously, I want to ask you a question. At the baptism, your brother and his friend had that baby with them. I was just wondering. I mean, I was going to ask, but... I have no idea how to ask."

"My brother's gay and that was his partner, not friend. They are foster parents and that was a crack baby that they had for awhile, but had to give him back to the drug addicted mother and now they have three Hispanic orphans."

Rob stares for moment before speaking, "We never had a minster quite like you before."

"Is my brother a problem for you?" Michael asks hoping not to lose the only real friend he had made since he moved to Shermanfield.

"No, but it is a little surprising. I kind of thought so that night and just couldn't think of how to ask."

Monday, Angel has lunch with Amber, Jessica, and Katie. She notices David, Jerry, and Becky sitting across the room watching her, but Angel doesn't care. She likes her new friends and her new life. She likes playing basketball and she even enjoys doing her schoolwork and getting good grades. She loves her new family and in a way, her first real family. She never had siblings and the Reverend is the closest thing she has ever had to a dad.

After school, as Angel heads for the locker room for practice, Cole catches her arm pulling her off to the side, "Hey Angel, my game is on Thursday this week which means that I'm free on Friday. What do you say that we go out on a real date? You know, one where both of our families aren't around the whole time."

"Really? Where do you want to go?" Angel's heart beats a little faster and her stomach flutters.

"I thought maybe we could go out to the mall. We can walk around a bit, eat at the eatery, and catch a movie," Cole suggests noticing that she is wearing the heart locket he gave her for her birthday.

Angel sees Becky glaring at her from down the hall, but she ignores her old friend. Cole is asking her out on a real date, "Yeah, sure, but I'll have to ask the Reverend. I haven't been out on a date since I lived in the parsonage. I'm not sure what he'll say. I'll tell you tomorrow if I can. I just know that the Reverend hated David the first time he laid eyes on him. One evening, David demanded that I meet him, but the Reverend figured out that was where I was going and said no. I tried to go anyway and the Reverend picked me up and threw me over his shoulder and carried me back into the house."

"Why did you date David?" Cole asks straight out.

"Once Mom went to prison and Grams was becoming sick, Becky and David were the only people I had in my life. I didn't think I had a choice. A lot of the time, they can be okay. David can be scary and mean, but he has another side. He did some nice things for me too," she defends her old friends.

"Are you still hung up on the guy?" Cole checks.

"No, I want something different now. Besides, I'm angry about what he did to the Donnelly's home, the Reverend's car, and our church. I'm also angry that they set me up as a drug dealer. Not only did they try to have me sent to a detention center, but they did it with what they knew would hurt the most because of my mom. That was so messed up. The Reverend and Sadie kept telling me that David would hurt me. They were right," Angel answers honestly.

"Okay, have a good practice. Break a good sweat," he leans in and gives her a quick kiss on the cheek.

Angel glances back down the hall catching Becky's eye a second before Becky turns on her heel and leaves. Angel goes to her locker before heading to the locker room.

Later, Michael arrives at the school to pick Angel up from practice. Turning off the engine, he leans back in the seat to wait. Cole is there to pick up his sister and knocks on the passenger's side window. Michael smiles inviting him to climb in. Cole opens the door and jumps in.

"Hey Reverend, I wanted to talk to you for a minute," Cole begins. "I want to take Angel out on a date Friday."

"Oh really?" Michael smirks amused that this young man would ask him.

"Look, my dad is concerned about her prior dating experience and I want you both to know that I get that Angel is trying to change her ways. I don't want to do anything that we aren't supposed to do. I just want to hang out," Cole attacks head on. "I thought that we could go to the mall to eat and catch a movie."

"Is your dad okay with this?"

"Yeah, we had a long talk, a really long talk. He said okay."

"Okay. Since the mall is forty minutes away, I would prefer that you go to a showing that begins between seven and seven-thirty so that you kids can make it back home at a reasonable hour," Michael stipulates.

"Okay, thanks," Cole smiles broadly.

The girls begin pouring out of the school. Cole opens the door waving to Amber who runs to the van.

"Hey Reverend," Amber greets, "What are you doing here?"

Michael finds the question odd, "I'm here to pick up Angel."

"Angel wasn't at practice. I thought she got sick or something," Amber informs him.

"She wasn't there?" Michael has a bad feeling.

Cole becomes nervous as well, "That doesn't make sense. I talked to her after school. She was on her way to practice. I told her to break a good sweat."

Michael jumps out of the van and Cole follows him. Michael paces around for a minute trying to decide what to do, "Do either of you know anything else, anything at all?"

The teens stare at him for a minute before Amber speaks up, "David, Jerry, and Becky stared at us all the way through lunch."

"I'm calling Dad," Cole announces pulling out his cell phone.

The coach comes out and stops to see what is happening. Michael quickly fills him in and then instructs the kids to stay put and wait for their dad while he runs around the building and the football field. The coach offers to run with him as an extra set of eyes and that if they did find something, it would be safer for two than one. Also, the coach has keys. They can search inside as well. Michael gives Cole his cell phone number so that they can reach him if they need to and to let him know when their dad arrives.

The coach and Michael slowly jog scanning the areas they pass. They spread out while staying within view of each other. Dan Haas notices the men and quickly joins them when he learns what they are doing. The three men carefully search around the building with no signs. They head out to the football field and track area. Michael's phone buzzes to let them know that Rob has arrived. Rob runs out to the field to join the search. They check under the bleachers and around the concession stands.

Soon, Haas leads the four men inside to take a look through the building. Cole wants to go with them, but he is forced to remain outside with Amber for a painful wait. Haas takes the men into the office and pulls up the computer links to the school cameras. They search the halls first for any sign only to see the custodial staff. Haas calls around on walkie talkies to the cleaning staff informing them of the missing girl. No one has seen anything or anyone.

Next the men run through the building checking in the restrooms and the locker rooms. All the teachers lock up the classrooms when they leave. Michael remembers the last assault happened in the boiler room. The men thoroughly search the basement where Angel ate her lunches for so long and had been attacked finding nothing out of place.

Michael thinks to check her locker. Haas knows where the secretary keeps the master key that bypasses the combinations. It takes a few minutes, but he finds her new locker number. Rob and Michael become upset to discover that her coat, book bag, and purse are still in her locker.

Sheriff Marsh arrives with an air of annoyance that quickly angers Michael. Rob inquires to where the other officers are, because they need to begin a full blown search. The first twenty-four hours are critical.

"Calm down, calm down," Marsh grunts, "We don't know that she is in any danger. She could have just run off."

Anger flashes through Michael, "Angel has never run off in the past eight months that I've known her and why would she? She is happy and she was just asked out on a date by Cole."

"You all seem to think that she can just completely change in a couple of months. The stress and pressure of being someone that she's not was bound to get to her. Besides, she has runaway before. A little over a year ago, the day after her mother had been sentenced, Angel took off. Mrs. Heckathorn came to me in a panic. I radioed all the surrounding area police to be on the lookout for her.

"Her grandmother called Becky Kolinsky, who didn't have her license yet. So Becky called their friend David. David drove around looking for her and found her hitchhiking. He brought her home. That was when the two of them became an item," Marsh reports.

"This is different. Angel didn't runaway this time," Michael insists.

"We don't know that," Marsh persists.

"Look," Rob steps in, "It is thirty-two degrees out here. If she ran away, why would she leave her coat and purse behind? Most runaways take a piece of luggage or a bag. She didn't even take her coat. I agree with Michael. Something is wrong here."

"Fine, I will call in more officers to search," Marsh reluctantly caves.

"Someone needs to check at Becky and David's houses. They might have taken her there or they at least need questioned," Michael orders.

"We don't have any reason to believe that David and Becky are involved," Marsh disagrees.

"Are you kidding me?! They framed her as a drug dealer, David assaulted her in school, they confronted her at her birthday party, and they vandalized my home and my church not to mention the picture of the dead angel hanging from a noose!" Michael blows up.

"You have to calm down before I run you in for disorderly conduct," Marsh warns. "Now, we don't know who vandalized the church and your house and we don't know for a fact that they had anything to do with the drugs. We can't just search their houses."

"We don't know any of that for a fact because you never bothered to investigate either incident," Michael accuses. "And we may not know these for a proven fact, but we definitely know it."

"Reverend Donnelly, I am going to have to ask you to leave the area before you get yourself into trouble," Marsh threatens.

"Gladly! I'm done searching here anyway. I have to go out there and find her, because there is no chance that you will. The last time she was missing that moron, David, found her, not you!"

"Just go home Pastor and let us do our job. We will let you know if there are any developments," Marsh orders coldly.

Michael storms off. Rob catches him before he climbs into the van, "Michael, wait. I know my boss is an ass, boy do I know, but listen to me. I'm looking for her and other officers are on their way. We will find her. Now go home. You are too upset to be running around. You could end up causing more problems than you help."

Michael responds, "Thank you Rob. I do trust you, but I'm not going home."

"Michael, wait. I need to fax out pictures of Angel to be passed out to the officers. Go home and get a current photo of her. Do you think you have one that would work?" Rob suggests.

"Sure," Michael nods, "I have some beautiful pictures of Angel from her party. They're on my camera. I can go home and print some off the computer."

Michael climbs into his minivan and pulls out. Rob exhales frustrated. He then instructs Cole to take Amber straight home and to stay there until he comes home. He orders Cole not to go driving around looking for her. If she is with David, seeing Cole searching for her could be deadly for Angel and Cole. Cole promises to take Amber straight home and to stay there.

As Michael drives home, he can't help pulling down the road to pass David's house. His curiosity and concern simply overpower him. The police may not have enough evidence to obtain a search warrant, but he is not a cop. He worries that if she isn't found soon, it will be too late.

A light in the living room can be seen. The police told him to stay out of this, but he just can't. He pulls into the driveway, approaches the door and knocks. He can hear people moving around inside. He pounds harder.

Jerry answers the door, "You again. What do you want?"

"Angel didn't come home from school today. I'm looking for her. Has she stopped by to visit?" Michael asks calmly.

"No, we haven't seen her since you stopped us from seeing her," Jerry sneers.

"Is Becky here? I'd like to talk to her or David please," Michael tries.

"Go away Preacher," Jerry starts to close the door in his face, but Michael pushes his way into the house.

"Hey, you have no right to do this. You're trespassing," Jerry accuses.

"Well, well, well, if it ain't the preacher. To what do we owe this honor?" David saunters into the room.

"Where's Angel?" Michael demands.

"You know Preacher; it seems to me that you have a strange obsession with Angel. I can't help wondering just how close you two really are. A girl like Angel could probably really spice up a boring life of a preacher," David leers.

"Shut your filthy mouth," Michael seethes with anger.

"Maybe she just couldn't stand living in your house anymore whether it was under your rules or under you," David suggests.

Michael shakes his head and then calls out, "Angel, are you in here?!"

David leans on a doorway with a smirk, "She's not here, so go away. This is my house and I want you out."

"I know that you know where she is," Michael persists.

"Get out," David repeats.

"Is Becky here?" Michael questions.

David reaches a hand behind his back and pulls a handgun from the back of his pants pointing it at him, "I said get out."

Michael freezes, holding up his hands, heart pounding, "Take it easy."

"You know, you really are full of yourself. You judge people and you tell people what to do and how they should live. You just assume that you know best. I think you're nothing but an asshole."

"I know. I read it on my car."

David laughs, but quickly becomes serious, "You took Angel away from me and now you are here asking for my help. I found her the last time she ran away, but I just don't care this time. Now, get out of my house or I will shoot. Don't test me. I hate you and I want you out of my house now."

Michael nods and slowly backs out of the house. Michael jumps in his van and drives to the sheriff's office where he finds Marsh sitting at his desk, not out looking for Angel.

"Did you bring the photo?" Marsh asks.

"No, I didn't make it home yet. I stopped to ask David if he knows where Angel is and he pulled a gun on me. Is the fact that he has a handgun enough reason to pull him in for questioning?"

"Reverend Donnelly, I told you to leave those kids alone. You had no right to go there. I will find Angel and you must go home," Marsh orders.

"How are you going to find her when you are here?" Michael accuses.

"Reverend, I'm sick of your attitude. Go home. We will look for her, but she'll probably turn up on her own."

"When I was in college, I attended a party at our frat house one night and got plastered. The next day I went to church and my minister noticed how out of it I was. He and his wife took me back to their house where I fell asleep. When I woke up, they gave me a nice dinner and a long lecture about drinking and other issues I was having at the time.

"When he dropped me back at the frat house, there were police on the front lawn and people everywhere. I went into the house to find that my parents had been called and a lead detective was questioning everyone. I was dumb enough not to tell my friends where I went and they reported me missing. Campus security and a large group of police were searching for me and questioning everybody they could think to question.

"Why was there such a big search mounted so quickly? Was it because I was some rich brat with a powerful father or was it because I was in a city with a quality police force? Is the problem here that Angel is a poor foster kid that no one seems to care about?"

Enraged, Marsh stands, "I am sick and tired of your smugness. You are disrespectful and full of yourself. You may be a minister, but you still act like a rich snob. Go home and allow me to do my job or I will put you in a cell," Marsh threatens.

"Don't bother yourself. I will use my connections to find someone qualified to search for a missing person," Michael snaps. "You couldn't find her if someone gave you a map."

"That's it," Marsh barks back. He takes Michael by the arm forcing him into the cell around the corner from his desk and confiscating his cell phone, "You just sit in there until you cool off."

Furious, Marsh slams a book down on his desk. This preacher already made him look bad in court and criticized him for not finger printing that box and for not taking statements from a bunch of high school students. Now he is going to call in the FBI telling everyone that the sheriff is too incompetent to find a missing teenager.

Frustrated, Michael sits on the cot. He hears Marsh call Sadie, "Hello, Mrs. Donnelly, this Sheriff Marsh. I need you to bring me a current picture of Angel... Thank you. Oh and you should know that I have your husband here in a cell... He needs time to cool off. He is rather out of control and out spoken." Marsh hangs up and calls to Michael, "Your wife is bringing a picture of Angel for me. If you can manage to behave yourself between now and then, I will allow her to take you home with her. Heaven knows I don't want you here."

Michael thinks about what the sheriff said. The sheriff is right. He is not reacting like a minister. He is reacting like a father, his father. The sheriff said that he was talking like a rich snob. He was talking like his father.

He promised to keep Angel safe. He knew that the picture on the church was a death threat, but he failed. He couldn't keep her safe. David took her and he has a gun. The sheriff refuses to even question him. Michael feels sick in the pit of his stomach. He wonders if she is already dead. The thought of Sadie being shot in front of Duffy's plagues his mind.

He remembers being tied up as Troy attacked Sadie. He hates that helpless feeling that returns easily by the mere thought of that afternoon. He feels helpless now and bows his head praying in earnest.

Chapter 29

Graham Worthington and his beautiful blond wife, Stephanie, attend a breast cancer benefit at the country club and are seated across from Michael's parents, James and Sophia Donnelly. Graham's phone begins to vibrate. Stephanie rolls her eyes annoyed that he answers his phone, but the powerful attorney always answers his phone. He quietly listens as Sadie quickly informs him about Angel's disappearance and the fact that Michael got himself thrown into jail.

"I'm on my way," Graham promises and shuts off his phone. "I'm terribly sorry, but an important client of mine just managed to get himself thrown in jail. I need to go."

Stephanie grabs his arm, "Oh no you don't. You just let your client sit in jail for a couple of hours. It would probably do him some good. I'm tired of being stood up. You promised to dance with me. You can go after the party."

Graham leans over whispering in her ear. Her eyes widen and she looks straight at James as she excuses herself, "I'm sorry, but we need to be going. Enjoy your evening."

They quickly head for the exit, when James and Sophia stop them. James asks Stephanie, "Why did you look at me that way? What's wrong?"

Graham and Stephanie look at each other for a moment and then Graham fills them in on what is happening over in Shermanfield. James and Sophia leave with them.

Rob arrives at the sheriff's office excited, "Marsh, I have something."

"Before you divulge information, you should know that your friend is around the corner," Marsh informs him.

Rob hurries to the cell to find his minister sitting on a cot, "What the hell did you do?"

"I lost my temper and I believe I have been channeling my father, shooting off my mouth," Michael admits.

"Anything else I should know?" Rob asks.

"I went to David's house looking for her. He denied that she is there, but he ran me off with a gun," Michael recounts.

"You idiot," Rob reprimands, "I told you not to run off half cocked. I told you to trust me or you would make things worse."

"I'm sorry. I have serious problems with feeling helpless," Michael feels like an idiot.

"Marsh, he has calmed down. Can I let him out?"

"Sure, what the hell," Marsh approves.

Rob lets Michael out and then goes to Marsh's desk where he sets up his laptop computer, "I have something. Angel disappeared in a short five minute space of time between talking to my son and not showing up for practice. I called the principal who came in and pulled up the video from the halls for me," he brings up the video which he had downloaded.

Rob narrates, "Here she is talking to Cole. Look here, someone is peeking around the corner. We can't know for sure, but that could be Becky. It's definitely a girl with long blond hair wearing a jean jacket. Cole gives her a peck on the cheek and walks away. Angel walks down the hall to her locker and notice that she has her purse on her shoulder. She opens her locker and looks down. Something has fallen out. She puts her books in the top of her locker and bends down to pick up a note. She reads it and looks all around. She places her purse in the locker, closes it, and runs down the hall. "

Rob pauses the video, "Now, she runs to the east side of the building, runs through the cafeteria and into the kitchen where there are no cameras. She must not have thought that she would leave the building, because she leaves her coat, but in the kitchen there is a door to the outside for deliveries. Now, according to Amber, Becky and David stared at Angel all the way through lunch so we fast forwarded through the time between lunch and Cole meeting Angel in the hall. Before seventh period, we have this."

Rob plays the video, "Here we have Becky pushing the note into the locker through the vents and she is wearing a jean jacket. Now, David is always seen with Becky by every teacher and student in that school and many students have witnessed David threatening Angel more than once. We have more than enough for a search warrant and instead of waiting for the judge, we have enough to bring them in for questioning now.

"The problem now, Michael, is that you already went to the house and confronted them. Chances are that if she had been there, they probably have moved her by now. From now on, you do what I tell you to do."

"Absolutely," Michael promises.

The door opens and Sadie runs to Michael. Rob leaves to attempt to pick up the teens. Michael fills Sadie in on everything that he knows. Sadie tells him that she has left their children with Jonel and that she had called Graham.

Michael turns to Marsh, "I'm sorry about earlier. My only excuse is that I was freaking out. I will call Graham and have him meet me at my house. If you think that you can use his help, call us there. We will get out of your way and allow you to do your job. Call if you need anything. I'm sorry."

Marsh nods accepting the apology. Sadie hands him several pictures of Angel that had been taken at the birthday party. Marsh pulls out a lovely head shot of her standing behind the cake before they sang to her. Michael and Sadie head home to pace and worry. Michael still doesn't trust Marsh, but he trusts Rob.

Soon, Rob arrives at the Donnelly home, "I hate to tell you this, but no one was at David's house."

Michael sits on the couch holding his head, "This is my fault."

"Don't worry about that now. I do know for a fact that Angel had been there," Rob holds up an evidence baggie containing the silver heart locket. "I found this in the driveway."

Sadie begins to cry and Michael rubs the back of his neck.

Rob sits on the recliner leaning forward, "Do you know where they tend to hang out? Do you have any idea where else they might go?"

Michael thinks hard, but shakes his head, "No, the only place I ever saw them together was out back in the pavilion."

Rob continues, "I stopped at Becky's house. Her mother is passed out drunk on the couch and her younger siblings are sitting on the floor in the same room watching TV. According to the kids, Becky never came home from school at all and apparently, that is not unusual. What is happening with the Heckathorn home?"

"It's empty. The nursing home will sell it to pay Garnet's bills. We allowed Angel to take her things and pretty much anything that she wanted to keep," Michael answers.

"I'm going to check out the pavilion and the field as well as the empty house across the street. You stay in here."

While Rob searches the area, Graham, Stephanie, and his parents arrive. They have never seen Michael like this, but they were not there the night Sadie had been shot. Graham offers to make some calls, but Michael tells him to wait to talk to Rob first. He doesn't want to go around Rob again.

Michael asks them to give him a minute and he will be right back. He runs out to his office to be by himself where he sits to pray again, "Dear Jesus, please help Angel. She is hurting and I can't find her. Please take care of her. Protect her from the evil in David. Help me to find her. I know that you brought me here to help her, but I've failed. I knew she was in danger, but I couldn't protect her.

"I messed up tonight. Rob might have found her by now if I hadn't gone there first. I'm so sorry. Please God, don't let them kill her. She was doing so well. She was just beginning to find herself and You. Please, tell me what I what I should do now."

Michael hears Rob return to the house and hurries back to the others. Rob had found nothing. He said that they may have to wait until morning to continue searching the area. With the amount of fields in Shermanfield, she could be anywhere.

"Are you saying that we have to just wait now to search for her body?!" Michael exclaims.

"No Michael, I'm not saying that. Please sit down. You need to stay calm. We have officers sitting on David and Jerry's house and at Becky's house. If they come home tonight we will grab them, but I don't know where else to go tonight."

"How can we find out who David and Becky's other friends are? Maybe they went to someone else's house," Michael suggests desperate not to give up and simply wait as he checks the clock, nine forty-five.

Sadie thinks, "Maybe we could ask Cole and Amber for the names of other friends and then get phone numbers and addresses from Mr. Moore. What about Garnet? She may have some ideas."

"I hate to upset her," Michael worries, "She is so close to death."

"Well, if Angel dies we have to tell her. If we talk to her now, she may be able to help," Sadie debates.

"I'm not sure that she paid that close of attention to who Angel hung out with or where she went," Michael states.

The phone rings. Rob grabs the portable which is setting on the end table to check caller ID. It reads, "Kolinsky."

Handing the phone to Michael, Rob quickly instructs, "It's somebody at Becky's. Stay calm and let whoever it is do the talking, just listen."

Michael nods as he answers, "Hello?"

He quickly stands turning the phone off, "She just said 'She's in the cemetery,' and hung up."

He begins to head for the door, but Rob grabs his arm, "Wait. Take it easy. It is pitch black out there. How many flashlights do you have?"

Michael rubs his forehead, "I have a big one out in the garage."

"I have one in my nightstand in case of power outages," Sadie offers.

"I have one in my trunk," Graham remembers.

"I have two," Rob states. "We will begin looking and I will radio for help and call for an ambulance."

"Will it take forty minutes for an ambulance?" Michael questions.

"No, our fire department has one. It will probably be here before we find her," Rob assures, and then turning to Sophia, "Mrs. Donnelly, you stay here in case anyone else calls. Michael has his cell phone."

The group quickly fetches their flashlights and then runs across the parking lot to the other side of the church to the cemetery. Michael is the first to reach the gate followed by Rob. Michael yells out to her, but hears nothing. Rob again, grabs his arm to stop him. As the others arrive, Rob begins to spread them out to carefully begin walking scanning their flashlights in all directions.

As they begin to search the vast cemetery, Sadie has an idea and calls out, "Michael! Look out there," she indicates a rather large statue in the distance with her flashlight. "That's a statue of an angel that Angel really likes. Do you think that she could be there?"

Michael breaks into a run for the statue dodging tombstones. As he comes close, he can see something long on the ground lying in the snow which looks like a body. He drops to his knees beside it, beside her. It's Angel. She's not moving. Michael thinks to himself "God, no, please no."

"She's here!" cupping his mouth with his hands, he shouts at the top of his lungs. She doesn't move or startle at the sound of his cry. He leans down touching her face. She is cold and her face is battered. A knot in his stomach tightens, "Angel, I'm here. Can you hear me? Sweetheart, open your eyes. Please open your eyes."

The others quickly arrive. Rob and Graham drop to their knees beside Michael. James takes Sadie into his arms holding her tightly. Rob exams her discovering her wrists and ankles are bound with duct tape. Michael cringes when he sees wanting to tear it off, but knowing all too well that would only hurt her.

Michael holds his breath as Rob covers her mouth and nose with his hand to check for breathing announcing that she is alive. Michael begins to reach for her to pick her up, but Rob stops him explaining that they don't know how severe her injuries are and to wait for the ambulance.

Angel lies there in the snow in only her pull over sweater and jeans. Michael takes off his coat laying it over her. Graham removes his as well covering her feet and legs. Rob gently lifts her face sliding his under it. The ambulance can be heard in the distance.

Michael leans in close, "Do you hear that? The ambulance is coming. Help will soon be here. You're going to be okay. Can you hear me?"

One of Angel's eyes flutters open looking at Michael while the other one is swollen shut. Michael smiles at her, "Hi sweetheart. I'm sorry it took so long to find you. We've been looking for you all evening."

Graham moves over as Sadie drops to her knees, "Hey, Baby. We're here. I love you. I'm sorry this happened to you. We love you so much."

Rob leans in, "Angel, I know who did this to you, but can you say it so I can go arrest them?"

Angel tries to open her mouth, but nothing comes out. Rob helps, "Was it David?"

Angel slowly nods her head just a little.

Rob continues, "Was it Becky?"

Angel nods again.

"Was it Jerry?"

Angel nods again.

James and Stephanie wave their flashlights at the paramedics as they weave the stretcher through the graveyard and snow. Sadie leans over lightly kissing the injured girl's cheek. Michael then leans down kissing her cheek as well. Everyone except Michael stands backing out of the way for the paramedics.

As one of the men kneels down to examine her, Michael stands and moves back. Angel softly cries out, "Dad!"

Michael drops back to his knees laying his hand over her bound hands, "I'm not going anywhere. I have to let these men take care of you, but I'm right here. I'll go on the ambulance with you."

The men place her on a board and put her in a neck brace. Michael does his best to stay out of their way and yet remain in her line of vision. Sadie is told that only one person can go on the ambulance, but James wraps his arm around her promising that they will be right behind it.

Marsh, who arrived behind the ambulances, turns to Rob, "I'll go arrest Becky, but David and Jerry are yours. Take Carter and those two over there with you. Charge them with kidnapping, assault, and attempted murder. She could have easily frozen to death out here."

Michael stands nearby listening. He and Rob lock eyes for a moment before Rob takes off running. Michael walks beside the stretcher trying to help light the way to the ambulance. He kisses Sadie before he climbs in with Angel watching as the paramedic begins working on his badly battered girl.

Chapter 30

Michael and Sadie sit cuddled together on an uncomfortable couch in a waiting room. Graham, Stephanie, and Michael's parents remain with them. Michael fears the doctor's report about the extent of her injuries. He attempts to push away the thoughts of Breanna Johnson, the fifteen year old who clung to life for hours after a car accident, but then died and the vision stuck in his head of her parents being told by the doctor that their little girl didn't make it. While he feels anxious to hear the doctor's report, he also doesn't want to hear it. Closing his eyes, he silently prays. His ears catch the quiet mumbling of Sadie and he knows that she too is deep in prayer.

Rob calls Michael's cell phone to let him know that all three suspects have been arrested. David's knuckles are all busted up and he simply sits staring coldly. Jerry has blood on his clothes as if he helped move her, but no signs that he had taken part in the beating. Becky is wailing and repeating over and over that she didn't know that it would be that bad. Becky's face also sports several nasty bruises. It appears that she attempted to help her friend when things became out of hand.

Dr. Vuppala, an older man from India, steps into the waiting room to speak with Angel's guardians. Michael and Sadie spring to their feet, holding their breath and each other's hand as they wait for the news.

"Angel's face is swollen and bruised, but no bones in her face are broken. She does however have a loose tooth and a chipped tooth. Her upper arms are bruised from being held too tightly. Her stomach is tender, but according to a sonogram, there isn't any internal bleeding. She does have two cracked ribs. It looks as if he kicked her while she was on the ground. Lastly, I'm sorry to have to tell you this, she was raped."

Michael closes his eyes and Sadie's chin trembles. James places his hand on his son's shoulder as Michael squeezes Sadie's hand. The doctor

225

assures them that there will be no permanent physical injuries and he expects a full recovery. The rest they will need to deal with one day at a time.

The doctor returns to Angel while Michael and Sadie cling to each other. Michael wants to let Rob know about the report, but holds his phone having difficulty repeating the words. Graham takes the phone from his friend's hand offering to make the call for him. Graham heard the report as well.

Sadie and Michael return to the couch. Sophia watches as a tearful Sadie whispers words of encouragement and comfort to her husband who seems to lean on every word. She promises that they can handle this, that they can get her through this. Sophia remembers a time when she did not want Michael to date Sadie. She had been so terribly wrong. Sadie is the perfect wife and partner for her son. She takes wonderful care of him.

A nurse enters the waiting room looking for someone named Sadie. Sadie and Michael both stand as the nurse informs her, "Angel is asking for you. We need to do a rape kit and she is scared. We asked if she wanted her mom and she said she wanted Sadie. You don't have to go in if you don't want to. It isn't pretty, but she is asking for you."

"Of course I'll go," she responds without hesitation. Sadie kisses Michael and then quickly follows the nurse into an examination room. Sadie sits on a small stool on castors beside a terrified Angel so that Angel can easily look at Sadie's face and takes her hand. Sadie soothes her the best she can flinching every time that Angel does, but she stays strong for her young girl. Angel cries, whimpers, and holds her breath. The horrible exam seems to be endless, but finally ends.

Sadie sits with her while Angel is given time to calm down. Angel whimpers, "I don't know if I can handle this. What am I going to do now?"

Sadie lightly rubs her arm, "You have to go through the emotions. Go ahead and cry when you need to, be angry when you need to, and be depressed when you need to. You have to take it one day at a time. Praying and leaning on God's strength will eventually help. Leaning on the Reverend and I will help. Talking to other people who have been through it will help.

"My friend Brenda, the one who helped DJ your birthday party, was raped by three frat boys when she was in college. When you are ready, you can always call her. We will take you for counseling and I liked going to Victims of Violent Crime organization. They teach about deciding to be happy again and techniques for relaxing your mind, when you feel ready for it.

"Tonight, just know that we love you and we will be there for you. We will get you through this. You will never forget tonight, but it will get better. I promise."

Angel nods giving Sadie a hopeful grin as tears spill. An orderly takes her to a room hooked up to IV's for pain medication and antibiotics. The day after pill they gave her causes cramping.

Once admitted into her room for the night, Michael finally returns to her side with Sadie. He hates seeing her so battered and wishes he knew how to comfort her as he takes her hand. She looks up at him with one eye purple and swollen almost closed.

"I was so glad to see you," Angel quietly smiles a crooked smile because of her fat lip.

"I was glad to find you," Michael smiles warmly at her.

Rob arrives to take her statement, "Are you up for giving a statement? I hate to bother you, but the sooner is better for gathering the most and correct details."

Angel nods.

"Would you be more comfortable if the Donnelly's leave?" Rob checks.

Angel shakes her head tightening her grip on Michael's hand.

"We know about them watching you in the cafeteria and that Becky watched you in the hall with Cole. We know that you found a note in your locker and went straight to the kitchen through the cafeteria," Rob gently helps her to start. "A nurse found the note in your pocket and gave it to me."

He opens the note and Angel looks away. Michael reaches for it and Sadie reads over his arm.

"My Dear Angel, Meet me in the school kitchen after school or I will take one of your new sweet little sisters. Love, David."

A chill runs down Michael's spine as Sadie's fingers dig into his arm. Angel faced this bravely to protect Robin and Rachel. He had seen the footage from the school hall. Angel had not hesitated.

"What happened in the kitchen?" Rob asks.

Angel's voice is raspy, "David, Jerry, and Becky were waiting for me. Becky said that they were tired of my preacher's kid act and it was time for me to get off my high horse. They said that it's a pathetic joke that I'm hanging with the popular crowd. They said that they wanted me to go with them. I said no. I said that I like my new life and that I was going to go to practice. David stepped in front of me. I stood up to him and said get out of my way. He backhanded me and I fell down on the floor. I heard Becky scream. He told her to shut up.

"He yanked me back up, wrapped his arms around me and dragged me out of the kitchen door to his car which was parked right there. Jerry opened and closed doors for him. I swear I fought. I swear that I kicked and jerked around and tried to scream, but he covered my mouth."

"We believe you," Rob assures her, "One look at you and we can tell that you fought back and that you were brave."

"David forced me into the backseat and Becky and Jerry got in the front. Jerry drove me to their house because their dad is away again. He's a trucker and is gone a lot. David dragged me into the living room. He started going on and on about Cole. He accused me of cheating on him even before the preacher forced me to break up with him. He said that Becky told him about seeing me flirt with him at the mall before Halloween and he hit me again.

"Then he asked me why I was so willing to leave him for Mr. Popularity after he had been there for me. He loved me and he doesn't know why I am so willing to walk away just because my preacher said to and why was I willing to replace him with some smug jock.

"I stood up to him. I stepped right up to his face and demanded to know why he was willing to frame me so that I would have been sent to detention center and how could he make me look like drug dealer. He knew that would hurt me and he didn't care. I asked him what kind of evil person could vandalize a church or the home of a loving family. Grams is dying and was going to put me in foster care, but now I'm living with a loving family. Why can't he be happy for me?

"He hit me again and told me how dare I think that those high and mighty people are so above him. He said that I was a fraud and didn't belong there. He said it is a joke if I think Cole wants more than just one thing from me. Then he said that he was going to remind me who my real boyfriend is. That's when he dragged me to his bedroom by the back of my hair. Becky tried to stop him, but he hit her too.

"Jerry held onto her as David dragged me away. I could hear her screaming to stop it. Anyway, you know what he did next and I don't want to talk about that."

"Okay, you don't have to," Rob comforts her. "What happened after?"

"He told me to stay there and he went out in the living room to have a beer. I hurt too much to try to crawl out of the window. I just laid there thinking that I would try to get out the window when I felt better in a minute. I think I fell asleep; I'm not sure. Then David came back in the room jumping on top of me and covering my mouth with his hand. He had a gun in his other hand." Angel begins to tremble and squeezes Michael's hand tighter. It takes a moment before she can continue. Her next words fill Michael with guilt.

"He told me that the preacher was here and that if he found me, if I yelled for him, that he would shoot and kill him. I heard the pounding on the door. David said that he meant it. He would love to blow off his head. I heard the pounding louder and I think someone answered because I could hear the Reverend's voice, but I couldn't make out what was being said.

"David put the gun in the waistband behind his back and sauntered out of the room. I could hear the Reverend and David arguing," she begins to cry. "I was so scared that David would kill him anyway. Then the Reverend yelled for me, asking if I was there. I wanted so badly to yell I'm here, but I just bit my lip and rolled my face into the pillow. Then I heard him leave. I was relieved that he left, but upset that he was gone at the same time."

Michael's chest aches knowing that he had made her ordeal that much worse for her, "I'm so sorry Angel. I should never have gone there. I should have waited for the police. I was so desperate to find you that I didn't realize that I would make it worse for you. I just wanted to find you."

"Don't be sorry. I was happy that you were looking for me. I was happy that you knew where I was. I knew you left because of the gun and I knew that you wouldn't give up. I knew you would come back for me. I figured you'd go get Mr. Monroe.

"David came back in and said that you were gone. He asked what the deal was between us. He accused us of doing disgusting things. I told him that I think it is sad that the only definition of love that he had was sick and perverted. I told him that I loved the Reverend and his family and that it wasn't sick; it was beautiful.

"He hit me again and then told me that I would never see you again. He told me to get dressed. Then he duct taped my hands and feet together. He dragged me through the living room with Becky begging for me. He put me in the backseat and then went and forced Becky in the car to watch. I thought he was going to take me out to a field and shoot me. Then he drove, but I couldn't see out the windows. Then he stopped and pulled me up to see the parsonage and church and my old house. He told me that he brought me home.

"I thought for one minute that maybe he loved me enough to leave me there. I thought that he was going to leave me where you would find me. I could see the light on in the window and there were cars in the driveway. But then, he drove on and into the cemetery. He said that this seemed like a fitting place to leave me. He said, 'Here Angel, what better place to put you than by this angel. They can find your dead frozen body right here so close to home. Then he kicked me a couple of times. It was such a sharp pain. I could barely breathe.

"I heard him threaten to kill Becky if she ever told what happened tonight. He said to look at me and know that he would kill her too if she breathed a word of this to anyone. Becky dropped to her knees beside me crying 'I didn't know that any of this was going to happen. I'm sorry. I'm so sorry.'

"Then they got in the car and left. I was so cold and I thought I was dying. You would be proud of me Reverend. I prayed."

"I am proud of you for all kinds of reasons," Michael boasts.

"I think I fell asleep, because the next thing I remember is the Reverend talking to me. I thought it was in my head for a minute, but he was there. Reverend, how did you find me?"

"Becky called me and told me that you were in the cemetery. She risked her life to save you."

Angel cries.

"Angel," Rob informs her, "Becky told us everything that happened tonight. Once she was in the police station, she sang like bird. She told us that you were in the cemetery by the angel. I told her that we already found you and took you to the hospital. She was relieved.

"She claims that she thought that when they took you from the school, they were going to force you in the car and take you to David's house to talk and yell at you. She never expected the violence.

"We gave her a deal. We told her that if she testifies against the others and if you back up her story, we won't press charges on her. She definitely has the bruises to prove that she had been hit as well. So how do you feel about Becky not being charged?"

Angel thinks for a moment, "She never hit me once and she tried to stop them several times. I saw her get hit. She really didn't mean to do anything but force me to talk. I was ignoring her and she was so jealous of Amber. She was just so hurt," Angel agrees.

When Rob leaves and Angel notices that it is after midnight, she assures Michael and Sadie that they can go home, but they have no intention of leaving. They tell her to just go to sleep. Around three thirty in the morning, Angel wakes up to find both Michael and Sadie asleep. A nurse had brought a parent's cot and Sadie is asleep on it. Michael sleeps slumped over in a chair. Angel feels surprised that they are both willing to stay all night with her.

Angel struggles to sit up and put the side rail down. Her cracked ribs and bruised stomach hurts and her face stings. She raises the bed to help her sit up which wakes Michael.

"What are you doing?" He inquires.

"I have to go to the bathroom, but I can't seem to sit up," Angel mumbles embarrassed.

Michael puts down the side rail and gently pulls Angel to a sitting position. He helps her to stand and to keep her IV tubes from becoming tangled. He rolls the IV pole with her as she clings to his arm walking stiffly. Once in the bathroom, it is painful for her to sit and stand. The nurse left her a squirt bottle to use warm water to wash away the urine since wiping with toilet paper would hurt. Once she squirts herself clean, she sprays herself with an antiseptic spray with pain killer which is cool and feels nice. She struggles to stand clinging to a rail by the toilet to pull herself up.

As soon as she opens the door, Michael is there to support her as she shuffles back across the room. He helps her back into bed tucking her in. He takes a special pad which becomes cool when he breaks it in half and crushes it and then hands it to Angel who reaches under the blankets to place it in the hospital issued net panties.

"Thank you Reverend," she mumbles.

Michael sits down next to her on the chair leaning his elbows on the edge of the bed, "You know sweetheart, when I found you in the cemetery, you called me Dad."

"I did?" Angel looks down embarrassed.

"I was thinking. I believe that many foster kids call their foster parents Mom and Dad. I know you have a mom already, but a lot of people call more than one person mom. Cole and Amber call their birth mom and Jonel, Mom.

"Anyway, if you want to, you can call us Mom and Dad," he offers. She shrugs shyly, so Michael continues, "It might be awkward at first, but you'd get use to it; whatever you want. Now go back to sleep sweetheart."

"Okay, goodnight, Dad," she tries it out awkwardly and he smiles warmly at her.

In the morning, when Angel wakes, Michael is on the cot and Sadie is in the chair. Angel pushes the button to lift the head part of the bed. Sadie wakes and smiles at Angel, "Good morning baby. How are you doing?"

"Okay. Last night the Reverend said that I could call you Mom and Dad," Angel informs her.

"I think that's a good idea, dear," Sadie agrees.

"So, what happened to your friend, Brenda?" Angel asks.

"Our sophomore year of college, Brenda, Colleen, and I went to a frat party without our boyfriends. We didn't cheat, but we were flirting and having fun. Brenda disappeared at some point. Colleen and I began to look for her. When we couldn't find her, we became scared. We went down to the basement where we saw a guy who looked as if he was guarding a door.

"I went up to the guy and started flirting while Colleen got down on her hands and knees and crawled behind the guy. I pushed him over her and we ran through the door he had been watching. There were three frat brothers inside taking turns raping her. Two had already finished and the last one was pulling down his pants.

"The one from the hall came in and closed the door. We were scared to death. Colleen and I pulled out pepper spray and sprayed all four and quickly dressed Brenda. The buttons on her blouse were missing. I was wearing a jogging bra the kind that some women wear to run in public, so I took off my top and gave it to her. The four guys still tried grabbing at us and we had to kick and shove our way out."

"Wow, you were there? And you said another time in college that your boyfriend knocked you down the stairs and you broke a bunch of bones. So you woke up with a broken hip and had to sit in a wheelchair?" Angel remembers the story.

"I never told you the whole truth about what happened," Sadie begins.

Michael sits up, "Sadie, I don't know if you should talk about that right now."

"She's old enough to handle this," Sadie continues, "I dated Troy for five years and I was within six months of our wedding, when I found out that I had gotten pregnant."

Angel looks shocked and she sits up a little more as Sadie goes on, "I thought that it wasn't that much of a scandal. I was twenty two and engaged, but Troy went ballistic. He didn't want a baby yet and wanted me to get an abortion. I said no and he made me an appointment. I went home to my parents. They said that I could come live with them until I had the baby, finished my student teaching, and got a teaching job.

"I went back to school and over to see Troy. We had a big fight. I told him that I would not have an abortion and I would not marry him. That's when he pushed me down the stairs causing a miscarriage."

"Wow," Angel stares.

"I swore off men and went three years on my own until the bishop appointed the Reverend to my church. I was attracted right away, but still refused to date him. You have met him. Have you ever noticed how stubborn he is?" Angel chuckles softly as Sadie finishes her story, "So to make a long story short, I told him I absolutely would not date him and within a year, I married him.

"My hip still hurts sometimes and I have a big scar where Troy shot me. Sometimes I still have nightmares. These things change a person, but I promise you can be happy again. Victims of Violent Crimes organization helped me. Brenda used to go with me to meetings. God and family can give you the peace and support you need. Michael, the kids, and I are your family. We will help. We love you."

Angel lies back with a small smile, "Thanks Mom."

Chapter 31

Angel's attack had been the end of February and she struggles to recover, suffering from depression and mood swings. Michael and Sadie patiently take care of her, driving her for counseling every week. They both take turns tutoring her with her school work, Michael focusing on math and science while Sadie covers language arts and history. Angel has difficulty caring about her work, but her grades hold at B's and C's for her third nine week report card.

Students at school know about the attack and feel sorry for her. Many avoid her because they don't know how to handle the topic or how to deal with her, but Amber remains a good and constant friend. Also, her friends from the youth group, Jessica and Gina, remain by her side. However, Angel feels uncomfortable around Cole and is not ready to date. Cole kindly gives her the space she needs at his father's suggestion while he makes it clear to her that he still likes her and acts friendly towards her.

Michael is unable to talk her into going on the youth group's ski field trip and goes with the others in the group, leaving Sadie to care for her and the other children.

The teens don't go to trial for Angel's brutal attack. With both Becky and Jerry singing like songbirds, David gives up and pleads guilty. Since Jerry is only fifteen and he isn't the one who inflicted the beatings, he is convicted as a juvenile and will remain in the juvenile detention center until he turns twenty one. David is convicted as an adult and is sentenced to life with no chance of parole for twenty years, having never once expressed any remorse for any of it. Becky walks free with the Donnellys not pressing charges and the prosecutor making a deal for her testimony against the other two.

At the end of March, Sean calls Michael. The past two months have been difficult for them. The ten year old didn't like that they were living with a gay couple and was very protective of his siblings. He wanted to take care of the baby himself and didn't want Sean and Jeremy touching the baby. He even became angry and called them fags.

Jeremy comforted Sean to just give it time and be patient. It took over two weeks, but the boy began to trust them. They bonded with the baby while the kids were at school. Carletta came around quickly and told them that her brother loved soccer. Jeremy took Donzel to sign ups for spring soccer and promised him that he would take him to some college games. In return, Donzel told them that Carletta had been in a dance class for tap, jazz, and hip hop. Immediately, Jeremy began looking around for a dance studio.

Their constant attentive care finally got to Donzel. Donzel, who had always eaten cold cereal or Pop Tarts for breakfast, is surprised that Jeremy always makes them toast, eggs, and cuts up fresh fruit. When Donzel sat at the dining room table doing his homework, Sean would stop and offer help only to be turned down, but Carletta went to them for help. One night while struggling with an algebraic concept, Donzel quietly asked Sean if he understood math. Sean sat down with the boy for half an hour and helped with his homework.

The next day, the case worker came for a scheduled visit. To Sean and Jeremy's surprise, Donzel only spoke favorably about his foster parents. That same night, Jeremy found Donzel in his bedroom looking at a professional eight by ten portrait of their mother taken with her three small children. Jeremy offered to hang it in the living room. Donzel watched with amazement while Jeremy took down an expensive painting over the mantel and hung their family portrait in a prominent place in the home. Sean arrived home and commented that their mother was beautiful with kind loving eyes.

Donzel seems to be coming around. The night before Sean called Michael, at dinner Donzel brought up the fact that they don't go to church. The children had been brought up active Catholics and that next year should be Carletta's First Communion. Sean asks Michael what he thinks they should do.

"I think you should find out which parish you live in, sign them up for PSR, and take them to mass on Sunday mornings," Michael confirms.

"PSR?" Sean asks.

"It's the parish school for religion, you know, the Catholic equivalent of Sunday school. I know that you and Jeremy aren't that comfortable with going to church, but apparently it is important to them and you don't want to hurt that. Actually, you two might do well in the Catholic Church. They are bigger than mine and they don't tend to be all up in each other's business. You can come and go and no one will probably bother you. If anyone stares, oh well, you get stared at other places anyway and it's only one hour a week. Also, we were raised in the Episcopal Church, when we went. That isn't that different from Catholic.

"The only problem is that you won't be able to take communion there, not even if you take classes. Homosexuals can take communion in the Catholic Church, but only if you're not active. If you are sexually active, you must be married and you can't be married. Since you live with Jeremy, you would never be allowed, sorry. If you ever want communion, I can give it to you. Our church conference didn't really commit to a position either way. We go with the 'don't ask; don't tell.' You could still enjoy the rest of the service and attend for the kids' sake."

"I wasn't sure as a minister, how you would feel about me going Catholic," Sean admits.

"Why? It's a Christian faith with beautiful rituals and a rich history. There are only two things that I have against the Catholic Church. One, I don't like the closed communion. Everyone who wants it is welcomed to partake in my church and secondly, if I was a pastor in the Catholic Church, I wouldn't have Sadie and the kids. I can't imagine my life without them for even a day." Sean agrees and Michael adds, "You and Jeremy will love First Communion. You will get to dress your little girl up like a mini bride and give her a big party. My family will be there and I'm sure Carol would come in a heartbeat."

Sean agrees stating that knowing Jeremy, he will go all out.

After the call, Jeremy and Sean have a discussion about taking their children to church and plan to begin this weekend. They are determined not to allow anyone to bother them.

In the beginning of April, Grams passes away in her sleep. Angel takes it hard. Michael gives her a lovely funeral. Sadie plays the organ and sings. Amber, Jessica, Gina, Cole, and Jonel sit with Angel and her new little siblings during the service. Michael's parents, Sean, and Carol's families attend. Sadie's parents attend as well. Grams had been a member of the church for over thirty years and many of the congregation's members attend. The fact that the church is full touches Angel.

Angel knew this was coming, but was still surprised when it happened. Grams had a will which left everything to Rev. Donnelly to take care of Angel and she left Angel to the Donnelly's since she had custody. By the time Tara, her mother, is freed from prison, Angel will be at least nineteen.

Two weeks after her grandmother's death, the Donnelly's prepare to celebrate Easter. Michael and Sadie buy all four of their children new outfits to wear even though Angel is not excited about the purchase. Thursday night, Angel sits in church staring blankly during the Maundy Thursday service which celebrates the Last Supper. At the end of the service, Michael has all the lights turned out and then Amber and Angel come forward in the darkness to help Michael strip the altar of everything except a gold cross which the Reverend covers with a black veil. When they finish, a small spotlight hits the cross while the sanctuary is dead silent. Then the light goes out.

For some reason that Angel can't explain, that moment and all of her emotions hit her and she ducks out a side door running to the Reverend's office. The lights in the sanctuary come back on and the congregation leaves in silence. Usually, Michael would walk outside to greet people, but he saw Angel run and looks for her instead.

After quickly searching through the church, he discovers her sobbing with her head down on the conference table in his office. Sitting next to her and rubbing her back, he coaxes her to tell him why she is crying, but she insists that she doesn't know. Michael lovingly assures Angel that he understands. The service is emotional and her emotions are on her sleeve. Michael simply waits with her and then walks her home.

Good Friday, Angel walks over to church with Sadie. She wanders around before the service and hangs around Michael as he prepares. Michael looks nervously through the door at the crowd gathering in the sanctuary. Angel watches as he takes a brown lunch bag and spills small, flat, black nails into an offering plate.

"What's wrong?" Angel asks.

"Well, as it turns out, the Baptist minister is sick and canceled his Good Friday service. He suggested coming to ours instead, so we have quite a few Baptists out there. I have these nails that I press into each hand and I say 'Remember Christ's sacrifice,' but now I'm worried I'll run out." Michael looks around as the time for the service to begin nears. He shrugs, "Well, I guess I'll leave it in God's hands." Angel watches as Michael closes his eyes, holds his hand over the plate and prays, "Dear Jesus, please do not allow the nails to run out. Make the nails in this plate be enough for all of Your people who have gathered here tonight."

Angel stares at him in disbelief, "Do you think that will really work?"

Michael shrugs with a smile, "It worked with the fish and bread."

Michael hurries to the back and Angel sits in the pew with her little siblings and Jonel's family. Angel's mind wanders around throughout the service until Michael blesses the nails and people come forward to receive a nail. Michael presses a nail in the palm of each church goer as he repeats, "Remember Christ's sacrifice."

After the service comes to an end, Sadie does not play a final hymn. The congregation again leaves in silence. Angel stands outside waiting around. Once Sadie heads home with the children, Angel runs back inside to the front of the sanctuary to look in the plate of nails. Astonished, Angel stares in the plate. It looks as if the Reverend hadn't given away any nails. She swears that the same amount remains in the plate even though he had handed out so many.

Michael walks up behind her, "I know. I'm just as shocked. I prayed that I wouldn't run out, but I never expected to still have that much when I was done either."

"Is this a trick? Did you add these just to get at me?" she accuses.

"Of course not, sweetheart, miracles happen every day. We just don't always notice them. Most of the people here tonight don't know that this happened, just you and me. God is powerful."

"The fish and bread, I never understood that story. Jesus prayed over the fish and bread and the rest appeared magically? Wouldn't that have scared the people back then?" Angel inquires.

"No, I don't think it was a magic trick. I think a young boy overheard Jesus and the disciples discussing the lack of food and offered all that he had to help. Touched, Jesus loudly blessed the food and the sweet boy who offered all he had for all to hear. This either shamed or encouraged others who were sitting around to offer what they had. You see, some people didn't have food, but others were prepared. I believe that everyone sitting around pulled their resources and then the disciples passed it out to everyone and had leftovers. Maybe Jesus did magically add to the pot as well. It's hard to say."

"That makes sense. So what happened with the nails?"

Michael shrugs, "I guess God answered my prayer. Good Friday is a powerful day in the year of the church. God is all powerful and all knowing."

"Then why didn't He protect me? Grams said that she had been praying for me harder than she had prayed in a long time. You have been praying for me since you met me and you asked the church to pray for our youth group and the teens who vandalized the church. After all of that, God didn't protect me. I still got all beaten up. Why?" Angel demands with tears in her eyes.

Michael sits on the steps in front of the altar patting the space beside him invitingly. Angel sits beside him as he begins, "Angel, when God gave man free will, it opened the door for much evil and good people have been fighting that evil ever since. God does not cause bad things to happen and he doesn't always stop bad things from happening. However, He can help you heal and He can bring you peace. He can help you make important decisions and He can step in to save you.

"Grams knew that she couldn't take care of you much longer and that you would probably sink in the foster care system. She prayed for a miracle that someone would come to take you in. God brought us here just in time to take you in. Sadie and I both said no at first because we already have three small children and the parsonage is so small, but Sadie and I both felt a strong push to bring you into our home. We began to figure out how to make it work and we both decided that we wanted to bring you home. Neither of us has ever regretted our decision. We both think of you as a blessing.

"The night you disappeared, I was frantic. When I got back to the parsonage and it looked like we weren't going to find you that night, I went to my office and prayed, begged God for help. Despite David's death threat, Becky found the courage to call me from her house before the police picked her up. Honey, if Becky hadn't spoken up, you probably would have died during the night. You have no permanent physical damage. Your body has healed. I am praying for your emotions to heal next, but it takes time."

"Dad, what does it mean to be saved?" Angel asks in a whisper.

"It simply means that you accept Jesus as your Savior and take Him into your heart. Give your problems to Jesus and find peace in your heart through Him."

"How do I do that?"

"Just pray. Tell God how you feel and accept Jesus as your Savior."

Feeling uncomfortable, Angel awkwardly stands and walks in front of the altar. Taking a deep breath and looking all around, she kneels, bows her head, and begins to pray silently. Michael doesn't move, but watches without making a sound. After a few moments Angel looks over her shoulder at Michael, "Is that it?"

"Yep."

"Now what?"

"We can go home or if you want, I could pray for you," he offers.

She nods and bows her head again. Michael goes to her placing his hands on her head and prays. He can feel her trembling. Once he says "Amen" she stands and wraps her arms around his waist.

"I love you Angel," Michael kisses the top of her head.

"I love you too, Dad. You know, I always wished I had a dad and I even prayed for a dad. I guess God does answer prayers."

"Yes he does."

The two walk home. Before they reach the house, Angel tells Michael that she feels better inside, better than she has felt in a long time.

Saturday, Michael spends the day away from home delivering communion to the shut-ins. Angel helps Sadie clean and prepare food for Easter. Michael's family and their friends from Ambrose are all coming. Angel and Sadie hide and prepare the Easter baskets for the three little ones. Angel even helps fill her own basket with candy. When Sadie sends her to check on the children, Sadie adds a couple of presents to surprise Angel.

Angel even helps Michael and Sadie that night arrange the beautiful lilies all over the front of the church. Using a series of risers of varied heights, they create an angled cross made of lilies in front of the altar. Angel is quite impressed. This Saturday Angel feels happy, truly happy for the first time in two months.

Sunday morning, Easter morning, Angel appears radiant in her Easter dress with a genuine smile. Everyone notices how beautiful she looks, especially Cole who dares to compliment her. Angel freely chats with Cole and enjoys his company. Angel revels in the celebration and the fact that she no longer feels awkward around Cole. Amber comments on the difference. Angel doesn't tell a sole about being saved on Good Friday. She feels it is private and only shared it with Michael and Sadie who keep it in confidence.

The Donnelly children enjoy playing with their new cousins, Donzel, Carletta, and Anton who are thriving in Sean's home. The boys are dressed in brand new suits and Carletta is dressed in a pink dress covered with lace and ruffles with a matching hat carrying a rather large pink fluffy stuffed rabbit. Anton clutches a fluffy blue duck with big black tear shaped eyes.

Sean informs Michael that he had been right. No one seems to bug them about being a gay couple at the Catholic Church which does seem familiar to him since he had been raised in the Episcopal Church. At first they felt uncomfortable, but now are actually beginning to enjoy the services.

Sophia and James hand out Easter eggs to all of their grandchildren and foster grandchildren which are filled with tickets to an amusement park and professional baseball games. One of Angel's eggs has the same tickets, but one contains a hundred dollar bill. Sadie's egg holds tickets for a musical play which will be shown in a nice theater on Playhouse Square in Cleveland. Michael rolls his eyes and sighs, but says nothing.

Chapter 32

After school on the first Monday of May, Angel sits on the patio's glider rocking back and forth in the warm air enjoying a spring day happy that the spray paint had all been removed. Cole pulls up in the church parking lot and comes down to the patio sitting on a bench by the picnic table.

"Hi Angel. I was just thinking that with everything that happened, we never had that first real date. If you're not up for it, I understand, but I was wondering if you would like to go with me to my senior prom. It's in two weeks."

Angel shyly smiles, "I'd love to go."

They visit for awhile before he heads back home. Angel runs into the house excited finding Michael and Sadie in the living room, "Dad, Mom, guess what. Cole just stopped by and asked me to his senior prom. Can I go?"

"Of course you can go. Oh, yea! I get to take you shopping for a gown," Sadie claps her hands.

"Those gowns are pricey," Angel frets.

"We have another check for you coming this week. It will be plenty to buy you everything you want for the dance, a gown, and shoes with a matching purse. You can borrow anything you want in my jewelry box," Sadie offers.

Angel hugs Sadie. Angel has been feeling freer to hug Michael and Sadie. As they discuss the prom, Peter crawls over using Angel's legs to pull himself up to standing. She leans down offering him her fingers so he can walk and stumble around while happily babbling.

Later that evening, Michael walks home from a Bible Study at the church noticing someone sitting on a swing in the playground. He walks over, taking a closer look.

"Hello Becky," he greets her as he approaches.

"I'm sorry. Do you want me to leave?"

"No," he assures her. "You're fine. I haven't seen you that much since you came to the house in February to tell Angel you were sorry."

"I've stayed away from here so she can get better. She made it clear that she doesn't want me around anymore," she pouts.

"Angel forgave you. We know that you didn't mean to hurt her that night," he reminds her.

"Even before that awful night, she was finished with me."

"She is finished with that lifestyle. You know, you could do better too," Michael points out, but Becky only huffs. Michael continues, "I know you have it hard at home, but your future is up to you. You could do better in school too. You just have to pay attention in class and do your homework. There isn't that much. You'd be surprised that your homework wouldn't take as long to do as you think. You're a smart girl. All Angel did, was dress nicer, do better in school, and join an extracurricular activity."

"That's just not for me," Becky stares at the ground shoving the dirt around with her foot.

"Well, how do you know until you try? Anyway, you're always welcome to come to church or to attend a Youth Group meeting. They have fun. You don't have to attend church services to be in the Youth Group. Think about it. They meet Sunday evenings at seven until eight thirty.

"You can find happiness for yourself. You don't have to smoke and drink like your mother. You don't have to have sex to have love. If you want to be loved, you need to love yourself first. You need to find some kind of peace in your chaos. That's where God comes in," he preaches.

"What has God ever done for me?" Becky spits.

"He gave you life and you have survived your life so far. You see, God hasn't caused your life to be like it is. He doesn't cause bad things to happen and He doesn't stop bad things from happening. We have free will and sometimes other people's free will can hurt us. You take Jesus into your heart and He will give you strength, guidance, and peace. I know that the Bible is too big to just sit down to read, difficult to understand, and can be intimidating. But if you're ever curious, just start with the four small Gospels, Matthew, Mark, Luke, and John."

"Stop preaching at me," Becky complains.

"I can't help it. I'm a preacher," Michael shrugs. "I'll tell you what; I have a book of Bible stories written for older kids where someone simply wrote out stories for easy understanding. It's not the whole the Bible, but just a bunch of short stories for easy reading. They're in my office in the church. If you ever want one, stop by and I'll give you one that you can keep."

Becky rolls her eyes, "Whatever." She stands and saunters away.

The next afternoon, Michael works in his office. Grace calls through his door that there are two ladies here to talk to him. He tells her to send them in and is surprised to see Sadie and Jonel enter the office.

"Since when does my wife need an appointment?" he leans forward on his desk folding his hands.

"Rev. Donnelly," Sadie explains taking a seat across from his desk with Jonel, "I am not here as your wife. I'm here as a business woman with a proposal."

"Uh oh, what are you two up to now?" Michael teases.

"You know, starting in September, we are going to have to drive twenty minutes one way to the nearest preschool. Oh, by the way, Kim Weaver said we can car pool with her. We can take Rachel and Jenna and she will pick them up."

"Where exactly is this heading?" Michael cuts to the chase.

Jonel jumps in, "I have my accounting degree and when I met Rob I was working as a manager at a department store at the mall. As you know, Sadie has her degree in early childhood with experience in first grade. During college, she spent her summers working at a daycare. We would make perfect partners to begin our own preschool."

"You want to start your own preschool?"

"Yes, but this is a business arrangement. We want to rent the educational unit of the church for five mornings a week. We would need to purchase better tables and chairs and more playground equipment and cots for naps as well as bring the building up to code," Sadie presents.

"Where would you get the money to start up?" Michael questions.

"I have some money in my savings," Jonel offers, "and I found someone to buy in with me as a silent partner. Sadie won't try to buy in, because we don't know how long she will be here and she doesn't have it. I will basically hire her. I will keep the books and manage the school and Sadie will take care of the curriculum, rules, consequences, and choosing the supplies. We would hire the teachers together and Sadie can teach a class."

Sadie proposes, "We would start as just a preschool and not a daycare. We could have a class or two for just three mornings a week for three year olds and a class or two for five days a week for four year olds. We know that we can't get this ready in time for this fall. We have a year to work all of this out and set up. Then, by the following fall, Cassie will be in third grade, Robin will be is second grade and Rachel will be in kindergarten. Peter will be two and I'd probably need to find a sitter for some mornings and you can watch him some mornings."

Jonel states, "We know that you can't simply give us permission. We will have to approach the Pastor/Parish committee, the church trustees, the finance committee, and church wide discussions with votes. We are simply lobbying for your support in this matter."

"Who are you going to for financing? You aren't going to my family are you?" Michael worries.

"No," Jonel informs him, "Ernestine Smith has a small fortune in the bank. We have already been talking to her and she is interested."

"Ernestine?" Michael doesn't hide his shock, "You want to work with Ernestine?"

"She talks rough, but she has a heart of gold somewhere in there," Sadie comforts, "You just have to be a duck."

"A duck?" Michael asks.

"The oil on duck feathers allows water to roll right off its back. You have to not take Ernestine's comments too seriously, but just let them roll off your back," Sadie illustrates to which Michael smirks.

"Okay, you have my support. You can take it to the next Pastor/Parish Committee to start looking into it. I'll put you on the agenda," he promises. "Jonel, do you mind if I talk to Sadie for a few minutes?"

"Not at all," Jonel stands, "I'll talk to you later Sadie."

Once Jonel leaves, Michael comes around and sits in the chair close to his wife, "How long have you been thinking about this."

"Jonel and I started talking about it since last week when we registered Rachel for that preschool that's so far away. You have your business degree. You could help us some," Sadie explains.

"Baby, this is a major undertaking. I thought you only wanted to live here as short a time as possible. I thought you wanted to move after two years. Well, we almost have one year in here," Michael reminds her.

"We can't move next year. Angel will be ready to start her senior year. She has been through enough. She doesn't need to start over in a new school, new town, new friends, and church for her senior year. Robin loves her riding lessons and she has Cassie. Rachel has Kim's daughter, Jenna to play with next year. We will probably end up here at least four years or more. Don't you think?"

"Sadie, are you accepting Shermanfield as your home?"

Sadie smiles, "Yes dear, I feel like I'm home. I'll even write my letter of resignation to Ambrose Elementary."

"First you're the church organist, then Sunday School Superintendent, then you took in Angel, and now you want to start a badly needed preschool. I believe that God sent me here for the express purpose of getting you here."

He pulls her to him, kissing her lovingly, when Grace knocks on the door.

Michael sits up sighing, "Come in."

"There is another young lady here to see you," Grace announces.

"I'll see you later," Sadie kisses her husband on the cheek and leaves.

Michael looks up to see Becky enter his office, "Well, hello there. Is there something I can do for you?"

"You said you had a free book for me," Becky reminds him in a raspy voice.

Michael goes to a cabinet and pulls out the book of Bible stories aimed at teens, plus a Bible, called Extreme Faith, with pictures of teens on bikes and skateboards on the cover.

"Thanks." She takes the books without looking at him.

"You're welcomed here anytime. If you ever need me for any reason or you want to talk or ask me questions about what you read or if you need my help, call me." He hands her his card. "I know you know my house number, but that has my cell phone and the church number."

She snatches the card and quickly leaves. Michael returns to his desk offering a silent prayer for this young lost soul.

Saturday, the week before the prom, Michael and Sadie are cleaning the living room. They pull the couches and the recliner into the center of the room finding a mess underneath the furniture: crayons, pencils, lollipop sticks, candy wrappers, hair clips, missing puzzle pieces, pieces of popcorn, and a plastic Easter egg with candy still inside.

Peter furniture cruises, holding onto the furniture to help him walk along the edge of the couch, as the girls sit, listening to a lecture about throwing the trash away where it goes and not eating in the living room. Angel helps with the cleaning cheerfully. She is in a good mood because Sadie bought her a beautiful prom gown last night and made an appointment for Kim Weaver to do her hair next week in her beauty shop garage.

Someone knocks at the front door. Sadie and Michael look at each other thinking of course someone would show up when their living room is trashed. Angel answers the door inviting the pop-in guest into the living room. On his knees behind a couch, Michael looks around the side to see his parents walking into the room.

"Hello son, down on your knees praying?" his father jokes.

"Yes Dad, I'm praying for a clean living room," Michael teases as he stands to greet his parents. "I'm surprised to see you."

He kisses and hugs his mother. The happy grandparents hug and kiss each of their grandchildren including Angel. Angel tells them excitedly that she is going to the prom next week. Robin shares that her riding lessons have started up again. Rachel brags that she is riding a two wheeler with trainer wheels instead of her tricycle. They rave about Peter walking while holding onto the furniture. He stomps his feet with his wide open mouth smile sucking up the attention.

James requests, "Angel, will you take the little ones out back to play for a while? It's beautiful out there. Go play instead of cleaning while we talk to your parents."

Angel picks up Peter and the girls follow her out of the house. Michael pulls a couch back a little so that they can sit.

"Is something wrong?" Michael inquires.

"No, it's nothing like that," James sits. "Your mother and I have been talking a lot lately and we just feel we need to talk with you."

"Okay, what's on your mind?"

"Son, when I found out that you had applied to a seminary, I reacted badly. I wanted so much for you. I never wanted to watch you struggle and do without," James begins.

"You mean living in a tiny house with one bathroom, no housekeeper, a rusty van and four children?" Michael smirks.

"Yes son. The thing is we are proud of your accomplishments and your family. We can tell you are happy. We were very impressed watching the way you and Sadie handled that awful night you found Angel in the cemetery.

"We are still your parents and we wish that once and a while you would allow us to help you. We haven't tried to help because we knew that you wanted to do things on your own and we respected that. We liked building the room for you and your mom loves providing the riding lessons. I don't want to have to fight with you about every gift like the van."

"What do you want to do?" Michael asks suspiciously.

"We simply wish that you felt freer to ask for help when you need it and you would let us do things for you now and then. In return, we would ask you first. I want to be able to discuss things with you without you becoming angry," James stipulates.

"I'm sorry I was angry. You were right. There was a snowy day that Angel and I were almost in an accident and the traction control kicked in. It works very well. Robin really loves her riding lessons. Thank you," Michael admits, "So, what exactly do you have in mind now?"

"This summer, we want to take you and your family to Disney World," James announces. Michael rolls his eyes as James continues, "You loved Disney World when you were young. Your girls are at that magical age for it and I bet Angel has never been there. What about you Sadie? Have you ever been there?"

Sadie cocks her head, "I only went once and it wasn't with my family. I went my senior year of high school with the marching band."

Michael looks at his wife and thinks about his kids, "Let's go to Disney World."

Sophia excitedly hugs him, "We will pay for everything, the flight, hotel, meals, tickets, and souvenirs."

"Okay, but don't go crazy with the souvenirs. Our house is small," he laughs.

"Can we take you out to supper tonight?" James requests.

"I don't have to make supper?" Sadie sits up straight, "Well, if you insist."

They call the kids back to the house to wash up and change for supper. Once they are outside heading for the cars, Michael announces, "Hey kids, Grandpa and Grandma want to take us to Disney World this summer."

The kids begin screaming and jumping up and down. Michael opens the garage for the kids to climb into the van. James walks in looking over the bikes as the girls continue their celebration.

James points at Angel's old rusty ten speed bike, "What is this?"

Angel walks over to look, "That's my bike."

"What? This is not a bike," he shakes his head and then returns to his car opening the trunk. He lifts out a bright blue twenty-one speed Schwinn sidewinder. "This is a bike."

Angel's eyes grow wide, "This is for me?"

"We are seriously behind on spoiling you," James laughs setting up the bike for her to look over.

Michael whispers in his dad's ear, "So you're going to check with me first, huh."

James waves his hand, "Oh, this is just a bike." James then reaches into his wallet slipping Angel a fifty dollar bill to help with the prom.

Sunday morning, Sadie plays the prelude as Michael walks to the front of the church. Robin sits with Cassie and Jonel. Amber, Cole, and Angel sit up front with Rachel and Peter. Michael looks over his congregation. He feels connected with his people. He, like Sadie, finally feels at home as if he is where he belongs here at Grace Church in Shermanfield.

Michael welcomes his congregation and gives the announcements followed by a time for the people to greet each other. Then Sadie begins the opening hymn. As the people sing, movement up in the balcony catches his attention. Becky is sitting up there by herself. Michael remembers back in college that when he began attending church, he would sit quietly in the back by himself. He looks up at the young girl and thinks to himself, "It's a start."

Manufactured By: RR Donnelley
                     Momence, IL USA
                     April, 2010